PENGUIN

HANG

SHIRLEY JACKSON was born in San Francisco in 1916. She first received wide critical acclaim for her short story "The Lottery," which was first published in *The New Yorker* in 1948. Her novels—which include *The Sundial, The Bird's Nest, Hangsaman, The Road Through the Wall, We Have Always Lived in the Castle,* and *The Haunting of Hill House*—are characterized by her use of realistic settings for tales that often involve elements of horror and the occult. *Raising Demons* and *Life Among the Savages* are her two works of nonfiction. She died in 1965.

FRANCINE PROSE is the author of more than twenty books including *Blue Angel,* a finalist for the National Book Award, and the nonfiction *New York Times* bestseller *Reading Like a Writer.* She is a former president of PEN American Center, as well as a member of the American Academy of Arts and Letters and the American Academy of Arts and Sciences.

SHIRLEY JACKSON

Hangsaman

Foreword by
FRANCINE PROSE

PENGUIN BOOKS

PENGUIN BOOKS

Published by the Penguin Group
Penguin Group (USA) Inc., 375 Hudson Street,
New York, New York 10014, USA

USA I Canada I UK I Ireland I Australia I New Zealand I India I South Africa I China
Penguin Books Ltd, Registered Offices: 80 Strand, London WC2R 0RL, England
For more information about the Penguin Group visit penguin.com

First published in the United States of America by Farrar, Straus and Young 1951
This edition with a foreword by Francine Prose published in Penguin Books 2013

LIBRARY OF CONGRESS CATALOGING-IN-PUBLICATION DATA
Jackson, Shirley, 1916–1965.
Hangsaman / Shirley Jackson ; foreword by Francine Prose.
pages ; cm.—(Penguin classics)
ISBN 978-0-14-310704-0
I. Title.
PS3519.A392H27 2013
813'.54—dc23
2013002349

Printed in the United States of America

For my children:
Laurence, Joanne, and Sarah

Contents

Foreword

In the fall of 2010, I taught a college literature course I decided to call "Strange Books." For the reading list, I chose the fifteen strangest books I could think of, starting with the stories of Gogol and Kleist and ending with Robert Walser's *Jakob von Gunten* and Bruno Schulz's *Street of Crocodiles*. All of these books were, and have remained, among my favorite works of fiction.

One of the reasons I regret not having read Shirley Jackson's *Hangsaman* until now is that I wish I could have added it to that list, on which it so clearly belonged.

Hangsaman is indeed a very strange novel, but what it shares with the others on my list (works by Jane Bowles, Henry Green, Wallace Shawn, and Roberto Bolaño, among others) is not only oddity but beauty, originality, a certain visionary intensity, and the ability to make us feel as if we have been invited into a private, very intimate world with striking similarities to our world, whatever that might be.

The book is so full of surprises that it's daunting to write about without the fear of spoiling them, so let me try to explain, a bit generally, what Shirley Jackson does so well. She writes brilliantly about consciousness—how the mind reacts to, adjusts, embraces, or recoils from experience. More specifically, she reminds us of what it's like to be seventeen years old, developing an adult consciousness, and at the same time being exquisitely, even painfully, aware of that development process. The everyday reality of Jackson's teenage protagonist is repeatedly interrupted by bursts of awareness and alienation so complex that it would be reductive to call them "out of body" moments.

I kept thinking of my favorite Elizabeth Bishop poem, "In the Waiting Room," whose speaker—waiting for her aunt to be released from the dentist's chair—is shocked by a startling apprehension of reality, of the physical world, and of the deceptively simple but ultimately mysterious fact of her own existence.

In addition, Jackson's heroine, Natalie Waite, is a psychically fragile flower, which adds several layers of nuance and an element of danger to what transpires in the book. How will this shaky sapling withstand the gale winds blowing around her, at home (where she lives with her hilariously vain, pompous, self-important writer-father; her neurotic, miserable, absent alcoholic mother; and a brother who has wisely absented himself from the entire situation), or away from home at the expensive and exclusive college in which she enrolls in the second section of the novel. Well-mannered, cliquish, privileged, the girls at Natalie's school are at heart little better than the proper townspeople who ritually sacrifice their human victims in Jackson's most famous story, "The Lottery."

At moments Natalie sounds a bit mad, and at others coolly rational and incisive. "Strange, Natalie thought, in all his wisdom my father never found from my letters that I get along badly with people; I suppose it's the first thing my mother fears, just as she is afraid that I have been visited with all her sorrows, because those she is better able to heal in me than she could in herself. It seemed that perhaps her father was trying to cure his failures in Natalie, and her mother was perhaps trying to avoid, through Natalie, doing over again those things she now believed to have been mistaken" (163–64).

But finally what makes Natalie's consciousness so consistently interesting is the fact that Jackson is such a good writer. She's an elegant prose stylist who expands and compresses language into complex, cadenced sentences, occasionally reminiscent of Henry James, of whom Jackson was apparently a fan. She uses words in new and unexpected ways that seem precisely right—the "asthmatic" buses wheezing at the bus stand. And she's acutely observant of how the world looks through Natalie's eyes. Here, for example, the exterior of a movie theater provides a mini-narrative within the larger narrative:

> the movie now being shown inside was old, and apparently past any redemption by adjective, so that the management had simply, resignedly let the pictures into the frames outside the theater, and were now presumably hiding away somewhere inside, beyond reach of irate patrons. One of the pictures showed a glorious scene between a man in a cowboy hat and uncomfortable pistols, who backed against a door to face a darker, equally weaponful villain; in the background a damsel wrung her hands and all three seemed to turn anxiously to the camera, which alone could justify the violent emotions they ravished themselves to feel. It was plain from the picture that it was near the end of the day; the sun was setting dramatically outside the backdrop window; the hero had the look of one who would shortly remove his guns and his spurs and go home in a car he had bought but could not afford; the heroine seemed to be thinking, under her beautiful look of fear and concern, that perhaps she should keep the children out of school until this chicken-pox scare was over.
> (191)

I suppose you could say there is social satire in the novel, but these expertly orchestrated and often terribly funny scenes go deeper than what the word *satiric* normally conjures up. Near the novel's beginning is a scene so intense, so well done, and so absolutely awful that after a while I realized I was holding my breath until it ended:

Natalie's blowhard father is helping her with her writing: private tutorials during which he involves her in a seductive conspiracy against her mother, who, they agree, is uninterested in Natalie's notebooks (in which Natalie has written about her mother) or in Mr. Waite's articles. He says, "I never could have found anyone else so unsympathetic as your mother, and so helpful" (10). They share a laugh about that. Now Mr. Waite has given Natalie another assignment, to write an essay about *him*. He modestly critiques it ("'Not handsome, Natalie. That I absolutely disclaim.'" [12]) and they

proceed to discuss it—in a highly civilized and totally blood-
curdling way.

Over the past weeks, I've been reading aloud to friends the
heartbreaking, hilarious rant of Natalie's mother, who, each
Sunday, is forced to host parties to which her husband invites
large but unspecified numbers of people. During one such
gathering, Mrs. Waite gets drunk and retires to her room to
complain about her marriage and her awful husband:

"It all starts so nice," Mrs. Waite said, twisting her face into
a horrible look of disgust. "You think it's going to be so easy.
You think it's going to be good. It starts like everything you've
ever wanted, you think it's so easy, everything looks so simple
and good, and you know that all of a sudden you've found out
what no one ever had sense enough to know before—that this is
good and if you manage right you can do whatever you want to.
You keep thinking that what you've got hold of is power, just
because you feel right in yourself, and everybody always thinks
that when they feel right in themselves then they can start right
off fixing the world. I mean, when I used to listen to him talking
about what kind of people we were, then I used to *believe* him."

"Mother . . ." said Natalie.

"First they tell you lies," said Mrs. Waite, "and they make
you believe them. Then they give you a little of what they promised, just a little, enough to keep you thinking you've got your
hands on it. Then you find out that you're tricked, just like
everyone else, just like *everyone,* and instead of being different
and powerful and giving the orders, you've been tricked just like
everyone else and then you begin to know what happens to
everyone and how they all get tricked. Everyone only knows one
'I,' and that's the 'I' they call themselves, and there's no one else
can be 'I' to anyone except that one person, and they're all stuck
with themselves and once they find out they've been tricked,
then they've been tricked and maybe the worst of it is that it isn't
like anything else; you can't just say, 'I've been tricked and I'll
make the best of it,' because you never believe it because they let
you see just enough about the next time to keep you hoping that
maybe you're a little bit smarter and a little bit . . ."

"Mother," Natalie said. "Mother, please stop. You're not making sense."

"I *am* making sense," Mrs. Waite said. "No one ever made sense before" (34–35).

The middle of the book's three sections suggests what I suppose one could call an academic novel. It's funny, as they often are, institutional pretenses and pretensions being so easy to make fun of. Though again, Jackson digs deeper, and is at once odder and more thought-provoking than surface mockery or humor. Here is how she captures the ethos of Natalie's newly founded college:

Anything which begins new and fresh will finally become old and silly. The educational institution is certainly no exception to this, although training the young is by implication an art for old people exclusively, and novelty in education is allied to mutiny. Moreover, the mere process of learning is allied to mutiny. Moreover, the mere process of learning is so excruciating and so bewildering that no conceivable phraseology or combination of philosophies can make it practical as a method of marking time during what might be called the formative years. The college to which Arnold Waite, after much discussion, had decided to send his only daughter was one of those intensely distressing organizations which had been formed on precisely the same lofty and advanced principles as hoarier seats of learning, but which applied them with slight differences in detail; education, the youthful founders of the college had told the world blandly, was more a matter of attitude than of learning (47).

As in "The Lottery," Jackson is attuned to the hideously discordant frequencies of power and group dynamics. While the citizens in "The Lottery" act communally in a single, unpredictable way, the students at Natalie's college act in little groups and in various predictable ways. Yet the results are no less brutal, if not so literally bloody.

In a series of expertly orchestrated scenes, two monstrous spoiled-brat students, Vicki and Anne, one of whom is having an affair with their English professor, conspire to torment the English professor's sad pretty wife, herself a former student. (Readers will gather that this was written at a time before changing academic mores made this sort of thing less common, at least on the surface.) Jackson assumes that we will register, without excessive prompting, how much *Hangsaman*'s unfortunate academic couple resembles a younger version of Natalie's parents—just as we have noted the irony of Mr. Waite's questioning Natalie's "whole attack in regard to the problem of description" (12) when in fact Natalie possesses almost preternaturally precise descriptive powers.

Natalie is lonely at school. And because of who she is, and because of what kind of novel this is, her loneliness is terrifying. The dangerous power of awareness, quotidian social brutality, loneliness, and existential fear propel *Hangsaman* toward the edge of becoming a psychological thriller, rather like one of Patricia Highsmith's, only less physically violent, funnier, more lyrical, imaginative, and interior.

I hesitate to reveal very much about the final section. Let me simply say that Natalie makes an extremely strange new friend. From this point on, we are tempted to read quickly to find out what will happen and at the same time hold ourselves back from reading too rapidly, because the sentences are so good, and because there are so many extraordinary scenes, including (to name just one) a meeting with a one-armed man who asks Natalie to butter his bread in a cafeteria.

The final sections generate yet another sort of tension, partly because they are seeded with traces of the occult; Natalie and her new friend are heavily into the tarot. And though by that point I was willing to follow the novel pretty much wherever it took me, I would have been disappointed to see it go any number of the ways I could imagine it going. In fact, the ending is a sort of triumph, absolutely in character with the rest of the book—the work of an author who not only writes beautifully but who knows what there is, in this world, to be scared of.

Another reason I regret not having read *Hangsaman* earlier, besides not being able to teach it in my "Strange Books" class, is that I'm sorry to think of all those years (the book was first published in 1951) when I could have been recommending it. It's a mistake I will try to correct, starting now.

Hangsaman is a wildly strange, strong, and original novel. Read it.

FRANCINE PROSE

Hangsaman

Slack your rope, Hangsaman,
O slack it for a while,
I think I see my true love coming,
Coming many a mile.

Mr. Arnold Waite—husband, parent, man of his word—invariably leaned back in his chair after his second cup of breakfast coffee and looked with some disbelief at his wife and two children. His chair was situated so that when he put his head back the sunlight, winter or summer, touched his unfaded hair with an air at once angelic and indifferent—indifferent because, like himself, it found belief not an essential factor to its continued existence. When Mr. Waite turned his head to regard his wife and children the sunlight moved with him, broken into patterns on the table and the floor.

"Your God," he customarily remarked to Mrs. Waite down the length of the breakfast table, "has seen fit to give us a glorious day." Or, "Your God has seen fit to give us rain," or "snow," or "has seen fit to visit us with thunderstorms." This ritual arose from an ill-advised remark made by Mrs. Waite when her daughter was three; small Natalie had asked her mother what God was, and Mrs. Waite had replied that God made the world, the people in it, and the weather; Mr. Waite did not tend to let such remarks be forgotten.

"God," Mr. Waite said this morning, and laughed. "*I* am God," he added.

Natalie Waite, who was seventeen years old but who felt that she had been truly conscious only since she was about fifteen, lived in an odd corner of a world of sound and sight past the daily voices of her father and mother and their incomprehensible actions. For the past two years—since, in fact, she had turned around suddenly one bright morning and seen from the corner of her eye a person called Natalie, existing, charted, inescapably located on a spot of ground, favored with sense and feet and a bright-red sweater, and most obscurely alive— she had lived completely by herself, allowing not even her father access to the farther places of her mind. She visited strange countries, and the voices of their inhabitants were constantly in her ear; when her father spoke he was accompanied by a sound of distant laughter, unheard probably by anyone except his daughter.

"Well," Mr. Waite customarily remarked, after he had taken his stand as God for another day, "only twenty-one more days before Natalie leaves us." Sometimes it was "only fourteen more days before Bud goes off again." Natalie was leaving for her first year in college a week after her brother went back to high school; sometimes twenty-one days resolved itself into three weeks, and seemed endless; sometimes it seemed a matter of minutes slipping by so swiftly that there would never be time to approach college with appropriate consideration, to form a workable personality to take along. Natalie was desperately afraid of going away to college, even the college only thirty miles away that her father had chosen for her. She had two consolations: first, the conviction from previous experience that any place becomes home after awhile, so that she might assume a reasonable probability that after a month or so the college would be familiar and her home faintly alien. Her second consolation was the recurring thought that she might always give up college if she chose, and simply stay at home with her mother and father; this prospect was so horrible that Natalie found herself, when she thought confidently about it, almost enjoying her fear of going away.

Thus, at nine-thirty of a Sunday morning the Waites had breakfasted together. Mr. Waite felt with complacence the touch of the sunlight on his head; Bud, stirring in his chair, sighed with the deep resignation of a boy fifteen years old who is going back to high school in fourteen more days; Mrs. Waite, looking deeply into her coffee cup, spoke with the soft, faintly wistful intonation she kept for her husband. "Cocktail olives," she said. It was as though she were deliberately setting him off, because Mr. Waite stared for a minute and then said emphatically, "You mean I have to make cocktails for that crew? Cocktails for twenty people? Cocktails?"

"You *couldn't* very well ask them to drink tea," Mrs. Waite said. "Not *them*."

Natalie, fascinated, was listening to the secret voice which followed her. It was the police detective and he spoke sharply, incisively, through the gentle movement of her mother's voice. "How," he asked pointedly, "Miss Waite, *how* do you account for the gap in time between your visit to the rose garden and your discovery of the body?"

"I can't tell," Natalie said back to him in her mind, her lips not moving, her dropped eyes concealing from her family the terror she hid also from the detective. "I refuse to say," she told him.

Mr. Waite spoke patiently. "You serve cocktails," he said, "you're always making them. With ordinary highballs everyone can make his own. They will anyway," he added, driving home his point.

"*I* didn't invite them," Mrs. Waite said.

"*I* didn't invite them," Mr. Waite said.

"I called them," Mrs. Waite said, "but you made out the list."

"You realize," the detective said silently, "that this discrepancy in time may have very serious consequences for you?"

"I realize," Natalie said. Confess, she thought, if I confess I might go free.

Mr. Waite shifted his ground again; by now he and his wife knew one another well enough to substitute half-hearted disagreement for a more taxing marital relationship, and an aimless, constant argument where either one took any side was to them a familiarity as affectionate as the ponderous sympathy of a Victorian household. "God," Mr. Waite said, "I wish they weren't coming."

"I can cancel it," his wife said, as she always did.

"I could get some work done for a change," Mr. Waite said. He looked around the table, at his wife gazing into her coffee cup, at Natalie regarding her plate, at Bud watching out the window some presumably enrapturing adolescent dream. "No

one ever *looks* at anyone else in this house," Mr. Waite said
irritably. "Do you realize I'm two weeks behind in my work?"
he demanded of his wife. He enumerated on his fingers. "I've
got to review four books by Monday; four books *no* one in
this house has read but myself. Then there's the article on
Robin Hood—that should have been finished three days ago.
And my reading, and today's paper, and yesterday's. Not to
mention," Mr. Waite added ponderously, "not to mention the
book."

At the mention of the book, his family glanced at him briefly,
in chorus, and then away, back to the less choleric plates and
cups on the table.

"I wish I could help you, dear," Mrs. Waite said artificially.

"Are you aware," the detective demanded sarcastically of
Natalie, "that you are retarding the course of this investigation by your stubborn silence?"

"Listen," Bud said abruptly, "*I* don't have to come to this
thing, do I?"

His father frowned, and then laughed rudely. "What were
you planning to do instead?" he asked; if there was a note of
thunder in his voice his family ignored it through long familiarity.

"Something," Bud said insolently. "Anything."

Mr. Waite looked down the table at his wife. "This son of
mine," he explained elaborately, "has such a distaste for the literary life that he prefers doing 'something—anything' to attending a literary cocktail party." An epigram obviously occurred to
him and he tried it out cautiously. "A literary cocktail party
holds few attractions for one," he began slowly, feeling his way,
"who is at the same time too untaught for literature and too
young for drink."

The family considered; Mrs. Waite shook her head.

"Adolescence is a time when—" she suggested finally, and
Mr. Waite took it up: "When one is too untaught for literature
and too young for drink."

"Too old for literature?" Natalie asked.

Bud laughed. "Too smart to get anywhere near it," he said.
They all laughed, and the sudden family gesture was so

pleasant to them that they immediately took steps to separate themselves from one another. Mr. Waite left first; still laughing, he slid his napkin into the ring which was composed of two snakes curiously and obscenely entwined ("nothing to sit at table with," Mrs. Waite called it) and rose, saying, "Excuse me," to his wife as he did so. A moment later Bud eased himself from his chair and was, by a typical sliding grace, able to reach the door ahead of his father. "After *you*, sir," Bud said grandly as he held the door for his father, and Mr. Waite bowed formally and said, "Thank you, young man." They went down the hall together, and Natalie and Mrs. Waite could hear Bud saying, "As a matter of fact, I'm going swimming."

Terror lest she be left alone with her mother made Natalie almost speechless; as her mother opened her mouth to speak (perhaps to say, "Excuse me," to Natalie; perhaps she was as much troubled by being left alone with Natalie) Natalie said quickly, "Busy now," and went with little dignity out of the French doors behind her chair and down the flat steps into the garden.

She did not really prefer the garden to several other spots in the world; she would rather, for instance, have been alone in her room with the door locked, or sitting on the grass by a brook at midnight, or, given an absolutely free choice, standing motionless against a pillar in a Greek temple or on a tumbril in Paris or on a great lonely rock over the sea, but the garden was closest, and it pleased her father to see her wandering morning-wise among the roses.

"And your age?" said the detective. "Occupation? Sex?"

It was a beautiful morning, and the garden seemed to be enjoying it. The grass had exerted itself to be unusually green just beyond Natalie's feet, the roses were heavy and sweet and suitable for giving to any number of lovers, the sky was blue and serene, as though it had never known a tear. Natalie smiled secretly, moving her shoulders stiffly under her thin white shirt, agreeably conscious of herself going from the flat line of her shoulders all the way down to her feet far below, so that she was, leaning back with her shoulders against the solid intangible of the air, a thin thing, a graceful thing, a thing of steel and subtle padding. She breathed deeply, satisfied.

"Will you talk now?" the detective demanded, his voice rising a little, although he kept it still under iron control. "Do you think that you alone can stand against the force of the police, the might and weight of duly constituted authority, against *me*?"

A lovely little shiver went down Natalie's back. "I may be in danger every moment of my life," she told the detective, "but I am strong within myself."

"Is *that* an answer?" the detective said. "What if I told you that you were seen?"

Natalie lifted her head, looking proudly off into the sky.

"The housekeeper," the detective said, dropping his voice into a vicious, slapping murmur. "She has testified—under oath, mind you, Miss Waite, under oath—that she saw you enter the house fully fifteen minutes before your screams summoned the household to the study where you stood over the murdered body of your lover. Well, Miss Waite, well?"

"I have nothing to say," Natalie said, barely able to form the words.

"What becomes of your story now?" the detective went on ruthlessly. "Miss Waite, what becomes of your precious statement that you were alone in the garden?"

"I have nothing to say," Natalie said.

"Tell me, Miss Waite," the detective continued remorselessly, his cruel face closer to Natalie's, his voice soft and evil, "tell me, do you doubt the word of the housekeeper? Do you dare to say that she lies? Do you believe that she is unable to estimate time?"

"Ten o'clock, Natalie," Mrs. Waite called from the French doors.

"Coming," Natalie called back. Because she almost always ran instead of walking she cleared the steps with one long bound—like a deer, she thought in mid-air—and went in through the French doors. "Where's my notebook?" she asked her mother as she passed, and did not stay for an answer; her notebook was on the hall table where she had left it that morning when she came down to breakfast. With her notebook in her hand, she knocked on the study door.

"Come in, my dear," her father said.

He looked up, smiling at her across the desk as she came in. "Good morning, Natalie," he said formally, and Natalie said, "Good morning, Dad." It was a fiction of theirs that these little meetings began the day for both of them, although before meeting in the study they usually breakfasted together, and pursued privately their personal morning occupations; Natalie watching the morning from her bedroom window and making hasty notes about it on her desk pad, combing her hair so that it fell carelessly along her shoulders, putting on the secret little locket she always wore; her father awakening and looking at himself in the mirror and smoking his first cigarette of the day and, presumably, somehow dressing himself.

"You look very fresh this morning, my dear," Mr. Waite said, and Natalie said to him solemnly, "I've been thinking a lot today," and he nodded.

"Of course," he said. "Brilliant sunshine, seventeen years behind you, the infinite sorrows of growing up on your shoulders—one *must* think."

Sometimes, these mornings in the study, Natalie was uncertain whether or not to laugh at her father's statements. It was difficult, usually, to tell if his remark was a joke because it was a point of conduct with him not to laugh at his own jokes, and with herself the only audience Natalie had only her own reactions to depend on. She was serious this time, because, although her father's expectant air seemed to indicate that this *had* been a joke, his pointing out that she had seventeen years behind her had given her a sudden sense of the immensity of time; seventeen years was a very long time to have been alive, if you took it into proportion by the thought that in seventeen years more—or as long as she had wasted being a child, and a small girl, silly and probably playing—she would be thirty-four, and old. Married, probably. Perhaps—and the thought was nauseating—senselessly afflicted with children of her own. Worn, and tired. She brought herself away from the disagreebly clinging thought by her usual method—imagining the sweet sharp sensation of being burned alive—and turned expectantly to her father.

"Well," he said. He was looking down at the papers on his desk. "Have you brought your notebook?"

Silently Natalie passed it across the desk to him. There was always this moment of dismay, when the words she had written crossed her mind remorselessly and the thought of her father reading them made her hesitate with an urgent desire to be off, out of the study, anywhere. Then the moment passed, and she said as she handed him the notebook, "I did it last night. After you were all in bed."

"Up all night writing again?" her father asked indulgently. He began to turn the pages of the notebook slowly, savoring them.

"I went to sleep about three," Natalie said. Her father was bitter about people who moistened their thumbs as they read, and used such vulgarity as a symbol for much of the reading public, but he was probably unaware that as he turned the pages of Natalie's notebook he wet his lips slightly with his tongue, although he kept his fingers away from his mouth as he always did.

"This has always been a favorite of mine, Natalie," he said, stopping at a page. "This one about the trees. 'Lined up against the sky' is good, very good. And the one on your mother." He chuckled, and turned another page. "I hope she never sees it," he said, and looked up at Natalie with a smile like a child's.

"She's never interested in my notebooks," Natalie said.

"I know," said Mr. Waite. "Nor is she interested in my articles." He laughed and said, as though in compensation, "I never could have found anyone else so unsympathetic as your mother, and so helpful."

This time Natalie laughed with certainty. It was a statement very true of her mother.

"Now," her father said. He stopped at the current page in the notebook, and deliberately hesitant, looked up at Natalie and smiled, turned to select a cigarette from the package on the desk, and made an elaborate ceremony of lighting it. "I'm a little bit worried," he said. "I'm not really sure I dare read it."

"It was the hardest thing I had to do yet," Natalie said. Her father looked at her with a quick frown, and she thought and then said, "It was the hardest thing I have had to do, so far."

"Can't be too careful," her father said. He braced his shoulders, and bent his head down to the notebook.

While he read, Natalie, her initial nervousness over (once she had given him the notebook each morning her step was taken; it was irrecoverable then, and she had only to wait for it to be returned to her), surveyed the study freshly, as she did every morning. It was a deeply satisfying place. The books which stood expectantly on the shelves around the room had the fulfilled look of books which have been read, although not necessarily by Mr. Waite; the leather chair still held the marks of Mr. Waite's ample bottom, the ashtray beside it already this morning touched with ash. The room was used, perhaps worn, and had nothing of abandon about it; it was relaxed, as though nothing now could surprise it, once Mr. Waite had given into it the care of his own alarming self.

"This is good," Mr. Waite said abruptly. He laughed aloud, and said again, "This is good. Here, where it says, 'He seems perpetually surprised at the world's never being quite so intelligent as he is, although he would be even more surprised if he found out that perhaps he is himself not so intelligent as he thinks.' Too many words, Natalie, and I think you became intoxicated with the first half of the sentence, and only tacked the second half on to make it come down the way it went up. It could be said more neatly, I believe. But it's sound, very sound. And I like, 'He has a great reputation for generosity, although no one has ever known him to give anything to the *poor*.' You've really extended yourself." He sat back and looked at her cheerfully, as she had known that he would. "I am more than pleased," he declared. He fell again to reading, laughing occasionally. "Of course," he said after a minute, "you realize— in fact, I believe I told you this when I gave you the assignment— that I cannot afford to quarrel with anything you have written here."

Natalie said, "Maybe I took advantage of that."

He shook his head. "I know you did," he said.

He read again, and Natalie looked around the study; the corpse would be over there, of course, between the bookcase with the books on demonology and the window, which had heavy drapes that could be pulled to hide any nefarious work. She would be found at the desk, not five feet away from the corpse, leaning one hand on the corner to support herself, her face white and distorted with screaming. She would be unable to account for the blood on her hands, on the front of her dress, on her shoes, the blood soaking through the carpet at her feet, the blood under her hand on the desk, leaving a smeared mark on the papers there.

"Oh, no," her father said. "Not handsome, Natalie. That I absolutely disclaim."

"But it's modified," Natalie said. She chose her words with mischief. "I particularly say that the handsomeness is largely arrogance; that so few people are really arrogant these days that such a person gives the impression of beauty. I liked that idea."

"It's an unusual thought," her father said consideringly. "I'm not sure but that you're too young for it, though." He gave the notebook a little push, to get it away from the edge of the desk so he could put his elbows down. "Now," he said.

Natalie settled herself, watching him.

"In the first place," Mr. Waite said, choosing his words carefully, "I'm going to quarrel with your whole attack in regard to the problem of description. No description can be said to describe anything—and I've told you this before—if it's in mid-air, so to speak, unattached. It's got to be tied on to something, to be *useful*. You have apparently neglected this in today's work."

"But I thought you said—" Natalie began, but her father held up his hand; he disliked being interrupted.

"Apparently, I say," he went on. "I don't think that you yourself quite realize the *work* you have given to this little sketch. Under any other circumstances your weighting of it would be meaningless, but I gave you this on purpose to try you out, and you did exactly as I expected." He paused, thinking. "Understand," he said finally, "I am not finding fault with your interpretation. You are of course completely free to write whatever you please about me or anything else. I am *interested* in seeing you write what you please, and in encouraging you to write more. But you *must*, if you are ever to be a *good* writer, understand your own motives."

He stopped, and made again his elaborate ceremony of lighting a cigarette. Then he folded his hands on the notebook and looked frankly at Natalie, the cigarette burning handsomely in the ashtray, the line of smoke framing his head on one side, and the squareness of the window shaping nicely on the other side.

"I am not a vain man," he began slowly. "I do not hold myself in undue estimation. As a matter of fact, my own description of myself would be *much* harsher than yours. You do not mention my pettiness, for example, although you hint at it in your statements about"—he consulted the notebook—"the fact that I 'substitute words for actions.' You overlook one of my outstanding characteristics, which is a brutal honesty which frequently leads me into trouble—an honesty so sincere that, applied to myself, it gives me a picture I cannot be proud of, although you name me as a proud man. My honest picture of myself has led me to aim less high than many of my contemporaries, because I know my own failings, and as a result I am in many respects less successful in a worldly sense. They, without knowledge of their own shortcomings, were able to conquer blindly, while I, always hesitating through doubt of myself, lost my chances, and fell. You do not mention—and I am using that same brutal honesty on myself now—that I am not always so kind to my family as I should care to be, because I am perhaps too much concerned with my own emotions at the expense of theirs—although, to speak with bitter truth, I am a person not gifted with great emotions and consequently, while I can never be sentimental, I can never be great." He seemed about to go on in this strain, which was a favorite of his, but then recollected himself, and said wryly, "I reveal myself more with every word. I *am* honest, Natalie, and sometimes ashamed of it."

"I always am, when I'm honest," Natalie said.

"Are you?" he asked with interest. "Do you know when you're being honest?"

"Usually," Natalie said. "If I'm surprised at myself for saying or thinking it, it's honest."

He laughed and nodded, and then said, "You teach me as much as I teach you, my dear." They were both quiet for a minute, counting over their individual virtues, and then he went on, his voice confidential. "Natalie," he said solemnly, "you know by now that it is natural for girls to hate their fathers at some point in their growth. Now I submit that at this time of your life you are growing to hate me."

"No," Natalie said. She stared at him. "Of course I don't hate you," she said. The remark had come so in a context of discussion that it was a moment before she thought to say, "I love you."

He shook his head sadly. "When you were born, and when Bud was born, I realized, even though your mother did not, that there would come a time when you would both rebel against us, hating us for what we represented, fighting to get free of us; it's a reaction so natural that I am ashamed to think that now I have a pang, a twinge, when I recognize it at last; it has been slow in coming, but I am as unprepared for it as I have ever been. Natalie, you *must* remember that it is natural, that hatred of me does not imply that *you* as a person hate *me* as a person, but only that the child, growing normally, passes through a stage when hatred of the parents is inevitable. That is your stage now." He held up his hand again as Natalie tried to speak and then, when she subsided, dropped his hand back to the pages of Natalie's notebook, which he touched as he talked, fumbling with the pages which held her assignment for that morning.

"That does not mean," he continued thoughtfully, "— although, remember, this is actually a new experience for me as well as for you—that does not mean that I am not able to help you, or advise you, or sympathize with you; it only means that we must recognize now that you are a growing girl and I an old man, and that a basic sex antagonism, combined with a filial resentment, separates us, so that we cannot always be honest with one another as we have been up to now."

If it's happening why does he tell me? Natalie thought briefly, and heard from far away the police detective demanding, "Are you prepared to confess that you killed him?"

For a long minute her father looked at her, obviously expecting some answer which she was unable to give; Natalie, her mind moving swiftly, went back over what he had said: what had there been, for instance, which indicated what she was to say? Had he asked a question, perhaps? Made a false statement she was to correct? Praised her, to hear her disclaim modestly?

"Well," her father said at last, and sighed. "It is not necessary to discuss it in detail, my dear. You will soon know more about it than I do. And I shall learn from you."

He sat back in his chair, and stared reflectively down at the desk, his eyes reading absently the lines of Natalie's notebook. "Handsome," he said, and laughed. "Oh, Natalie, my dear." And he shook his head helplessly.

It was a dismissal. Nothing was to be further identified. As Natalie rose, her mind already moving ahead to the garden, to lunch, to the length of the day stretching ahead, her father pushed the notebook impatiently across the desk.

"You will be at the party this afternoon?" he asked, accenting the "you" just enough to make Natalie remember Bud's refusal to come.

"I guess so," Natalie said lamely because she was wondering where Bud found the courage to announce publicly that he was not bound by family plans.

"Try to help your mother, if you can," her father said. "Entertaining is difficult for her." He smiled up at Natalie, his mind already going on to more important things, the deep complex ideas that were his own work. "A fundamental hatred of people, I believe," he added as Natalie went toward the door.

On Sundays the Waites regarded themselves as living in a carefree, bohemian fashion, although for the other six days of the week they lived like everyone else. Mrs. Waite was not allowed

the services of her maid on Sundays, and on Sundays the
Waites usually entertained, with what Mr. Waite confidently
referred to as potluck, although it was Mrs. Waite who dealt
with the pot—the only reason the Waites were able to keep a
maid at all. Mr. Waite customarily invited anyone who pleased
him over for Sunday afternoon at his house, and Mrs. Waite
was expected to provide various manner of refreshments for
Mr. Waite's casual guests. This included, usually, one or another form of small sandwiches and canapés for any number
of people—since Mr. Waite was never able to remember
whether he had or had not invited any given person—and buf-
fet supper afterwards; Mrs. Waite had thus established for
herself a strict eight-o'clock Sunday bedtime, retiring at about
the time Natalie and Bud were released from Sunday bondage
and Mr. Waite was settling down with his convivial guests.

Natalie and her mother spent Sunday mornings, after Natalie's visit with her father, in the kitchen preparing for the day's
guests; Mrs. Waite thought of this as good training for her
daughter, and Natalie, telling her father about her mother, had
once remarked, "She makes the kitchen like a room with a
sign saying 'Ladies' on the door."

The kitchen was, in fact, the only place in the house that
Mrs. Waite possessed utterly; even her bedroom was not her
own, since her husband magnanimously insisted upon sharing
it. He shared also the dinner table and the services of the radio
in the living room; he felt himself privileged to sit on the porch
and to use a bathtub. In the kitchen, however, Mr. Waite
amusedly confessed himself "inadequate," and so Mrs. Waite,
one day a week, was allowed a length of time unmolested except
for the company of her daughter. Perhaps, even, Mrs. Waite
felt that in these hours that they shared the kitchen, she and
Natalie were associated in some sort of mother-daughter relationship that might communicate womanly knowledge from
one to the other, that might, by means of small female catch-
words and feminine innuendoes, separate, at least for a time,
the family into women against men. At any rate the kitchen
alone with Natalie was the only place where Mrs. Waite talked
at all, and probably because she talked so little elsewhere she

made her conversation in the kitchen into a sort of weekly chant, a news bulletin wherein all that Mrs. Waite had thought or wanted to say or felt or surmised during the week was aired and considered, in combination with Mrs. Waite's refrain of reminiscence and complaint. Natalie admired her mother at these times, and, although she would go to any length to avoid even the slightest conversation with her mother in the living room, she enjoyed and profited by the kitchen conversations more than even Mrs. Waite suspected.

This morning Mrs. Waite's initial momentum came from her Sunday casserole which, incredibly complex and delicate, would be devoured drunkenly in a few hours by inconsiderate and uncomplimentary people. When Natalie came into the kitchen her mother was leaning over the sideboard, slicing meat beautifully thin with the butcher knife. "Natalie?" she said without looking around. "Did you hear him?" she went on, without assuring herself that it *was* really Natalie and not Mr. Waite come to announce that the house was on fire. "Did you *hear* him? He's an old fool, he really is." She held her breath to cut daintily around a bone, and then went on. "Sometimes I think he must be an awful fool, to think people are taken in by his pretensions. Paranoid," Mrs. Waite announced with satisfaction. "Paranoid. My father used to laugh when he came, he really did. Paranoid. Natalie, I wish Ethel would leave dishes the way I leave them. Little ones inside big ones. It's impossible to believe that anyone can put dishes away in this sort of insane arrangement; she piles them all together without thinking of size or safety. Used to laugh. Sometimes I think he only married me because my name was Charity and it was the fashion then for people like your father to sing songs like 'Buffalo Gals' and dance a Virginia reel. Charity. *My* father knew what he was doing."

Natalie's Sunday morning work usually began with the salad greens. She washed lettuce and carrots, tomatoes and radishes, cleaned them and set them in cold water to be made into salad at the last minute. With both hands full of lettuce leaves, now, she stood at the sink watching the waterfall of the cold water running from the faucet through the clear green of the lettuce. It was incredibly beautiful until her hands began to chill.

"Too lazy to do anything for himself," Mrs. Waite said. "Imagine a grown man taking up square-dancing in New York City. I remember my mother, a real scold *she* was. Her voice up *here* all the time, and I sometimes think your father would profit by her, although before she died she did get pretty quiet without my father. I always used to wonder how people made happy marriages and made them last all day long every day. Seemed to me my mother wasn't happy but then of course I didn't know. Natalie, see that your marriage is happy." She turned and looked earnestly at Natalie, the knife resting against her palm. "See that your marriage is happy, child. Don't ever let your husband know what you're thinking or doing, that's the way. My mother could have done *any*thing, anything she wanted, my father would have let her, even though probably he wouldn't have known. Of course, by the time he died she was too old." Mrs. Waite took the thin slices of meat and began to arrange them in the baking dish. "I remember Sundays at home," she went on.

"You want me to hardboil eggs?" Natalie asked softly.

Mrs. Waite thought, looking around at the kitchen as though the casserole or the lettuce had an opinion she was waiting for. Finally she said, "I guess we'd better, Natalie. Can't ever tell how many will come." She smiled as she went on, "Sundays at home, we never knew how many were coming. Sometimes we'd go to my grandmother's, or to one of my sisters'. All my sisters married before I did, Natalie, there's something for you. *They* could have told me. Or else they'd come to our house. We never knew. They were like a flock of birds—one would take off for someplace, and then the rest would follow. All big men, small women. My uncles—when I remember them I see them sitting on Sunday afternoons, sometimes in one house, sometimes in another. Take my uncle Charles; I usually remember him sitting in the red chair in our dining room—we had to bring chairs in, they'd be so many at table—or else in the old brown mohair chair he kept by the fireplace in his own house. Aunt—what was her name, Natalie? Who married Charles?"

"Helen," Natalie said.

"Helen," Mrs. Waite said. "Well, she used to hate that chair, except I always used to think then that she only made such a fuss because she knew wives always hated their husbands' old dear things and she was afraid no one would respect her if she let him keep the chair without a fuss. Except I don't think she ever paid much attention to doing it seriously." She slid her knife through the piece of cooking butter on the plate, and began to slice an onion. "Fancy African masks," she said. "Cheap dirty silver jewelry. Old blues records you wouldn't want to know the words of if you *could* hear them. Anyway, I always remember that uncle sitting in that chair. I guess all young girls—more water there, Natalie—get to hate where they're living because they think a husband will be better. What happens is that a husband's the same, usually. When I met your father he had a lot of books that he said he read, and he gave me a Mexican silver bracelet instead of an engagement ring, and I looked around at my uncles sitting in their old goddam—your father taught me to say goddam, too, and a lot of words else I could tell you if I wanted, although I *do* believe I've outgrown *that* part of it—chairs and I thought being married was everything I wanted. Only of course it's the same, only now it's strangers for Sunday dinner, and your father will be sick all tomorrow if he smokes anything stronger than cigarettes. Let's have a potato salad. I told Ethel to boil extra potatoes yesterday."

Natalie had discovered that by a slight pressure on a back tooth she could make a small regular stirring pain that operated as a rhythmic counterpoint to her mother's voice; she would not for the world have told her mother that she had a cavity in her tooth, but it was a pleasant change in her body since the day before, and she enjoyed it.

"Ice cream," Mrs. Waite said. "We always *used* to have ice cream."

"Tell me," the detective said insistently, leaning forward, "tell me how it was done; you may rely on my not using the information against you."

"I don't know," Natalie answered silently. "I don't remember."

"I can promise you," the detective said with great dignity, "that I am a reasonable person to confide in. I can be trusted absolutely."

"I don't remember," Natalie told him.

"Of *course* you remember," the detective said impatiently. "No one can live through such things and not *remember* them."

"Natalie," Mrs. Waite said, her hands quiet for a minute while she stared at the wall before her, "what will I do when you're gone?"

Embarrassed, Natalie carefully turned down the flame under the boiling eggs. "I'll be back a lot," she said inadequately.

"A mother gets very lonesome without her daughter," Mrs. Waite said. "Especially when it's an only daughter. A mother gets lonesomer than anything in the world."

One of the things which Natalie most disliked about her mother was Mrs. Waite's invariable trick of putting serious statements into language that Natalie classified as cute. Mrs. Waite, too long accustomed to seeing her most heartfelt emotions exposed, discussed, and ignored, had long since fallen into protecting herself by stating them as jokes, with an air of girlish whimsy which irritated both Natalie and Mr. Waite as no flat statement of hatred could have. Because of this, Natalie—who had sometimes thought of running to her mother with a voluntary expression of affection—said briefly, "You'll find something to do."

Mrs. Waite was silent. She had set the casserole carefully into the oven and turned her attention to the silverware before she began again, very timidly, "And at home when we had no dishes for all those people we used to ask one of the aunts to bring along . . ."

Lunch on Sundays was a pick-up meal; Mrs. Waite had over the years prevailed upon her husband to accept the fact that the oven would not hold at the same time an unusual meal for his friends and the correct nourishing lunch he believed his due. Although in most ordinary matters Mr. Waite would far sooner have sacrificed his friends than himself, in the question of his hospitality and the probable Monday conversations about it, Mr. Waite was willing, with objections, to forego his own comfort, always believing that it was a temporary measure due to Mrs. Waite's inefficiency and that the next Sunday would see him sensibly fed. Since it was his custom to greet regular occasions with regular remarks, Mr. Waite habitually observed over his Sunday peanut-butter sandwich, "This is not food for a grown man."

On Sundays Mrs. Waite had an answer for him, probably because originally she had had all the week to prepare it; she habitually answered, "*You* make the dinner and *I'll* make the lunch."

Standing at the kitchen table next to her father, Natalie looked peacefully at the scene of competence around her. The dishes used in the morning had been washed, the breakfast cups and saucers put away, and the company cups and saucers set out instead. The family napkins, suspended for the present lunch and dinner, reposed on the kitchen mantel to be brought out again on Monday. The very familiar kitchen things—the plant which Ethel kept beside the sink, the smaller teakettle, the plastic-handled tableware—were all pushed back and set aside before the company preparations. Natalie, because her mother and father were bickering, transplanted herself to an archeological expedition some thousand years from now, coming unexpectedly upon this kitchen and removing layers of earth carefully from around the teakettle—"This may have been a cookpot," someone said wisely, and someone else added, "Or of course a chamber pot; we have no notion as yet of the habits of these peoples." Further excavations—perhaps three or four days later, and after serious quarrels between the junior and senior members of the expedition, one force maintaining that it would be more sensible to move on; this was an infertile spot for discovery and besides the air was bad—might yield the skull of Natalie, and one, holding her precious head in his hands, turning it over and examining it intimately, might remark, "Look, here, at these teeth; they knew *some*thing of dentistry, at any rate—see, here's one filled, with gold, it appears. Had they any knowledge of gold, do you remember? Male, I should say, from the frontal development." At that time, of course, Natalie reflected with contentment, her life would be done. There would be no further fears for Natalie, no possibility of walking wrong when you were no more than a skull in a strange man's hands. "And see," another voice called from the end of the kitchen, "see, here, these very strange objects—ornaments, I'd judge. And look here, at these two skeletons here—see, look *here*, they had *children*."

The garden belonged exclusively to Natalie; the rest of the family used it, of course, but only Natalie regarded it as a functioning part of her personality, and she felt that she was refreshed by ten minutes in the garden between the arbitrary pleasures assigned her by other people. If she sat on the grass at the foot of the lawn, her back against a tree, she could look out over fields that seemed soft at this distance, into mountains far away, since her father had sensibly enough chosen a picturesque location in preference to her mother's choice of something that might *grow* something; thus, at the back of the house, there was a kitchen garden ineffectually tended by Mrs. Waite, which yielded a regular crop of dubious radishes and pallid carrots, and the rest of the land about the house—some three acres of it—was allowed to run to meadow, or vacant-lot, standards. Natalie's garden was in front of the house, and was tended by a gardener who refused to touch the kitchen garden, and this part of the property ended uncertainly in a sort of cliff—if you looked at it from far enough back—below which ran the south road. Behind the house, behind even the kitchen garden, Mr. Waite had graciously permitted trees to grow unmolested, and when Natalie was younger, before the garden and the view from the cliff had taken such a hold of her, she had delighted in playing pirate and cowboy and knight in armor among the trees. Now, however, for some reason only remotely connected with knights in armor, the tree on the grass belonged to her, and she ignored the trees below as dark and silent and unprovocative.

The sight of the mountains far away was sometimes so perfectly comprehensible to Natalie that she forced tears into her eyes, or lay on the grass, unable, after a point, to absorb it—she was, of course, adequately hidden from the windows of the house—or to turn it into more than her own capacity for containing it; she was not able to leave the fields and mountains alone where she found them, but required herself to take them in and use them, a carrier of something simultaneously real and unreal to set up against the defiantly real-and-unreal batterings of her family. There was a point in Natalie, only dimly realized by herself, and probably entirely a function of her age, where obedience ended and control began; after this point was reached and passed, Natalie became a solitary functioning individual, capable of ascertaining her own believable possibilities. Sometimes, with a vast aching heartbreak, the great, badly contained intentions of creation, the poignant searching longings of adolescence overwhelmed her, and shocked by her own capacity for creation, she held herself tight and unyielding, crying out silently something that might only be phrased as, "Let me take, let me create."

If such a feeling had any meaning to her, it was as the poetic impulse which led her into such embarrassing compositions as were hidden in her desk; the gap between the poetry she wrote and the poetry she contained was, for Natalie, something unsolvable.

Lying on the grass on Sunday afternoon, while her mother and father debated over their guests for the day, she rested her cheek on her arm and lost herself in contemplation of the fields and mountains below her; the sun behind the mountains was, to a Natalie not quite used yet to the triteness of miracle, a calendar gesture, the overdone and typical scene of a grown-up world; she had seen so many bad pictures of suns behind mountains that she allowed herself to find the sun itself ludicrous and unnecessary. But the mountains, relieved of the pressure of the sun, were dark and shadowy, and the fields, still lighted by the sun, were clear and green, and Natalie, lying with her cheek on her arm, felt herself running, lighter than anything she had ever known, running with great soft steps across the world. Her feet brushed the ground—she could feel it, she could feel it—her hair fell soundlessly behind, her long legs arched, and the breath came cold in her throat. The first to awaken, the first to come, misty, into the world, moving through an unpeopled country without a footstep, going up the mountains, touching the still-wet grass with her hands.

The mountains, full-bosomed and rich, extended themselves to her in a surge of emotion, turning silently as she came, receiving her, and Natalie, her mouth against the grass and her eyes tearful from looking into the sun, took the mountains to herself and whispered, "Sister, sister." "Sister, sister," she said, and the mountains stirred, and answered.

She saw her brother coming from the house and into the garden, and spent a brief moment of wonder at his presence; from his sudden great resemblance to herself, she thought that perhaps he did not know she was there and was coming to sit and look at the mountains, but he was looking for her, she knew then; he called, "Nat? Nat?"

"Here," she said, and saw him turn his head toward her, but the trees hid her and he came on, saying, "Where are you?"

When he found her and sat down beside her she saw with satisfaction that he had not been here before, because he took a minute to look out over the cliff before he said, "Mother said you were to come in and get dressed."

"You going swimming?" she asked him.

She could see him making up his mind to say something, and knew from the way his face took on a new expression that it was something he had long ago determined to say when he got an opportunity; it was never possible for her to tell whether his face was so familiar because it strongly resembled her own, or because she saw it three times a day across the table. "Listen," he said finally, and pulled irritably at the grass. "You *want* to go to this thing this afternoon?"

"I don't know," she said. "I don't mind."

"Because, listen," he said. Any kind of positive statement

was so much an invasion of his own privacy that he almost stammered, and turned red. "I'd *take* you swimming," he said.

There was nothing to say except "No," and yet it was impossible to say that. Natalie tried not to look at him, and yet his face was—so much like her own, she was sure—so unhappy at the thought of taking her swimming, that she stared at him and he turned and frowned. "Well?" he said. "You *want* to go or *don't* you?"

"Golly," Natalie said. She pulled at the grass in her turn. "No, I guess," she said. "Dad wants me to stay," she added hastily.

"Sure," he said, relieved. "Dad wants you to stay."

I wonder what he ever thinks about, Natalie thought. "Anyway," she said defensively, "these are very important people, some of them."

"What are *they* good for?" he demanded contemptuously. "Poetry?"

They were quiet for a minute while the sun removed its last light from them and a cold wind came up over the cliff from the fields below. Then Bud twisted himself to his feet and said, "Mother says for you to come get dressed," and started off back toward the house. "Better hurry," he called back over his shoulder. "They'll be here pretty soon."

"Well," Mr. Waite said genially. It was four o'clock and the casserole was in the oven, the Sunday liquor was set out in the pantry, the ice was freezing dutifully in the refrigerator, the long living room was in order, with ashtrays located at approximately the points at which Mr. Waite's friends were most apt to drop cigarettes, and chairs readied for the brief, inconclusive sittings of Mr. Waite's friends. The books they were likely to want to consult during discussion (*Ulysses*, C.S. Lewis, *The Function of the Orgasm*, the newest English homosexual novel, *Hot Discography*, an abridged *Golden Bough*, and an unabridged dictionary) were set in the small bookscase near the windows; Mr. Waite's own books—the one he had written and the ones he had articles in, as opposed to the ones he referred to—were hidden modestly, bound in green leather, upon the mantelpiece. "Well," Mr. Waite said, with the satisfaction of a country squire surveying his horses and his dogs and his shooting preserve, and he added, as though to his gamekeeper, "Looks fine, all of it."

"Everything *seems* to be ready," Mrs. Waite answered nervously. She had inherited, probably from that indefatigable hostess, her mother, the hostess's conviction that some vital factor has somehow been forgotten (perhaps because no one wanted company in the first place?), so that it would turn out suddenly that there were no cigarettes in the cigarette boxes, or that the magazines would all prove to be an issue old, or that the dust on the table *had* been overlooked after all, or that, suddenly at dinner, Mrs. Waite would have to turn her stricken face to her dumfounded husband as it occurred to them both simultaneously that the dinner wine had been forgotten and lay, unpurchased and unchilled, on the shelf at the store.

"Casserole, salad," Mrs. Waite said, flexing her fingers as though she were counting, or perhaps as though with remembered motions her fingers would recall all that they had done, and by neglected motions point out the forgotten fact, "coffee, pie. Rolls. Cigarettes, candy, pretzels. Please don't let them drop cigarettes on the carpet, it's bad enough as it is. Natalie, are you dressed?"

Natalie moved into the range of her mother's blinded eyes, and said, "I have on my blue dress."

"Good," said her mother. "Did you comb your hair?"

As though I could forget to comb my hair, Natalie thought happily. I am seventeen, after all, and a party is a party even if it *is* all grown-ups. And anyway I spend so much time looking into my mirror . . .

"Are *you* dressed?" Mrs. Waite said, in so many years she had not found a usable name for her husband.

"Of course," he said, and he might have added, A party is a party . . . He had chosen to dress himself in a fuzzy tweed jacket and he looked very literary indeed; no amount of poise could forsake him in this jacket. It was almost equivalent to a brace of pistols and a pair of jackboots; Mr. Waite was arrayed for his own interpretation of a street brawl.

The doorbell rang.

"Oh my God," said Mrs. Waite. "Casserole, rolls, coffee . . . will you get it or shall I?"

"I'll get it," said Mr. Waite, in a tone which implied very strongly that he did not believe that Mrs. Waite could find the door by herself. As he disappeared into the hall, Mrs. Waite said to Natalie, "I'll just look at the kitchen," and ran the other way.

Natalie stood in the doorway between the hall and the living room, thinking, This is a party and I'm here already and I must remember that my name is Natalie.

The first guests were a disappointment; they turned out to be an enormously fat person named Verna Hansen, and her brother Arthur; Mr. Waite had invited them, not believing they would come, in a spirit of neighborly conviviality, since their house was nearest the Waites', and their estate considerably larger. Partly because they were not proper guests—having been invited, as it were, on the wrong side of the blanket—and partly because he sincerely did not feel that any chair in the living room would hold Verna, Mr. Waite seated these guests on the lawn in wrought-iron chairs which were stronger than the living room chairs and substantially less expensive. He brought Natalie out to entertain them while he went off to fetch them drinks, and Natalie, introduced as, "My daughter and our assistant hostess," found herself, before she was really quite ready for a party, seated on the lawn in an iron chair, facing Verna. Arthur, with a brief and confusing remark about garden sprays, had wandered away, and Natalie, calling herself together, folded her hands and said brightly to Verna, "Isn't it a *lovely* time of day?"

Verna looked at her for a minute, glanced briefly at the doorway within which Mr. Waite had disappeared to find her a drink, and sighed. "Fine," she said shortly. "So you're Natalie?"

"Yes," said Natalie.

"Your father has mentioned you," said Verna, implying with

her tone many clandestine meetings with Mr. Waite, during which he very likely called upon his daughter's name in remorse. . . . "We shall be friends, little Natalie," she added. She looked fatter sitting down, but the wide lawn around her was becoming, and she wore it with dignity. Natalie, who with one part of her mind was reserving judgment on anyone who called her "little Natalie," was, with another part of her mind, vastly impressed by the extreme comfort and ease of Verna's manner; it seemed that all the effort of Verna's life had been spent and all the problems solved, so that Verna, having succeeded, had now to do nothing except sit fatly in the middle of other people's smooth lawns and call people, less fortunate, "little Natalie."

"I can help you get over the preliminaries," Verna said. She half-closed her eyes and thought. "I dislike all the beginnings of conversations where people ask one another as subtly as possible how old they are, and what their names are, and how they are feeling these days." She added all this suddenly, opening her eyes as though recalled from her preliminaries by the unexpected realization that little Natalie needed an explanation, being, as indeed she was, unused to Verna's ways. "I *like* people," Verna said, and she made it sound as though she ate them for dessert. "First of all I shall tell you everything I can think of about myself, and then you will tell me about yourself." She opened her eyes again, and smiled, and Natalie began feverishly searching her mind for trivial secret thoughts with which to pay for this condescension. "I am older than you are, little Natalie. I am perhaps fifteen years older—a great deal, counted in experience. I have known many people, known them well, known their hearts and their sins."

Irreverently, Natalie thought of saying, "That must have been very interesting," but refrained.

Verna sighed heavily. "My name used to be Edith," she confided abruptly.

Natalie blinked.

"Arthur wouldn't change *his* name," Verna said. "Little beast."

"I've often wanted to change my name," Natalie said untruthfully.

Verna shifted heavily, in a gesture which might have been leaning foward. "Do so, my dear," she said. "Do so, by all means, if you need to. You will be amazed at the difference a new name will make for you. Take Edith, for instance. Now, when I was Edith, I was coarse, and ugly, and thoughtless. I used to laugh very loudly. I used to accept people at their face value; when someone said to me, 'Edith, you ought to take more of an interest in yourself,' I was ready to believe them. It sounds incredible to *you*, doesn't it? But that was Edith, not Verna."

"Why didn't Arthur want to change his name?"

Verna shrugged violently. "Little beast," she said. "He likes being the same as he always was. *Now* he doesn't dare, but he thinks the same all right." She laughed softly, what was clearly her Verna laugh. "Little Natalie, never rest until you have uncovered your essential self. Remember that. Somewhere, deep inside you, hidden by all sorts of fears and worries and petty little thoughts, is a clean pure being made of radiant colors."

This was so much like the things that Natalie sometimes suspected about herself that she turned to Verna, swept by a rush of warm feeling, and said incoherently, "Verna, how do you ever know?"

Verna smiled sadly. "I know, little one," she said. Her eyes fixed somewhere over Natalie's head, she said softly, *"From too much love of living. From hope and fear set free, We thank with brief thanksgiving . . ."*

"There you are," said Mr. Waite heartily. He handed Verna her drink, and Verna was unexpectedly quiet as she drank.

"My dear," said Mr. Waite to Natalie, "I didn't bring you a drink."

Natalie was surprised. Although her father had made a great point of her being allowed to drink and smoke when she was sixteen, in the year since he had never before offered her a drink. She had learned to smoke, with some amused assistance from her mother, who gave her a cigarette case, but the furtive

terrors hidden in alcohol were as yet only vaguely glimpsed by
Natalie; she thought now with some shame of a secret passage
in her most secret diary (It began: "I hardly think that the taking of cocktails and such is a vice which I shall ever indulge in
more than very mildly, since it seems to me that any woman
interested in an artistic career dulls the fine, keen edge of her
understanding by an indulgence in any stimulant other than her
work." This diary was written for ultimate publication, but
Natalie of course intended to go over it very carefully first.),
and said shyly to her father, "I'd like to try, sometime."

"Help yourself," he said genially.

"Wine is a splendid thing," said Verna encouragingly. "Little Natalie and I," she said to Mr. Waite, "were discussing our
souls when you came."

"Indeed?" said Mr. Waite. He turned and looked at his
daughter. "Natalie?" he said.

"This is a child of great talent," Verna said, putting her hand
on his arm to attract his attention. "This is a chosen child." She
handed him her empty glass and said, "I am going to think a
great deal of this little Natalie."

"Do you suppose she'll *ever* go?" Mrs. Waite whispered to
Natalie; they were standing together in the doorway. Mr. Waite
and Verna were conversing politely on the lawn, and far away,
at the end of the garden, they could see Arthur, lost in earnest
contemplation of what seemed at this distance to be a dande-
lion. "I really think she's crazy," Mrs. Waite said.

Natalie was pretending to be a young girl standing in the
doorway of her own house next to her mother. If she tried to
look as much as possible as though she were seventeen, innocent, protected by her parents, beloved, sheltered here in this
house, then perhaps . . .

There was a slight movement in the hall behind her; Natalie,
her eyes fixed on Arthur, stood, seemingly unconcerned.

"She'll keep your father out there all afternoon," Mrs. Waite
whispered urgently. "I *know*."

"Really," Natalie was saying silently, "I don't know what
you mean."

"Do you pretend," the detective said, "that you are actually the daughter of these people? That they will acknowledge you?"

"Sir," Natalie said silently, "this is my mother. That is my father out there."

"And if I ask them?" the detective demanded. "You must be very foolish to suppose that you can rely upon the generosity of strangers."

"The next people who come," Mrs. Waite said, "I'll ask them inside. Then maybe once she's standing up she'll think of going home."

"And your name?" said the detective.

"My name is—" Natalie hesitated in her silent talk. She was about to change her name, was she not? But her hesitation had told against her; the detective was laughing.

"Yes?" he prompted sardonically. "Your name is?"

Mr. Waite rose from his chair on the lawn, and, taking Verna's empty class, came to the doorway where Mrs. Waite and Natalie were standing.

"Natalie," he said, his back to Verna, and grinned. "I hardly know you from her description."

"You'll have to get them *out* of here," Mrs. Waite whispered.

Mr. Waite had already donned his company manners which meant that his usual attitude toward his wife was subdued to a sort of tolerant dismay. "Why?" he asked. "Isn't there plenty of liquor?"

Mrs. Waite gestured helplessly; more people were arriving and she had planned to entertain them indoors; here was Mr. Waite, already too expansive to be reliable, calmly receiving and probably planning to seat these people out on the lawn, which had not been cleaned and which held only four iron chairs and would thus require more brought from the dining room, leaving less for company when they *did* move indoors, because unless you asked company to carry their *own* chairs, then the chairs would be left outside, and so it would rain, and the dining room chairs ... not to mention company sitting probably on the floor. "Oh, *please*," said Mrs. Waite madly.

"Keep calm," Mr. Waite said. "You'd be surprised how easy it is for people to have a good time."

"Easy for *you*, maybe," said Mrs. Waite, but her husband did not hear her; he had gone, hand outstretched, to receive his new guests.

At one point Natalie counted the people on the lawn and found that there were fourteen. She knew that many more than that had been invited, so it seemed wise to go and help her mother now, rather than wait until later when there might be someone she wanted to talk to.

In the kitchen Mrs. Waite, her almost-finished cocktail sitting on the sinkboard, was nervously dabbing cream cheese on crackers.

"They've almost finished *every*thing," she said, without turning around as Natalie entered. "*Why* don't I ever believe your father when he says he's invited all those other people?"

Natalie took the knife out of her mother's hand and began spreading cream cheese. "They're all having a wonderful time," she said. "Don't worry."

Mrs. Waite took up her drink, finished it in one swallow, and went over to the bottles on the shelf waiting to be produced later. She opened one with a twist of the top and poured whisky into her glass. "I *never* know what to do," she said. "No matter *how* much I get ready, there are always too many of your father's friends, and not enough food in the world to feed them all."

Natalie put one more cracker on the plate, considered piling more crackers on top, and decided it would look too lavish. "I'll just go on in and pass these," she said. "You stay out here quietly."

She had not yet had anything to drink, although it was not possible to pass Verna without being offered a "teentsy sip" of Verna's cocktail. Natalie had decided privately that later on, when the first excitement of the party wore off, she would try one delightful—alas, not forbidden—taste of spiritous liquor, although her allegiance to her art was still dominant. Therefore, when she went onto the lawn with the plate of crackers

and cheese, she tripped perfectly legitimately over the feet of
the man in the big chair, although she fortunately saved the
crackers and cheese. "My fault, madam," said the man in the
big chair.

Natalie, preoccupied with the balance of the plate, only
nodded.

"Daughter mine," said her father, who came to help her,
"has anyone yet corrupted you?"

Natalie smiled pleasantly, knowing from experience that it
was unwise to answer her father at one of his own parties,
since not even his family were at that time safe from practiced
witticisms, and she offered the plate of crackers to the man in
the big chair, saying, "You almost had this in your lap."

Her father came up behind her and said over her shoulder to
the man in the big chair, "*This* one is my daughter."

"A fine figure of a girl," said the man in the big chair. He took
a cracker in each hand, and Natalie went on carefully around
the group, presenting the plate to one person after another,
answering their questions and watching their feet.

"Natalie, when do you go to college?"

"Aren't you *growing*, though; you make me feel *ancient*."

"Aren't you looking forward to education, after all these
years with your father?"

When she got to her father Natalie put the plate under his
hand, and he looked up at her and smiled. A dark, pretty girl sat
next to him, a girl whom Natalie did not recognize. Her father
said to the girl, "This is my little daughter, my Natalie. Don't
you think she'll grow up to be a beauty?" He and the pretty girl
both laughed, and Mr. Waite, laughing, refused a cracker from
the plate.

Later, when Natalie had passed farther around the room,
she heard her father's voice rising above the rest.

"—The sacredness of human droppings," Mr. Waite was
saying. "Let me illustrate from my personal life. When Natalie
was a baby and used to play on the lawn, her mother ignored
the droppings of the dog and cat—"

"Only careful not to step in them," said the pretty girl next
to Mr. Waite.

"Only careful not to step in them," Mr. Waite agreed. "But when small Natalie fouled the grass, her mother carefully and laboriously cleaned it up with a paper towel—"

"It isn't any single thing I mind so much." Mrs. Waite sat up and took hold of Natalie's hands, and looked earnestly into her eyes; it seemed, somehow, as though this at last were really true, and now, with all the words she knew, Mrs. Waite could not find unused ones, or authentic ones, or words not debased by her lifetime of whimsy and lies, to tell Natalie that after all, this at last was really true. "It isn't any *single* thing," Mrs. Waite repeated earnestly, the tears on her cheeks. "It's just that—well, look, Natalie. This is the only life I've *got*—you understand? I mean, this is *all*. And look what's happening to me. I spend most of my time just thinking about how nice things used to be and wondering if they'll ever be nice again. If I should go on and on and die someday and nothing was ever nice again—wouldn't that be a fine thing? Wouldn't I have been cheated, don't you think? I get to feeling like that and then I think I'll *make* things be nice, and *make* him behave, and just *make* everything all happy and exciting again the way it used to be—but I'm too tired."

She lay back on the bed again, the tears still on her cheeks. When she had been eager to make Natalie understand the truth of what she was saying, she had not cried, but now, knowing from Natalie's timid smile and soothing pats that of course Natalie did not understand, she began to cry helplessly again. "I keep telling you," she said finally, sadly, "I keep *telling* you to watch out who you marry. Don't *ever* go near a man like your father."

"Would you like to go outside and walk in the garden for a while?" Natalie asked, hardly knowing what she suggested. "We could go out the back door."

"It all starts so nice," Mrs. Waite said, twisting her face into a horrible look of disgust. "You think it's going to be so easy. You think it's going to be good. It starts like everything you've ever wanted, you think it's so easy, everything looks so simple and good, and you know that all of a sudden you've found out what no one ever had sense enough to know before—that this is good and if you manage right you can do whatever you want to. You keep thinking that what you've got hold of is power, just because you feel right in yourself, and everybody always thinks that when they feel right in themselves then they can start right off fixing the world. I mean, when I used to listen to him talking about what kind of people we were, then I used to *believe* him."

"Mother . . ." said Natalie.

"First they tell you lies," said Mrs. Waite, "and they make you believe them. Then they give you a little of what they promised, just a little, enough to keep you thinking you've got your hands on it. Then you find out that you're tricked, just like everyone else, just like *everyone,* and instead of being different and powerful and giving the orders, you've been tricked just like everyone else and then you begin to know what happens to everyone and how they all get tricked. Everyone only knows one 'I,' and that's the 'I' they call themselves, and there's no one else can be 'I' to anyone except that one person, and they're all stuck with themselves and once they find out they've been tricked, then they've been tricked and maybe the worst of it is that it isn't like anything else; you can't just say, 'I've been tricked and I'll make the best of it,' because you never believe it because they let you see just enough about the next time to keep you hoping that maybe you're a little bit smarter and a little bit . . ."

"Mother," Natalie said. "Mother, please stop. You're not making sense."

"I *am* making sense," Mrs. Waite said. "No one ever made sense before."

"Mother, it's all right," Natalie said. "You had a little bit too much to drink and nothing to eat. I could bring you up some coffee."

"My own daughter," said Mrs. Waite bitterly. "I can't even tell my own daughter. If I were dead you'd listen to me."

"Now how could—" Natalie began and then saw that it was useless. "Shall I bring you some coffee?" she asked. "It won't take a minute, it's all hot downstairs." Downstairs, she thought, the party going on without me, people laughing and making noise while I sit up here in the silence and this thin bad voice going on.

"Listen," said Mrs. Waite, and, suddenly, she rose and leaned on her elbow and looked sternly at Natalie. "You listen to me," she said. "You're my own daughter and the only person in the world I have any right to tell these things to. In another week— in another hour—it might be too late for me even to try telling you. Now you *listen*.

"All these years your father has been trying to get rid of me. Not rid of *me*—he doesn't care if I hang around the house, cooking and saying, 'Yes, sir,' when he opens his fat mouth. All he wants is no one to think they can be the same as he is, or equal to him, or something. And you watch out—the minute you start getting too big, he'll be after you, too."

"I think you ought to go outside for a while," Natalie said nervously.

"With *me*," her mother continued, "it was because I didn't have anyone. He picks out the one way he can frighten you most, you see, and I didn't have anyone at all, because my family didn't understand me any more after I went off with your father, and I used to lie awake wanting my mother and she wouldn't have me because I was different by then. And he'll find the way he can frighten you, too, but it won't be because you don't have anyone because *your* mother won't turn you down. She *won't*, Natalie," Mrs. Waite said, beggingly, pulling at Natalie's sleeve, "she won't, she won't ever. I know what it's like Natalie, and I'll always protect you from them, the bad ones. Don't you ever worry, little Natalie, your mother will always help you."

An agonizing embarrassment kept Natalie from looking away. She looked at her mother and her mother looked at Natalie; it was at this point in her mother's drunkenness that Natalie always longed to say something sympathetic, and could never find the right, understanding words. Then suddenly Mr. Waite called from the foot of the stairs. "Natalie. Coming down?"

Mrs. Waite began to cry, and buried her head in the pillow. "Poor little girl," she said. "No mother."

A sort of intoxication possessed Natalie; this could surely not be the intoxication, she thought breathlessly, born of one weak cocktail sipped timidly in the kitchen. It was instead, and she was almost sure of this, the preliminary faint stirrings of something about to happen. The idea once born, she knew it was true; something incredible was going to happen, now, right now, this afternoon, today; this was going to be a day she would remember and look back upon, thinking, That wonderful day . . . the day when *that* happened.

"Let us go over the sequence of events once more," the detective said tiredly. He had leaned back and unbuttoned his jacket, and Natalie, who saw him more clearly than she saw the people on the lawn, thought that no matter how tired he was, he would not stop until he had from her what he wanted. "Let us start from the very beginning," the detective said.

"I've told you all I know," Natalie said silently. She could see her father across the lawn, leaning forward and smiling as he talked, his arm carelessly around the waist of the pretty, dark girl. Somebody began to sing; at occasional points in the song many people stopped talking and joined in with the singer, even Mr. Waite and the pretty girl, who laughed when they sang.

"One is one and all alone and evermore will be so," everyone sang.

"I'll sing you two-O," the single voice sang, clearly through the noise.

All around the lawn people were talking, raising their voices to override what someone else was saying, looking secretly at one another, frowning openly at one another, talking, laughing, talking. As though she had just come onto the lawn, Natalie heard suddenly the swell of sound that so surely meant "party." It rose and moved and eddied, individual voices rising for a second, laughter riding high over the rest, the thin sound of glasses rattling, so fine that it could be heard straight through the heavier noises. It was shocking, loud, and Natalie stepped back, and found herself almost stepping again on the man who had tripped her when she came in earlier with the plate of crackers.

"Bound we're going to kill each other today," the man said, smiling. He was alone now, and Natalie spared a thought for the odd recognition of the fact that his voice came clearly to her through the noise; in spite of the loudness of the party, which she could still hear, she knew exactly what the man was saying as though they had been alone, or, perhaps, as though his voice were in her mind like the detective's.

Two, two, lily-white boys, clothed all in green-O,
One is one and all alone and evermore will be so.

"Sit down," the man said pleasantly. "Tired?" he asked her as she sat in the empty chair next to him, and Natalie nodded.

"Now let me see," the detective was saying, and she could not quiet him now; his voice came to her as clearly as that of the man in the chair. "This morning you were in the garden, were you not? At about what time was that?"

"I don't remember," Natalie said. "Please leave me alone now; I want to think."

"Think?" said the detective. "Think? Suppose you think about the fact that you are very close to being in serious trouble?"

"Are you having a good time?" Natalie said inadequately to the man in the chair. All the polite things she had heard so many people say this afternoon fled her mind, and she could only smile vacantly at him and say something foolish like, "Are you having a good time?"

"Very nice," said the man soberly. "Are you?"

"Very nice," Natalie said. *"One is one and all alone,"* everybody sang, *"and evermore will be so."*

The man looked at her curiously and Natalie was provoked. Here he was, this man, in her father's house—in her *own* house—and he was staring at her and very likely laughing. Worse, he was old, she could see now, much older than she had thought before. There were fine disagreeable little lines around his eyes and mouth, and his hands were thin and bony, and even shook a little. Natalie formulated a thought which she intended to use forever after: "I like a man with nice hands," she told herself. "Nice hands are a particular beauty in a man." She tried to remember what her father's hands were like, and could only remember his doing things with them—lifting a fork, holding a cigar. She glanced quickly across the lawn and found that she could not see her father's hands—one was in his pocket reaching for a pencil, the other lost around the waist of the pretty girl.

"—And so I came," the man was saying. He looked at her as though he expected some appreciation of the point of the story he had been telling her, and, Natalie, still provoked with him, smiled politely. "I'm glad you did," she said, as her mother would have.

"You realize," said the detective weightily, "that you were seen at almost every moment?"

The man in the big chair offered Natalie a cigarette and she took it, hoping earnestly that she would not fumble it, would not blow out the match he was holding for her, would, at all costs, not look as though she had not often smoked publicly before. "Your father tells me," he said, holding the match, "that you're quite the little writer." As though he might have been saying, "a girl scout patrol leader," or, "top in your grade in algebra," and obviously meaning to make her sound less like her mother and more like a frightened girl not yet in college.

Natalie wanted to hurt him back, so she said, quite with the air of a silly girl not yet in college, "I suppose you probably want to write too?" She knew she had done right because he blinked, and she felt a new wild excited joy in the thought that here was Natalie, enough a woman of the world to keep her head during a conversation, to perceive and follow and employ the innuendoes of a man who had probably talked to many people, most of them women, and heard many answers and who could very likely read almost any meaning. Perhaps someday, Natalie thought quickly, chiding herself, I'll learn to talk for a longer time and not stop to think about it in the middle.

"—novel?" the man said.

This was hopeless; they were too far into their conversation for Natalie to say anything at all without losing all the ground she had gained; she would betray herself utterly if she asked him what he had said; she could hardly pretend she didn't care, or walk off, or turn her back; she could certainly not go back now and ask him if he were having a nice time. "I didn't hear you," she said suddenly, frightening herself almost to tears. "I was thinking about myself instead of listening."

> Four for the gospel-makers;
> Three, three, rivals,
> Two, two, lily-white boys, clothed all in green-O,
> One is one and all alone and evermore will be so.

"Thinking what about yourself?" the man asked.

Said the detective, leaning foward, "Have you given any thought to the extreme danger of your position? What about the knife?"

"About how wonderful I am," Natalie said. She smiled. Now I can get up and walk away, she thought, the faster the better. She started to get up, but the man got up first, and took hold of her arm.

"About how wonderful she is," he said as though to himself. "Thinking about how wonderful she is."

A little chill went down Natalie's back at his holding her arm, at the strange unfamiliar touch of someone else. Leading her by the arm, he moved to the tray where full glasses stood, took one and handed it to Natalie, and took another for himself.

> Five for the cymbals at your door,
> Four for the gospel-makers,

people shouted at them as they moved.

"Come along," the man told Natalie. "This I intend to hear more about."

"And the blood?" the detective said fiercely. "What about the blood, Miss Waite? *How* do you account for the blood?"

"One is one and all alone and evermore will be so."

"You will not escape this," the detective said. He dropped his voice and said, so quietly that she barely heard him, *"This* you will not escape."

The strange man led Natalie away from the crowd on the lawn and across the grass; after a minute the people and their voices (*"Six are the six proud walkers . . ."*) were removed into a background noise, distantly behind them in the night-filled garden. They moved slowly; Natalie was afraid to speak, not trusting her voice in the new silence, perhaps she was still turned to the noise behind and when she spoke it would be in a scream. In those few quick minutes the man walking next to her had changed so rapidly from one shadow, on the lighted lawn, to another shadow, in the dark garden, and her final statement to him had been so conclusive, that past "Are you having a good time?"—which now seemed even less appropriate than before—there was nothing to say.

He spoke, at last. Without the support of other noise, his voice was weak, and perhaps even older than it had sounded before.

"Now then," he said. "Tell me what she thinks is so wonderful about herself."

How far wrong, Natalie thought, can one person be about another? Perhaps in that little time I have grown in his mind and he is now talking to some Natalie he thought he had hold of by the arm. She felt the grass under her feet, the soft brush of bushes against her hair, and his fingers on her arm. It was no longer afternoon; the time had slipped away from under Natalie and while she had been behaving in her mind, under the lights, as though it were five o'clock, she found now in the darkness that it was much, much later, long past dinnertime, long past any daylight. She found that she was carefully carrying a glass in her hand, and she brought it up and sipped at it, standing still to do so.

"Tell me," he said insistently.

"I can't answer that," Natalie said.

"Do you realize," he said, amused, "that you made a perfectly outrageous statement? You *can't* refuse an explanation."

I wonder what I said, Natalie thought; she tried to remember and found that just as her feet were wandering over the grass, so her mind was wandering over the hundreds of words she had heard and spoken that day; it was not possible, she thought, annoyed, to sort out any one statement from that confusion and answer it; he was asking too much. "Where are we?" she asked.

"Near some trees," he said.

They had come, then, to the trees where Natalie had once encountered knights in armor; she could see them ahead, growing together silently. There were almost enough of them to be called a forest. Natalie could still, before reaching the trees, see the path under her feet; the darkness was then not yet absolute, but the light came by some unknown means, since there was no moon and the lights from the house could not reach this far; Natalie thought briefly that the light came from her own feet.

"I used to play in here when I was a child," she said.

Then they were into the little forest, and the trees were really dark and silent, and Natalie thought quickly, The danger is here, in *here*, just as they stepped inside and were lost in the darkness.

What have I done? she wondered, walking silently among the trees, aware of their great terrifying silence, so much more expectant by night, and their great unbent heads, and the darkness they pulled about her with silent patient hands.

When the man beside her spoke she was relieved: there was another human being, then, caught in this silence and wandering among the watchful trees, another mortal.

"Let's sit down here," he said, and without speaking Natalie sat beside him on a fallen trunk. Looking up as she did immediately, she saw immeasurable space, traveling past the locked hands of the trees, past the large nodding implacable heads, up and into the silence of the sky, where the stars remained, indifferent.

"Tell me what you thought was so wonderful about your-self," the man said; his voice was muted.

Oh my dear God sweet Christ, Natalie thought, so sickened she nearly said it aloud, is he going to *touch* me?

Natalie awoke the next morning to bright sun and clear air, to the gentle movement of her bedroom curtains, to the patterned dancing of the light on the floor; she lay quietly, appreciating the morning in the clear uncomplicated moment vouchsafed occasionally before consciousness returned. Then, with the darkening of the sunlight, the sudden coldness of the day, she was awake and, before perceiving clearly why, she buried her head in the pillow and said, half-aloud, "No, please no."

"I will not think about it, it doesn't matter," she told herself, and her mind repeated idiotically, It doesn't matter, it doesn't matter, it doesn't matter, it doesn't matter, until, desperately, she said aloud, "I don't remember, nothing happened, nothing that I remember happened."

Slowly she knew she was sick; her head ached, she was dizzy, she loathed her hands as they came toward her face to cover her eyes. "Nothing happened," she chanted, "nothing happened, nothing happened, nothing happened, nothing happened."

"Nothing happened," she said, looking at the window, at the dear lost day. "I don't remember."

"I will not think about it," she said to her clothes, lying on the chair, and she remembered as she saw them how she had torn them off wildly when she went to bed, thinking, I'll fix them in the morning, and a button had fallen from her dress and she had watched it roll under the bed, and thought, I'll get it in the morning, and I'll face it all in the morning, and, in the morning it will be gone.

If she got out of bed it would be true; if she stayed in bed she might just possibly be really sick, perhaps delirious. Perhaps dead. "I will not think about it," she said, and her mind went on endlessly, Will not think about it, will not think about it, will not think about it.

Someday, she thought, it will be gone. Someday I'll be sixty years old, sixty-seven, eighty, and, remembering, will perhaps recall that something of this sort happened once (where? when? who?) and will perhaps smile nostalgically thinking, What a sad silly girl I was, to be sure.

How I worried, she would think—would it have happened again by then? "I won't think about it," she said. "Won't think about it, won't think about it."

Get up, she thought, so that someday, as quickly as possible, with infinite speed, somehow, she might get to be sixty-nine, eighty-four, forgetting, smiling sadly, thinking, What a girl I was, what a girl . . . I remember one time; did it happen to me or did I read it somewhere? Could it have happened like that? Or is it something one only finds in books? I have forgotten, she would say, an old lady of ninety, turning over her memories, which would be—please God—faded, and mellowed, by time. "Oh, please," she said, sitting on the edge of her bed, "oh, please, please."

The most horrible moment of that morning, and of that day—horrible in itself by being, horrible with its sidelong (suspicious? knowing? perceiving?) looks from her mother and father, heavy amusement from her brother, horrible with remembered words and impossible remembered acts, horrible with its sunlight and its cold disgusting hours—the most horrible moment of that morning or any morning in her life, was when she first looked at herself in the mirror, at her bruised face and her pitiful, erring body.

She came down to breakfast dressed unfamiliarly in her old clothes; so much of her life had taken place in the blue dress she wore the day before that her old sweater and skirt seemed strange, the costume for some extraordinary Natalie part, which had lain for weeks in a stockroom, waiting for the chosen actress to put them on.

Perhaps a gladiator, entering the arena, might notice with some dull interest the sand underfoot, carelessly raked and still showing little hills and scuff marks which registered the brief passage of previous victims; Natalie, approaching her own breakfast table, observed absently that her napkin, folded by herself at breakfast the day before, was pulled carelessly

through the ring. Her mother's face, Natalie saw, was tired
and she looked at none of them; her father was red-eyed and
frowning. All of us, Natalie thought, and turned her eyes to
the table.

"Good morning, everyone," she said without cheer.

"Morning," said her mother wearily.

"Natalie," said her father without enthusiasm.

"Hi," said her brother; his voice was outrageously fresh,
and Natalie thought briefly, No one ever knows what *he's* been
doing.

We are a graceless family, she thought again, cringing away
from her own worn mind. "No egg, thank you," she said civilly to her mother, avoiding in time a look at the plate of fried
eggs. "Thanks," she said to her brother, who passed her the
toast without displaying any conspicuous interest in whether
or not she starved.

Her family's dullness lessened Natalie's own concern, and
she began to lose a little of the feeling that her face showed, as
the map of a country passed through by only one traveler and
charted with a single destructive route, any of the fears of this
morning, although when she relaxed even slightly the "Please,
please, please," still echoed maddeningly through her head.

"What would she do if she knew what I know?" Natalie asked
herself, staring at her mother from under her lashes; "What
would she know if she did what I did?" And from far within her
head came the echo, "please, please, please." Mrs. Waite, who
had hoped for so long to persuade Natalie of her womanhood
with words, having no better weapon at her disposal, sighed
deeply, and the silence at the breakfast table, which had been a
family silence before, became a family pause, a preparation for
speech. Who is going to speak? Natalie wondered; not me, certainly. She knew, incredibly, that if she spoke she would tell them
what had happened; not because she so much desired to tell, that
she wanted to tell even them, but because this was not a personal
manifestation, but had changed them all in changing the world,
in the sense that they only existed in Natalie's imagination anyway, so that the revolution in the world had altered their faces
and made their hearts smaller.

I wish I were dead, Natalie thought concretely.

Mr. Waite leaned back, so that the feeble sunlight, which had endured for a very long time, touched his hair impersonally. "Your God," he remarked bitterly to his wife, "has seen fit to give us a black and rotten day."

Anything which begins new and fresh will finally become old and silly. The educational institution is certainly no exception to this, although training the young is by implication an art for old people exclusively, and novelty in education is allied to mutiny. Moreover, the mere process of learning is allied to mutiny. Moreover, the mere process of learning is so excruciating and so bewildering that no conceivable phraseology or combination of philosophies can make it practical as a method of marking time during what might be called the formative years. The college to which Arnold Waite, after much discussion, had decided to send his only daughter was one of those intensely distressing organizations which had been formed on precisely the same lofty and advanced principles as hoarier seats of learning, but which applied them with slight differences in detail; education, the youthful founders of the college had told the world blandly, was more a matter of attitude than of learning. Learning, they had remarked in addition, was strictly a process of accustoming oneself to live maturely in a world of adults. Adults, they pointed out with professorial cynicism, were tough things to come upon suddenly. As a result, they concluded—and this may be found still in their catalogues, although much of the original thesis has been modified and watered down by their trustees—going to college must be, for girls and boys, something of a drastic experience.

Obviously, in any college which begins with the notion of education as experience, a certain amount of confusion must be allowed for before anything can be done about what is going to be taught. Should the student be free, for instance?

Should the teacher be free? Or should the concept of freedom be abandoned as an educational ideal and the concept of utility be substituted? Ought the students be allowed sentimental sciences like Greek? Or geometry? Should there be a marriage course? What, precisely, should be the attitude taken by the college with regard to a resident psychoanalyst?

The college had been in existence for perhaps fifteen years. Its founders had thought they were cutting their problems in half, originally, by eliminating men from the student body and women from the faculty. They had told one another honestly over beer in the clever apartments where the idea of the college had first seen light that they all of them believed in informality, that more information was derived from one casual conversation than from a dozen lectures, that education was after all a thing of give and take and should be a pleasure as well as a duty. Words like "mature" and "sustained" and "life" and "realistic" and "vision" and "humanities" were used lavishly. It was decided to construct the college buildings entirely of shingle and "the original beams"; it was supposed that modern dance and the free use of slang in the classrooms might constitute an aura of rich general culture. It was decided that anyone who wanted to study anything should be accommodated, although gym was not encouraged, and it was regarded as extremely fortunate that no one spoke up for microbiology before the fifth year of the college's life. It was ardently hoped that moderately odd students—such as perhaps even Negroes, or real Navajo Indians—might desire to enroll. It was unanimously voted that students should be allowed to drink, stay out all night, gamble, and paint from nude female models, without any kind of restraint; this, it was clear, would prepare them for the adult world. Any student was to be allowed to make any suggestion. The faculty members were to be drawn almost entirely from a group which would find the inadequate salary larger than anything they had ever earned; the first legitimately appointed Literature professor was a young man whose series of articles in a political journal had aroused much comment, since they were concerned with the illiberal overtones of a revival of Aristophanes. The music faculty were, to a man, intensely interested in the various usefulnesses of the percussion instruments, and without exception composed drum quartets to accompany the college dancers. A great deal was said about old English ballads, and one entire course with a large enrollment spent a semester studying "Frankie and Johnny." It was not believed among the science people that information came before experiment, except in the most extreme cases; "Theory is nothing, experience all," was a phrase used most effectively in the college prospectus. The people in the town near the college felt strongly that the college community was Communistic, and could not understand, when they thought about it, why so many rich people sent their daughters there.

Unfortunately, this state of mind, happy as it might be for the future adults of the world, did not in the last analysis profit the college. It was found that certain compromises with conservatism were desirable. Although the college catalogue continued to lean heavily on "expression" and "creative activity," the practice of both became more restrained, and some required courses were found necessary. Instead, for instance, of being allowed to dance as they pleased, students were now required to dance in patterns. Students who formerly waited on table for the joy of common effort were now paid small wages for their work. Instead of being allowed to gamble and drink freely, they were permitted to do neither on campus without the condoning presence of a faculty member or wife, the young man who resented Aristophanes having been dismissed after two years. The students indeed might stay out all night if their rigid schedules permitted, but only if an accurate address were left with the college officials. It had been found dreadfully necessary to install a sort of house resident in each living center; this person was called a "tenant," inhabited a faculty apartment, and was expected to exert a semi-official influence over the girls in the house and to invite them in to tea occasionally. These faculty apartments were much sought after, because they were inexpensive compared with what the students in the houses paid for their rooms, and because they were a more comfortable place for single faculty than the living centers devoted to faculty or the unusually perishable faculty houses.

Thus the college was, in brief, a place modern, authentic, progressive, realistic, honest, and humane, with decent concessions to the fact that it was supposed to be, and had to be, a strictly budget-balanced proposition, a factory in which the intake must necessarily match the outgo. It had a clean-shaven president who played golf and who made speeches to Women's Clubs in a mildly humorous vein, a board of trustees who came regularly to sherry parties and tours of inspection, a faculty with more-or-less accurate caps and gowns to wear at Commencement, and a set of alumnae ranging from the bold-eyed members of the first graduating class, who were almost without exception divorced and haggard women of the world, to the well-trained members of the most recent graduating classes, who came back comfortably to reunions with their small children.

It might also be noted that the "original beams" having been found to need constant repair, plastic brick had been substituted wherever possible.

It was, for Natalie, precisely a new start. The room was almost square, perhaps a little longer than it was wide, with only one window that filled almost the entire far wall. So far, completely blank and empty, it was expectant, almost curious, and Natalie, standing timidly just inside the door, in the wall opposite the window, looked at the bare walls and floor with joy; it was, precisely, a new start.

The walls and ceiling had been painted a dull tan, in the proper institutional bad taste, so uninspired as to be almost colorless, and the dark-brown woodwork and the smallness of the room made it seem cell-like and dismal. The uncurtained window showed the rain clouds; because the room was on the third floor it was lighter than many, but still Natalie had to turn on the light, a bare bulb in the ceiling which lighted with a string, in order to admire most fully the clear spatial beauties of her room. These were walls to be adorned with her pictures, or whatever else she chose to put on them (a fine of twenty-five cents for every nail hole, of course; graduation from the college not allowed until every blemish on the walls of the room, including marks left by scotch tape, had been paid for), the floor was readied for the movements of her feet, presenting itself as exactly right-angled at the corners and in respectful anticipation of anything Natalie might be inclined to set upon it (excepting, of course, scratches, which must be eradicated at the comptroller's office by the payment of a small fine) and the ceiling, bleak and neat in the unshaded light from the bulb, stood at attention over Natalie's head, setting her in a sort of package, compact and square and air- and water-proof, a precise, unadulterated, fresh start for Natalie, a new clean box to live in.

They—the unidentified, fearsome, unsleeping *they* of the institution—had furnished it, of course. They, along with their nightmare watchfulness, and their frantic concern over marring, possessed an unerring sense of the minimum in form and design, in material and workmanship, in color and quality, which a girl, paying her tuition and her room and board as expected, could endure in silence. The bed was narrow and its mattress thin enough for the sleep of exhaustion, never thick enough for the restless pre-exam sleep of worry. The sheets and pillowcases were piled neatly on the foot of the bed. Natalie had her own blankets in her trunk; her mother had chosen dark rose as most practical, and had indulged Natalie in a bright bedspread and matching curtains for this room.

For the first time, standing in this doorway of this precise room on the day she first saw the college, Natalie knew a certain pride of ownership. This was, after all, the only room she had ever known where she would be, privately, working out her own salvation. Briefly, she thought of long nights alone in this room (no one to notice her light, no one to tap on her door and ask was she all right, dear) and long afternoons spent at the narrow desk in the corner, writing whatever she pleased and perhaps making only silly pictures on paper if she chose. If she liked, she might lock her door. If she pleased, she could entertain here; if it suited her pleasure, she could shut the windows, open the windows, move the bed, upset the chairs, go in the closet and hide. A purely mechanical love possessed her; the number on the door—it was 27; a good number, owning a seven for luck and a two for work, and adding, triumphantly, to nine—belonged only to her; she might tell people, "Room 27," and know that her own dear possessions were surely inside. Tomorrow morning, she thought, and leaned back happily against the door, she would wake up in this room.

For the whole first afternoon that she was alone at college Natalie asked herself constantly, Is this meaningful? Is this important? Is this part of what I am to go home knowing?

They sat around the living room of the house, the girls who were to live in it, eying one another, each one wondering, perhaps which of the others was to be her particular friend, sought out hereafter at such meetings, joined in the terrible sacred friendship of these years. Each one wondering, perhaps, who it was just and right to be afraid of in the room: who, for instance, was to be the belle of the house, superior and embarrassing with her greater knowledge, her secrets? The ones who had been senior queens in high school stood out, the one or two who had been high school class historians were clearly marked, as were the students, the learners of facts, the ascetic amateur writers with their poems safely locked away upstairs; the hangers-on were there, eying the beauty queens, estimating clearly which one it were best to appropriate immediately. The poor ones, with their obvious best clothes, the smart ones, with their obvious right clothes, the girls who would teach the others to dance, the girls who would whisper inaccurate facts of life, the girls who would fail all their courses and go home ingloriously (saying goodbye bravely, but crying), the girls who would fail all their courses and join the best cliques, the girls who would fall in love with their professors, either desperately and secretly, or openly and disgracefully, the girls whose hearts would break and the girls whose spirits would break—a group of girls from whatever kind of homes, with whatever agonized mothers wondering, tonight, at home—herded uneasily together into one room to await the preliminary steps of an education.

They sat, murmuring, in the living room of the house they were going to live in, which was to replace whatever houses they had left that morning or the day before or the week before, the old houses still so clear in their minds and so much home, to be so soon replaced by this one, with its careful undistinguished furnishings, designed to be neither better than the worst homes left behind, nor worse than the best; the living room where the perfect college girl could entertain, circumspectly, her immaculate date. It was designed to form a reasonable and not too indicative background for any of the girls who lived in it (who would, of course, never have lived in it if they had not been that most clearly indicated of all types, the college girl), and thoughtfully chosen to harmonize with the best college fashions being shown in the smartest middle-price department stores (in all cities; ask for the College Shoppe or the Sub-Deb Salon or for Teen Tempos or Girlhood Styles, Incorporated: third floor, fifth floor, pen and pencil sets on the main floor, stationery); its discreet neutral walls, the green-and-gray-striped chairs, the helpless vases on the mantel, the picture over the fireplace, which may have been of a past president of the college or of a financial lover of education—all were so carefully devoid of personality that the room as a whole reduced conversation to the exact level which a well-bred girl would choose.

Natalie, accustomed to rooms and to company which were, as a complete unit, intended to bring out the maximum personality any given organism possessed, felt smothered by the room and by her companions. She sat in a corner, on the floor because when she came in after an uncomfortable farewell to her mother and father and brother, still carrying the money her father had pressed into her hand and the box of cookies her mother had nearly forgotten, more girls were sitting on the floor than on chairs and because by now all the chairs were taken by girls who had obviously exercised a freer choice than Natalie had; and she looked, trying not to seem looking, at the other girls in the room.

There was one directly opposite who had bright-red hair,

and who was laughing and talking with several girls around her; more girls were listening and edging nearer, and Natalie, drawing back from that side of the room, thought, *There* is someone I will know only slightly. The girl next to her had hair that grew in an ugly line across her forehead, and when Natalie risked saying, after rehearsing it for some minutes, "Do you know any of these people?" the girl said, "No," briefly, eyed Natalie for a minute, and then looked away. She is not looking for me, Natalie thought, and the girl on her other side was not looking for Natalie either; as Natalie turned to her, to repeat her question, she rose quickly and went to join the group by the red-haired girl. Will they all notice that I am sitting almost alone? Natalie wondered. Did the red-haired girl thank her fate every morning and night, when she looked at herself in her mirror, with a comb in her hand? Did the girl near Natalie bewail secretly the ugly line of her hair, and persuade herself that she was more aware of it than anyone else? Was someone regarding Natalie, identifying her by some extraordinary characteristic which Natalie did not know or had forgotten or had convinced herself that no one saw? Was it not possible that the girl over there, in the blue dress, had put the dress on that morning wondering if it would do for her first day at college? Because it would not, and had she spent the day concerned with it, or had she forgotten it immediately she put it on? Had the mother of the one in green told her not to forget her pills? Was the one with glasses afraid of waking in the night, alone? Which of them had come to college hoping secretly to meet a thin nervous girl named Natalie? Did she expect Natalie to recognize her first? And, worst of all, what terrible change were they all expecting so immediately, so fearfully? Was something going to happen?

Natalie had already discovered that it was not possible to think clearly in this bedlam, any more than it was possible to act clearly. All thoughts and actions were called for so quickly, were so subject to immediate and drastic change, that she dared not try to rise to go upstairs and find her room again, and she dared not estimate finally the probable characters of the girls in the room, for fear that, in either case, someone should look at her and laugh; suddenly, permanently, seeing her as, "That girl who . . ."

Then without warning the room quieted, and Natalie perceived that the red-haired girl was standing. "Shall I?" she said to someone sitting near her, as one who has intended to all the time and merely expects public confirmation; the girls around her nodded and spoke urgently, and the red-haired girl turned prettily to the room, spread her hands, and said, "Listen, everyone, we've all got to introduce ourselves to each other. After all, we'll be living in the same house for a long time." Everyone laughed as though, unexpectedly, she had voiced the hidden dismay of them all, and the red-haired girl said, "I'll go first. My name's Peggy Spencer, and I came here from Central High School in—"

The girl next to Natalie, the one with the unpleasant hair, leaned over suddenly and said to Natalie, "Isn't she cute?"

Cute? Natalie thought. "She certainly is," she whispered back.

Around the circle of girls, each one in turn announced her name and her immediate past record. Each one, speaking her own name in a voice she had rarely heard pronounce it, was more or less embarrassed; when Natalie's turn came, and the girl next to her had identified herself as Adelaide something or other from some school or other, and turned expectantly to Natalie, as one who sees an ordeal safely past and another up for the question, Natalie found herself surprisingly able to say clearly, "My name is Natalie Waite." *Is* it my name? she wondered then, afraid for a minute that she had appropriated the name of the next girl, or of someone she had met slightly once and remembered only in the recesses of her mind which seemed called upon unreasonably to function now, socially, and without experience. The name passed without comment, perhaps because no one was listening, actually, to any name other than her own.

After each, then, had with shame called upon herself to stand forth alone, the red-haired girl, without so much pretty confusion, said in the voice of one to whom amateur parliamentary procedure is familiar ("Well, of *course* it will be Peggy

Spencer for vice-president . . ."), "All right, then, since we're all frosh together, we ought to settle any problems we've got right now."

Frosh, Natalie thought, problems. Are the problems to be settled here? She wanted desperately to go to her room.

By the second day (waking up delightedly into the strange room, dressing alone without the certain knowledge of her mother moving downstairs, putting away her own things, selecting her own places for underwear in the dresser, books on the shelves, papers in the desk) she was able to find her own room without being puzzled by the stairs or the length of the hall. She had taken to staying around the floor bathroom at bedtime, with the rest of the girls, asking odd, uncertain questions of the others as they did of her, laughing at jokes whose inevitable point was the uncanny ability of new students to outwit old students, shouting meaninglessly at people she hardly knew. She knew the name of almost everyone on the floor; the red-haired girl, who was already running for some freshman office or other, nodded cordially to her whenever they passed on the stairs, the girl with the ugly hair sat next to her at breakfast one morning. It was thus possible to live—breakfast, lunch, dine, brush one's teeth, sleep, read—in an odd, random fashion, in this world. As one who wakens to find his city destroyed and himself alone in the ruins, Natalie found herself a rude shelter, food, and comfort, by a system almost scavenging.

It could have been a nightmare, but it was a frantic, imperative knock on her door. Natalie, fumbling, turned on her light and looked, as though it were important, at the clock: three o'clock. That meant it was the middle of the night, and her mind, suddenly concerned lest its own signal system be awry, moved quickly over obligations and commitments. No class at this hour, surely, no appointments. A fire, then? Something wholly beyond her own jurisdiction? A murder? Perhaps in the room next door? (A thought of the glories of innocent witness-ship crossed her mind, perhaps for future reference: "But *that* man is not a postman, Inspector; did you see the way he opened the mailbox?") Perhaps they were waking Natalie, as someone who might help, who was known to keep her head in emergencies, phone the doctor first, know always who was to apply the tourniquet, who the makeshift splint. Or, perhaps, waking Natalie as the obvious, destined victim? War? Pestilence? Terror?

"Initiation," called a long voice down the hall. "All freshmen out . . ."

"No," said Natalie, and reached for the cord of her light. Was she a freshman? So designated by those who did not know her name? Or had she been awakened by mistake—or *was* this meant for her? Natalie alone, then? (Her untrusted mind playing her tricks? A dream, so that she should stand in a moment, shivering and miserable, alone in the hall while doors opened up and down the length of the building and curious, mocking faces peered out, saying, "What *is* she doing?" and answering, "She dreamed, she dreamed she was a freshman and it was something called initiation, she keeps saying something about a murder, she keeps asking what her name is, she doesn't seem to know where she is . . .") "I *am* a freshman," she said aloud, and, quickened by a sudden excitement, she swung out of bed and into a bathrobe. "College," she told herself cynically, hurrying with the bathrobe cord, "initiation," stuffing her feet into her slippers. She opened her door, tentative at the last moment, to find the hall lights on and the hall full of nervous, curious, bathrobed girls.

"Where do we go?" someone asked Natalie immediately, perhaps assuming from her late exit from her own room that she had some special inside information.

"*I* don't know," Natalie said. "We better stay here."

"I understand," said someone, and giggled, "that they make us . . ." The rest of her words were most unfortunately lost to Natalie, whose arm had been seized by a temporarily authoritative hand, and whose ears had been seized by a voice saying, "Frosh? This way."

Resenting again the movie word "frosh" (and, to a certain degree knowing curiosity tempered with excitement, so that she thought consciously, in the midst of an unwanted fear, So *this* is why they always pick the middle of the night for things

to happen! and knew she had hit upon something very profound), Natalie followed the firm hand, and the rest of the
girls followed her. Behind her someone still giggled, someone
still said, "But where are we going?" Someone insisted nervously, "I'm not sure my *doctor* . . ."

"Where are we going?" Natalie asked the person leading
her; she discovered with strong embarrassment that this person was masked with a handkerchief over her face, tied approximately at the back of her head; this cops-and-robbers effect
conveyed to Natalie the fact that the night's escapade (she did
not phrase it to herself like this until much later, however) was
something these people might not care to do in daylight, with
their faces uncovered; there was about her conductor a faint
air of many people provoking one another, saying, "Go *on*, I
dare you . . . go *on*; you look *wonderful*; I will if *you* will,"
and the intoxication which comes of a deed hallowed in tradition but uncertainly remembered in detail.

"Shut up," Natalie was told, in answer to her question, and
she thought of how bold the lack of a face made one, and, perhaps, how not having a face of one's own might lead to univer-
sal peace, since a face was, after all, only . . .

"In here," said the faceless creature.

It was extraordinary how not having faces had changed the
bodies of the girls in the house. Falteringly, Natalie was able to
pick out two or three, but, reflecting that she had known them
at best only by their make-up and the way they did their hair,
she was forced to distrust her own judgment and to believe,
most charitably, the best of them. One, who seemed to have
constituted herself leader, remarked as Natalie, first in line,
was brought in, "Do you have any qualification for entering
here?"

They were sitting in a semicircle on the floor, all masked as
foolishly as the girl who had brought her, all wearing their
own pajamas, which surely their mothers, picking them out,
had not destined for such midnight purposes; or, indeed, had
they? Did the mothers of such girls encourage their superiority,
egg them on to masked acts? Did they, sending their daughters
off to college, remark, as last-minute advice, "And, dearest,

remember, when you get after the frosh . . . *do* please wear your blue-and-white-striped p.j.'s—they look the best, and they'll stand the splinters in that floor . . ."

"No, I was brought," said Natalie, and received for reward a push from the girl who had brought her, so that she fell clumsily against a girl sitting, and the girl said, very humanly, "*Cut* it out," and pushed back.

Now I *will* keep quiet, Natalie thought, knowing—and it was not, after all, any too soon to learn—the resignation of a perceptive mind before gleeful freed brutality—and let someone else get pushed.

"—for entering here?" the leader was asking the next girl.

"I don't know," said the girl uncertainly, and was pushed.

As that girl dropped down next to Natalie, she whispered, trembling, "I wish I'd never come."

"Me, too," said Natalie inadequately.

She found that she was thinking absurdly of Jeanne d'Arc; perhaps the next girl, or the one after that, would turn in contempt from the leader, and, addressing a dim figure in the background, drop to her knees and say, "You, Sire, are my king . . ."

After the first few girls, their mentor was tired of pushing them—perhaps she had worn out her rage, or her arms?—and they were allowed to seat themselves quietly. No one spoke, and beyond their mutual and spreading apprehension came the sure conviction among the freshmen that their superiors had exceeded themselves, that the "*I* will if *you* will" had begun to evaporate, with the laughter and the bad puns; that the torment they had devised extended perhaps to one or two girls and could not, for sheer bodily weariness, be repeated, over and over again, for twenty. Moreover, it became increasingly clear that the party had fallen flat, that the pure number of girls entering docilely had worn thin the viciousness in the voice of the leader, that she and her cohorts were going to skim over the last few girls, relying for their effect upon the first few, and, perhaps even with discomfort for themselves, let the business go to pieces now without further emphasizing their futility; the part of wisdom lay clearly in choosing the weakest first.

Natalie, at least, felt a grateful relief when, instead of calling upon her as the first girl, the leader waited until all the freshmen were in, and crowded uneasily onto the floor, and sitting or kneeling, then pointed to a girl in the middle and said, "You, there."

It crossed Natalie's mind then that if she had stayed in her room quietly and never heeded the call to frosh, she would have been overlooked, since no one seemed to care about those who did not come. With this in mind, Natalie turned cautiously and scanned the ranks of freshmen for the red-haired girl, but did not find her. Another instance, she thought regretfully (or at least remembered later that she had so thought), of ritual gone to seed; the persecution of new students, once passionate, is now only perfunctory.

The girl chosen was required to sit upon a low stool in what was, most of them now recognized, the center of the second-floor lavatory—the largest in the house, and the one with most floor space—and she was required further to give her name and her previous educational experience, as though that had not all been gone over before by people more qualified to know, and then the leader, hesitating and prompted, had chosen to confer with a colleague rather than to continue the questioning immediately. Then someone from the masked circle around the new students said, "Look, we're all allowed to ask questions, aren't we?"

"Sure," said the leader, with obvious gratitude.

"Then listen, Myrna," said the girl happily, from behind her mask, "you a virgin?"

Natalie saw the freshman blushing full-face and the upperclassmen blushing behind and above their masks, and thought, I hope they don't ask me, and, It's the girls with masks on their faces blushing too. Could it be, she wondered tiredly, that a mask is no protection at *all?*"

"Certainly," said the girl on the stool, surprised at the question, and blushing as well as the rest.

"Tell us a dirty joke, then," said someone else.

"I don't know any," said the girl, writhing, obviously repressing a seemingly forgotten story that came unfortunately to mind. "I don't listen to *those.*"

"Excused," said the leader. The girl came off the stool and retired, blushing and explaining, to oblivion among her friends; she had passed; she had at that moment taken on a protective coloration among the general run of girls in the house; she was not in any way eccentric, but a good, normal, healthy, American college girl, with ideals and ambitions and looking forward to a family of her own; she had merged.

"Next," said the leader. She gestured at random, and her gesture was answered with alacrity by someone who, seating herself on the stool, showed that she, and no other, was possessed of the information the masked girls wanted to hear, and that she was, in addition, prepared to lie valiantly to deprive them of it and to exalt herself in the eyes of the freshmen girls.

She gave her name in a pleased voice and eyed the circle defiantly, as though daring any of them to match her siren experience or to question it.

Natalie, who needed abruptly to establish her own position, leaned to the girl next to her and whispered, "I won't answer them."

"Shhh," said the girl next to her, bending forward to hear the victim on the stool, who was delivering the punch-line of a joke. The girls in the masks did not laugh, or at least did not show beyond the masks that they were laughing. "That's not very dirty," said one.

"It's the best I know," said the girl on the stool innocently.

"Excused," said the leader helplessly. Then, unbearably, unbelievably, she looked squarely at Natalie. "You," she said.

"No," said Natalie, but the desire to assume the stool, if not the confessional, drove her. Sitting in the center of light, with everyone watching her, she knew at once and for all time the hard core of defiance with which she might always face unknown faces staring; she knew with strength that it would be as easy, or even easier, to resist than to expose herself.

She gave her name (*was* it her name?) and then, when asked if she were a virgin—and this question, gaining adherents from the unkind and the merely curious, was being asked now by three or four voices at once, and even, Natalie saw from the high point of the stool, being echoed by the traitor freshmen themselves—said briefly, "I won't answer."

The worst she had expected was another push, but obviously everyone was afraid to push her with everyone else watching; no single girl there dared expose her own self ("Are *you* a virgin? Well?") with any untoward gesture by now; no single girl dared, however much she desired, take on the limelight; because perhaps by now one small gesture of resistance from the freshmen would have dissolved the upperclassmen into tearful dismayed people, without superiority, and tearing off their masks, saying, "It was *her* idea—I wouldn't have done it at *all* except . . ."

Someone said menacingly that she had better tell, and someone else said that if she didn't *want* to tell, well, that proved it.

"Tell a dirty joke," said the leader.

"I will *not*," said Natalie, who, like everyone else there, was more afraid of being found not to know dirty jokes than of being found to have a rich supply. "Don't you know *enough* jokes?"

"Bad sport," someone called, and then others took it up. "Bad sport, rotten sport, not fair."

What a silly routine, Natalie thought, not realizing, sitting there alone on the stool in the center of the ring of girls, how she was jeopardizing her own future in college, her own future for four years and perhaps for the rest of her life; how even worse than the actual being a bad sport was the state of mind which led her into defiance of this norm, this ring of placid, masked girls, with their calm futures ahead and their regular pasts proven beyond a doubt; how one person, stepping however aside from their meaningless, echoing standards, set perhaps by a violent movement before their recollection, and handed down to them by other placid creatures, might lose a seat among them by questions, by rebellion, by anything except a cheerful smile and the resolution to hurt other people.

"I won't," Natalie said, not knowing whom she was answering.

"Excused," said the leader.

Natalie, realizing that she must relinquish the stool and the light, said as she rose (and loud enough, she hoped, to carry to the fortunate girls still asleep, the red-haired girl and the others who had not answered the call), "I think this is the silliest thing I ever saw." Follow me, she prayed to the girls still sitting in the ring, follow me, stand up, and a new world is made; but no one, standing up beside her, or even raising her voice or her eyes, noticed Natalie by now.

"Dirty joke?" the leader was saying to the new girl.

"I don't know," said the new girl, blushing pleasurably. "Let me think."

Natalie opened the door, observed but not interfered with, and went out.

She went, alone and with a realization of aloneness, to her own private, untouched, room.

Dear Dad,

This is going to be my most ambitious letter to date, and *please don't criticize*, because I am writing fast and not stopping to correct, and even though that might be the way to get things down best, it makes for a lot of mistakes. Because this is going to be about the college. I know you saw it that first day when you and Mother and Bud brought me down, but at that time we were all strange and didn't know what it was like, and now, after over two weeks (and it seems like two years, really) I feel so much at home here that I don't really remember what it was like to live anywhere else, and I sometimes think of how that first day is all *you* know of the place, and you still see it like that, and I can't remember.

First of all, let me tell you about my house. I guess you saw most of it when I moved in—and by the way, that was the *only* time I saw it *that* way, like a stranger with her mother and father and brother, I mean, because right after you left it got all different and I started feeling like a college girl who lived here. Do you know what I'm trying to say? Anyway, the house you saw isn't the one, I think, that I live in at all. By now it's turned into something where girls are yelling and laughing and feeling somehow completely private, and sort of in a world of their own. It has four stories, and I live on the third, as you know. I have a little room, like all the other rooms they give to freshmen. The third- and fourth-year students can have double rooms or suites, but the freshmen and usually the second-year students have rooms alone.

Our house is supposed to be the best because it's attached to the dining room and kitchens, and the girls here only have to go down the stairs and down a hall to get their dinner. Some of the others have to come all the way across the campus, from the other houses we saw. The main part of the campus is a long lawn, where we sit on warm evenings, and I keep thinking about that lawn, because, when I saw it the first day I was with you and Mother and Bud, I kept thinking how I was ever going to find my way back across it and get to my own house, and now I think I know every tree on it, and I go up and down the paths every day. Almost all my classes are in the lecture halls in the big building at the end of the lawn, but one class—Langdon's English I—is usually held outdoors on the lawn or else in the living room of our house. Some of the girls here asked him to have the class here instead of in a lecture hall so he said yes and the college said OK. I like it better because you can sit in a comfortable chair and smoke and not in a lecture room. There's more noise, though, and girls keep opening the doors and starting to come in and then they always get scared and excuse themselves and run out.

I get up as early as I can in the morning, but it's usually just in time for my eight-o'clock class, which is music two days a week and philosophy another two. Classes last an hour and a half, and I get terribly sleepy along about nine o'clock, especially since I don't usually have time for breakfast and I get hungry too. Then at nine-thirty I usually go up to the campus store for a coke and doughnuts, and of course I usually run into my professors there, because somehow everyone always goes there between classes. Then at ten o'clock two days a week, after music, I go to French, which I *hate*. I would drop it only I'd have to take something like Spanish instead. They won't let you graduate without one year of language. Lots of people think Spanish is easier. And I have a sociology course two afternoons a week, and the other two afternoons, of course, is English with Arthur Langdon. That's supposed to be an hour and a half too, but it's usually longer because we all stay around talking to him. I guess he's the most popular person on the campus. He runs the beauty contest before the Senior Dance.

The meals are terrible. They have a kind of salad made of sliced bananas and peanuts, and it seems like we have it five times a week. Also liver. And the coffee is no good, which is why no one ever bothers to go to breakfast.

I played some tennis yesterday with a girl named Helen something. I went down to the courts to practice, and she was there and asked if I wanted to play so I said yes. I wasn't half good enough for her, and we only played one set. We're going to try again sometime when I'm more used to these courts.

I'm looking forward to coming home for a weekend but guess I'll be too busy for a while yet. I'm working hard and having a fine time, and I'm very glad to be here. We're starting *Romeo and Juliet* in English next week.

Tell Mother I am well and I think I am gaining weight. In spite of the bad food, I eat a lot more here than I did at home. Tell her I could use a box of cookies or a cake, lots of the girls get packages from home.

I guess there are about three hundred girls here. Some very nice ones.

Lots of love to everyone at home,
Natalie

It was almost dark outside; the one window of Natalie's room showed black when she had the light on, and pale when she had the light off. When the light was off the room was beautiful and shadowy, with the light from the window moving gently onto the bright bedspread, touching slightly the paper on the desk, coming to rest on Natalie's own hands and the page of the open book before her. When, reluctantly, she turned the light on again—feeling that to seem to be abed at this hour was somehow disgraceful, and indicated perhaps a guilty conscience or perhaps even loneliness—the window fell black and the bed became square and neatly made, and the corners of things became then apparent, from the corners of

the room to the corners of the book, and the feet of the desk
on the floor were somehow obscene.

She was not trying to study; the fact of study was still strange
to her, so that she read with appetite the freshman English textbook, and took novels from the library, and read with mild
interest and a wandering mind the textbook of biology (having
read, the first day, as had everyone in the class, the chapter on
human reproduction), and saw no pattern and no meaning in
the French text, the sociology book (past the chapter on pros-
titution), and regarded with blank contempt the book which
very likely held all the world's carefully alphabetical facts
upon the analysis of words—learned, very likely, and infinitely
careful about theories, but duller than words had any right to
be. For music, fortunately, she had only to arise at eight the
next morning with both ears still attached to her head; so long
as her ears *were* there, the fact that she did not use them to listen enthusiastically was unimportant to the music lecturer.
For philosophy she had long ago evolved a complex and—she
suspected—meaningless theory, which she kept by her in case
the professor should raise his old head, ever, and look in her
direction. "Sir," she meant to say brightly, "if Descartes *really*
means that he exists because his mind *thinks* he does, then
wouldn't it be true that . . ."

A knock on her door was as strange a thing to her as the fact
of the door itself; at first she thought, It is across the hall, how
clearly it sounds; then she thought, It is a mistake; she wasted
a minute thinking of someone looking at the outside of the
door steadfastly, as she looked at the inside, and meant to mark
the next day whether the panels outside were the same as those
inside; odd, she thought, that someone standing outside could
look at the door, straight ahead, seeing the white paint and the
wood, and I inside looking at the door and the white paint and
the wood should look straight also, and we two looking should
not see each other because there is something in the way. Are
two people regarding the same thing not looking at each
other?

The knock came again. "Come in," occurred to Natalie
then as reasonable thing to say, but the door was locked, so

she stumbled, hastily and spilling her book, off the bed and across the room and finally remembered how to turn the key and open the door.

"Yes?" she said blindly, now that the door was removed.

"Hello," said the girl outside; Natalie remembered, as though once the door was opened the world outside it slowly established itself, small section after small section—as though, in fact, it had not been prepared tonight for Natalie to open her door again, and had been caught completely unaware, and was putting a bold face on things and getting everything back together as quickly as possible, so that Natalie should not perceive it, looking through her door, and say, "Just as I thought; this confirms everything I have always suspected"—she remembered, slowly, seeing the girl's face before and then, that her name was Rosalind.

"Hello," Natalie said.

"Are you busy?" Rosalind said, leaning slightly to look over Natalie's shoulder and into her room. "I mean, I just thought I'd come over and say hello, but if you're busy . . ."

"No," said Natalie, surprised. "I'm not at all busy." She stood away from the door, and Rosalind came into the room, looking around curiously, as though she had not left one just like it immediately before, although perhaps Rosalind's bedspread was blue instead of patterned, and she had perhaps been reading different books, and the clothes in the closet would of course be different.

"I wanted to talk to someone," Rosalind offered; once in, she sat quickly on the bed and tucked her feet under her. "I saw your light on and thought that since we didn't know each other very well it might be a good time to come and make friends with you."

"I'm glad," Natalie said. She was happy at having been disturbed; her books would still be there after Rosalind left, and who knew what odd thoughts and notions Rosalind might have brought with her? Natalie sat uneasily on the desk chair, knowing it was her duty to speak, and able to think of nothing but the list of irregular French verbs she would not be able to remember half so clearly tomorrow. "I was just trying to do my French," she said, with an embarrassed laugh that she deplored.

"French," Rosalind said, and shuddered. "I'm glad I took Spanish."

"Is Spanish terribly hard?" Natalie asked politely.

"Listen," Rosalind said, obviously feeling that the amenities were over and it was time to get down to business, "do *you* know any of the girls around here?"

"No," said Natalie, "not very many." Not that I *want* to know them, she longed to add, I'm *very* careful about my friends, I dislike knowing lots of people, I don't make friends easily because I keep them for a long time, I make friends slowly and with discrimination, I devote myself to my studies . . . "Not any of them, really," Natalie said.

"That's what I thought," Rosalind said. "Did you *ever* see anything like them? I mean, they certainly aren't very *friendly*."

"I haven't really tried—" Natalie said.

"Peggy Spencer and *her* friends," Rosalind said disdainfully. "Helen Burton and *her* friends . . . and such a noise going on all night. I can't even *sleep*."

"I've never had any trouble getting to sleep," Natalie said eagerly.

"We ought to show them they're not so very special," Rosalind said. She lifted her chin and shrugged. "You go into one of their rooms and they're all there and they stop talking and say, 'Yes?' as though you were a beggar until you turn around and go and then you can hear them laughing after you shut the door. I don't think they're *that* important, I *must* say."

"I've never gone into any of their rooms," Natalie said, feeling that she had an end of this conversation to keep up.

"Well, you know what they say about *you*," Rosalind said. She looked at Natalie as though for the first time aware of the particular person she was addressing, calling to mind this person's special liabilities. "*They* say you're crazy. You sit here in your room all day and all night and never go out and *they* say you're *crazy*."

"I go out to class," Natalie said quickly.

"They say you're spooky." Rosalind said. "That's what they call you, Spooky, I heard them."

"Who?" Natalie said. "*Who* knows what I do?"

"Well, *I* think it's your own business," said Rosalind critically. "I mean, everyone has the right to live the way they want, and naturally none of *them* has any right to call a person names just because a person wants to live their own way."

Feeling a sudden quick warmth toward Rosalind for not having watched her, Natalie said, "All I want them to do is leave me alone."

"Well, *that's* what I say," Rosalind said, "but if you really don't belong to their little crowd, *naturally* they think you're crazy, and they never even stop to think that maybe you and I don't *want* to run around with people like *that*, and what I'd like to know is how does anyone get to belong with them if they look at you like you were a beggar and then laugh when you go out? Does it really seem *fair?*"

"What they think is actually not at all important," Natalie said with dignity.

Even as she spoke she knew her position, and her mind, racing ahead of her, was counting over its special private blessings: there was her father, of course, although he seemed, right now, far away and helpless against laughing girls, there was Arthur Langdon and the fact that she seemed, more than any other, to be comprehending and alert in his class, and had received a sort of recognition, as though they were kindred, from him—but then perhaps, she thought, frightened, perhaps not everyone thought of Arthur Langdon's regard as special. Perhaps he was not so valuable to these watching, laughing girls as other things Natalie had never heard of. But then, of course, there was always and beyond all laughter and beyond all scrutiny her own sweet dear home of a mind, where she was safe, protected, priceless . . . "They're trivial people, really. Mediocre."

"Try and get anywhere *without* them," Rosalind said cynically. "They're *every*thing."

Not everything, Natalie thought hastily, not quite everything. Not the place ten, fifteen, twenty years from now, the place of pure honor and glory, from which one perhaps looked down and said, "*Who?* What was the name, please? Did I ever meet you before? In *college?* Dear heaven, so *long* ago . . ."

"They get away with murder," Rosalind said. "Think any of *them* has to do what *we* do?" She put out her lip sullenly and began to swing one foot back and forth. Looking at her, Natalie saw clearly what had not seemed important before now: that Rosalind was squat and ugly, and had a drab dull face and a faint growth of hair on her upper lip. "Listen," Rosalind said, "you know that girl, the skinny one who's such a good friend of Peggy Burton's? The one they call Max, because her name's Maxine? Well, the reason *she* went away last weekend was because she had an a*bor*tion."

"Oh," said Natalie.

"Heard them talking about it through the door," Rosalind said. "And Peggy Burton—*she's* only been lucky. You know that guy of hers, the football player?" She nodded emphatically, and glanced slyly at Natalie. "I mean," she said, "not that I want to repeat scandal, but they're *all* like that. We ought to be thankful we don't have more to do with them. I mean, I'm *sure* the college people know all about them, and if you hang around with them, first thing you know they think the same about *you*."

"About me?" said Natalie. Far off, in the untouched, lonely places of her mind, an echo came: It isn't true, it didn't happen . . .

"Not that either of *us*," Rosalind said, and laughed lightly. "I mean," she said, looking again at Natalie, "I know about *me*, and I guess about *you*."

Pride caught at Natalie; here was this hideous girl attempting an alliance on the grounds that Natalie was—what? was there a word? (Innocent? Who was innocent—this girl with her nasty eyes? Chaste? Chaste meant no impure thoughts; virginal meant clear and clean and could not include this Rosalind with her low coarse face; untouched? Spotless? Pure?) Could I, Natalie thought, in the second when her eyes met Rosalind's, could I possibly associate on any grounds with this girl? Whichever way I speak, she will follow me. "It isn't true," she said.

"Of *course* it's true," Rosalind said indignantly. "Don't I hear them talking every night through the wall? Some nights they're in there giggling until I think I'll go crazy, things you and I don't even think about, much less talk about, and then when I pound on the wall you'd think *I* was the one, the way they yell back."

"I mean," Natalie said apologetically, "if *we* don't meddle with *them* . . ."

Rosalind shrugged. "I just think it's terrible," she said, "them thinking they're so good, and the things they do. What they don't realize is that no one *wants* to be in their crowd, for fear of having people think things about them."

Suddenly (and it gave a sudden clear picture of her decision to come here in the first place; suddenly, on a phrase, perhaps not even considered, so that she knocked on Natalie's door at random, because it was the third from the end of the hall, or because the door somehow resembled, in some mystic, impossible way, the door to her own room, far away at home) she rose, pushed her hair back with an unattractive gesture, and said wearily, "Anyway, I wouldn't want anyone knowing *I* had anything to do with them."

"Of course not," said Natalie helplessly; she answered the girl's leaving as she had answered her coming, without volition, without desire, without conviction.

"Listen," said Rosalind, as though it were a sudden idea, "let's go to breakfast together tomorrow. OK?"

"I have an early class," said Natalie hastily.

"So do *I*," said Rosalind. "I'll come and knock on your door about seven-thirty. You be ready."

"I don't know if I'll have breakfast before class," Natalie said. "I always wake up so late—"

"I'll see that you're up," Rosalind said. "We'll show them they're not the *only* people in the world. OK?"

From Natalie's secret journal:

Dearest dearest darling most important dearest darling Natalie—this is me talking, your own priceless own Natalie, and I just wanted to tell you one single small thing: you *are* the

best, and they *will* know it someday, and someday no one will
ever dare laugh again when you are near, and no one will dare
even *speak* to you without bowing first. And they *will* be afraid
of you. And all you have to do is wait, my darling, wait and it
will come, I promise you. Because that's the fair part of it—they
have it now, and you have it later. Don't worry, please, please
don't, because worrying might spoil it, because if you worry it
might not come true.

Somewhere there is something waiting for you, and you can
smile a little perhaps now when you are so unhappy, because
how well we both know that you will be happy very very very
very soon. Somewhere someone is waiting for you, and loves
you, and thinks you are beautiful, and it will be so wonderful
and so fine, and if you can be patient and wait and never never
never never despair, because despair might spoil it, you will
come there, someday, and the gates will open and you will pass
through, and no one will be able to come in unless you let them,
and no one can even see you. Someday, someone, somewhere.
Natalie, please

In the class named philosophy, Natalie appeared two mornings a week, although it was not proven that Mr. (Doctor by
ambition, although his thesis—"The Probable Intention of the
Subjunctive in Plato"—had not yet found a completion) Desmond noticed, particularly, whether or not Miss Waite had
chosen to attend any given morning. Under her father's tender
care, Natalie had been formally introduced to both Plato and
Aristotle, but had never, until now, been required to digest
such ideas reduced to the probable, or diagram, level of the
schoolgirl mind. The man—that would be Mr. (to be Doctor)
Desmond—who taught this class, and who had named it philosophy, obviously felt that anyone who had spent years studying his subject should by rights end up as something rather
better than a man trying to teach ideas to girls, or at least as
something more reconciled; he was bitter and impatient, and
made his own intimate friend Plato as disagreeable as possible,
perhaps to keep the uneager girls from intruding unwarily into
some secret philosophical circle, where bitter men who taught

philosophy drank deeply of clear wine with the Platos and Berkeleys, the Descartes and the Hegels, and commiserated with one another over the fate of philosophers: *philo*: love; *sophia*: wisdom.

"Nothing," the philosopher might remark at sometime after nine in the morning, fingering his gray tie, or touching with uncertain fingers his pockets, or merely eying unenthusiastically the penciling girls in the front rows, "nothing," he would say thoughtfully and with some relish, "*nothing* in the world exists in a perfect form."

Nothing in the world exists in a perfect form, Natalie wrote in her notebook, feeling as she wrote that there just *might* be something.

"How about a vacuum?" the girl next to her said unexpectedly.

There was a silence. The professor (so soon to be Doctor Desmond) stared, repeated to himself: What about a vacuum? and raised his eyebrows slightly.

"Well," he said, his surprise not yet demonstrated to his own satisfaction, "*what* about a vacuum?" One heard—or rather, perhaps, only Natalie heard—the faint murmur as Plato leant to Descartes, Dewey asked Berkeley, "*What* did she say? What *was* it?" the learned teachers of philosophy all raising their eyebrows and smiling at one another, telling one another perhaps, "Science . . . science."

"Well," said the girl next to Natalie, who was suddenly discovered by both Natalie and the girl on the other side of her to be a clumsy creature, given to raw blushing, and undoubtedly not finely drawn in mind, "I mean, when you say there's nothing perfect?"

"Nothing in the world exists in a perfect form," the professor murmured, watchfully. "Yes, I said it."

"Well," the girl said; she stared straight at the professor; to confound a professor of philosophy midway through the first month of the first semester of your first year . . . "Well," she repeated, "I mean—what about a vacuum? I mean, *that's* perfect, isn't it?"

Natalie perceived that one of the junior members of the

philosopher's circle (William James?), overeager, anxious to establish himself among the select, hurried with his joke, and was hushed by the others, and drew even a shade of a frown from the Bishop himself; would these impetuous young fellows never learn their equivocal standing?—and the professor, at whom the student was staring entranced, looked quickly, once, around the class, opened his mouth, and smiled.

There was, on alternate mornings, the class named history of music, and here the professor was a man equally thwarted, but happy about it nevertheless; he was ridden by a sort of genius, and felt strongly that it was far more valuable for college freshmen to participate two mornings in the week in the intricate, subtle, unendingly lovely convolutions of a genius mind than to concern themselves tidily with dates and composers, the whole-tone scale, the *castrati*.

"Listen," he told them one morning, too soon after breakfast, and he held up one finger of one long hand in a graceful eloquent gesture, "this morning I shall play for you . . . "

He selected, with the quick decisive motions of a man captivated by a thought he cannot elude, a volume from the stack on the desk; although his air was one of unpremeditated desire, he had nevertheless remembered to procure in advance copies of the music to pass among the girls in the front row. Natalie, who sat at the end of the front row nearest the piano, was thus able to follow the music and the professor's playing together, and found it perhaps as little instructive as anything she had ever heard; she was accustomed to listen to music rarely, and then in strict solitude, with her eyes shut and various odd glories in her head; she could read barely enough music to perceive that the professor consistently played a sharp where a double-sharp was written. To confound a professor of music midway through the first month of the first semester of the first year . . .

At the end of the class Natalie stopped at the desk where the professor was modestly disclaiming the shrill feminine compliments on his playing; when he turned to Natalie with his smile ready, she said meekly, "Please, may I ask you something?"

Where did you study? Is it a natural talent? Why do you not compose? The continuing smile on the professor's face showed Natalie that she had not made her question quite clear. "I mean," she said, "here—" she had the book open, her finger on the spot, all ready "—you always played a sharp and isn't this a double-sharp? I mean," she added, in the face of his uncomprehending smile, "I just wondered, while you were playing."

"Playing very badly, by the way," he said, still smiling, and raising one hand gracefully against the low voice of protest, in which Natalie, to her eternal recognized cowardice, found herself joining. "No," he said, "I really *did* play badly. One knows."

"But—" Natalie said, her finger on the book.

"This girl," he said, his hand on Natalie's arm, his face turned toward the other girls, "this girl listens to music, as—how shall I say it?—as an artist. Perhaps music has a meaning for her beyond what it has for the rest of us."

Perhaps it has, Natalie thought; I am fairly beaten. Desiring to retire with an understanding grin and a knowledgeable look, she turned when the professor spoke to someone else and went softly away, no one turning to look after her.

At the beginning of her second month at college, one day Natalie turned a corner suddenly (where was she going? what was she running from? She was never able to remember afterwards, since at the moment the incoherence of her life dissolved and she became again a functioning person, somewhat later than the red-haired Peggy Spencer, perhaps, but still much sooner than many of the girls around her) and crashed into someone who, picking her up, said, in the voice of one who was not confused but knew these many corners perfectly, "I'm terribly sorry; I should have looked where I was going."

"My fault," Natalie said. She had not dropped anything, otherwise she could have hidden her face searching for it on the ground. As it was, she was forced to observe that she had run into a woman, who was a woman as surely as Natalie was a girl, since where Natalie was unconnected and vague, this other was purposeful and compact. "You all right?" the woman asked the girl. "You're new, aren't you?"

Natalie, blessing her for avoiding the hateful word frosh, nodded and looked up. A pretty woman. "New," Natalie confessed, "and confused. And frightened, I guess."

"Everyone is," the woman said. She hesitated, and Natalie, who was these days forming estimates about people because she feared speaking to them, imagined that the woman had had a destination and was wondering if it would wait while she helped Natalie; the desire to be helpless and the pride against being helped by a woman who might be, after all, inadequate, made Natalie say dismissingly, "I suppose I'll get over it." She pretended to be ready to walk on, but, blessedly, the woman decided suddenly, and turned to walk with her.

"I was new here recently," the woman said and smiled. "I'm Elizabeth Langdon," she said. "My husband teaches English. I used to be a student." And that's all she knows to tell me about herself, Natalie thought, and said, "Oh, yes. I believe I'm in one of Mr. Langdon's classes. At least," she added doubtfully, for fear of being thought by his wife to have a crush on Mr. Langdon, "I *think* it's his class."

"Is he short, with a mustache?" the woman asked, as though it were of some importance, "or dark? Curly hair? Blond with glasses?"

"Dark," Natalie decided, remembering the slim figure which moved gracefully before the class, speaking with humorous informality of Shakespeare; suppressing quickly and emphatically the recollection of her own vague daydreams ("Miss Waite? I don't suppose you remember me? Well, I'm Arthur Langdon; I want to tell you that your performance of Portia was . . ."). "Of course, it must be Mr. Langdon. It's just that, being so new here . . ."

"Of course." The woman sounded relieved, still giving the impression that the point had been important. "Has he begun to quote Suetonius yet?"

Natalie suddenly wanted to make a good impression on the wife of the slim figure who might, at any moment, quote Suetonius. "My father," she said, "says that people only quote when they can't make a point any other way."

"I see," said Mrs. Langdon; Natalie thought that perhaps

she was storing the remark away to use on her husband later. ("Dear, I understand that people only . . .") "How do you like it here?" Mrs. Langdon asked.

It was, of course, not the first time Natalie had been asked; she laughed with embarrassment and then, changing her mind for some reason in midstream, said uncomfortably, "I don't know yet. I mean, I have so much yet to learn."

"Like not running around corners?" said Mrs. Langdon, and paused, smiling, in their walk. "This is where we live," she said. "It's a faculty house—observe the architecture, done by a fellow faculty member, since deceased, observe the college stonework and the handy-man air about the drainpipes. Students," she added soberly, "are to feel free to call upon faculty members for assistance and advice, although it is recommended that they do not visit a faculty home without specific invitations having been issued." She smiled again, and Natalie smiled back. "No one pays much attention to that sort of thing," Mrs. Langdon said. "Won't you come in?"

"Thank you," Natalie said; could it be true that she was so casually invited into Arthur Langdon's house?

As the door closed behind them Natalie hesitated in the small hallway; the fact that this was certainly the house where Arthur Langdon lived seemed somehow to color the air of it, and was that not a trace of his pipe smoke? It could be that as Natalie stood in the hallway her feet were set precisely in Arthur Langdon's footprints. It was undeniable, also, that he had at some time touched this doorknob.

Elizabeth Langdon, her own door closed behind her, had changed, as a bird stepping again inside its cage is no longer a creature of circle and parabola, but a hopping thing; Elizabeth pushed off her hat and slipped her coat from her shoulders and, preceding Natalie into a light living room, dropped her hat and coat on a couch. "Take off your things," she said with a gesture. Seemingly she had accepted Natalie inside her house as a person, something more than the mere student Natalie had been outside the house. Natalie saw dimly, as she fumbled with the buttons of her coat, a succession of meetings with Elizabeth Langdon outside her house, of formal questions after one's health and dutiful laughter, of civility and disinterest and courtesy, of Elizabeth Langdon denying politely anything she might ever have said inside.

"It's so nice here," Natalie said. Although she had already glanced quickly around the room (wondering, as she did so, with a fast secret look at Elizabeth Langdon, What is it in here she finds so alarming? Will *I* be happy here? Will I ever know these things well?), she made now a great performance of looking around, letting her eyes stop suitably long at the Hayter etching over the mantel, taking in gratefully the blended colors of the slipcovers, the curtains, the rug. There were books, and she estimated them and the Langdons by her own secret process (the proportion of bright jackets to dull bindings) and found them dubious—too much yellow and red, too little calf. It occurred to her that she would probably like the Langdons very much, while privately deploring Elizabeth a little.

"I *can* offer you a drink, you know," Elizabeth Langdon said; she had been busied hanging up their coats and now backed out of the closet, her hair rumpled. "Would you like a cocktail? Martini?"

Natalie realized how *very* indelicate this all was. She had been in college not more than a month, and this woman had certainly no business offering her cocktails, or even speaking to her so. "Thank you very much," said Natalie, thinking, *She* must be *terribly* lonely. Her problem was illustrated directly with the question of sitting down: as a student, she should certainly not seat herself while a faculty wife stood; as a guest, she certainly could. The only solution was to lift the whole situation into a never-never land where neither rule applied, so Natalie, with dogged informality, followed Elizabeth into the small kitchen.

"May I help you?" Natalie asked.

"Nothing to do," said Elizabeth, her head now buried in the refrigerator. "Arthur keeps a pitcher of martinis already made. I can't make them," she added, drawing out her head, "and he's always too tired when he comes back from class. Olive?"

"Thank you."

"God *damn*," said Elizabeth. She leaned back, trying to see

the top shelf of the pantry. "No more," she s
and laughed at Natalie. "We've got to have o
fruit juice glasses. There's only one cocktail glass
ken and of course I have to give that to Arthur."

Natalie, who was not really completely certain of
ence between a cocktail glass and a fruit juice glass,
moment to wonder about the oddness of saving the la
for Arthur, before she said, "Mother never lets me d
glasses at home because I always drop them." Why did
that? she wondered again, it isn't true. Now I'll just have
remember it so I won't tell her in a few minutes that I nev
break anything.

They took their cocktails into the living room again, walking cautiously and not speaking. Then, when Natalie had low-
ered herself tentatively into an overstuffed armchair, with her
cocktail correctly on a coaster and a cigarette offered and
declined (Natalie was afraid to smoke until she had solved the
problem of who was going to light whose cigarette; it was difficult for Natalie to get up from the overstuffed chair and walk
across to Elizabeth with a match, but it was unthinkable that
Elizabeth should stand up from the couch and walk across to
Natalie with a match. It occurred to Natalie that she could
light a cigarette after Elizabeth was well started on hers, taking
one from her pocket with an absent-minded air, as one who
smokes without thinking, and lighting it carelessly, holding the
match a trifle too long while she talked), Elizabeth leaned back
on the couch, looking at Natalie smilingly, and said, with an
air of having all the time in the world to get to more important
subjects, "So you're one of my husband's students?"

"I believe I am," Natalie said cautiously—best not to appear
too anxious.

"Do you like it here?" Elizabeth asked.

It was still not a question Natalie was entirely equipped to
answer. She decided finally that the least she could do was reply
again to this determined friendliness in an open manner, and
so she looked at Elizabeth and smiled and shrugged. "I don't
really think I like it very much yet," she said. "No one seems to
pay much attention to anyone else."

ded, choosing to take this statement as one of

true," she said. "You'll find as you get on that
ss and less attention to you, and you get used to it.
everyone here is so much interested in themselves
own concerns, and no one cares about anyone else
tion or teaching the young or helping anyone else, but
y care about is getting as much as they can as fast as
an."

hat did I start? Natalie thought. "I suppose that's a good
cription of education," she said, feeling her way. "Except that
ven if you learn *that* much, it's something."

This was lost on Elizabeth; she was staring into her cocktail glass, her long fair hair falling softly down on either side of her face, her eyes intent. When she looked up suddenly, as Natalie finished speaking, she smiled and said, "I suppose I'm more bitter because I used to be a student and now I'm a faculty wife."

"I should think that would just give you twice as many friends," Natalie said, wondering if it was friends they were talking about.

Elizabeth shook her head; Natalie thought that the motion would spill her drink and then saw that Elizabeth's glass was empty. Hastily Natalie took up her own glass and sipped. "It means I have almost *no* friends," Elizabeth said, now watching Natalie drink. "You *can't*, you know. I mean, girls I used to know as students are in their last year now, and it's very hard for me to talk to them. And of course all the other faculty wives are too old for me."

"You didn't finish college before you married?" asked Natalie with interest, *here* was an achievement to be envied.

Elizabeth shook her long hair again. "I never wanted to come in the first place," she said. "I'm *only* about three years older than you are."

And yet she can sit here and serve cocktails, Natalie thought. "I'm seventeen," she said.

"You see?" said Elizabeth. "I was twenty-one my last birthday."

Should *I* tell her she doesn't look it? Natalie thought. "I think you're terribly pretty," she said, shocking herself deeply by this statement, which was not in her usual repertoire.

Elizabeth smiled again, her smile this time deepening with pleasure, her eyes shining. "I think that's *nice* of you," she said. "Another cocktail?"

Natalie looked at her half-finished glass. "I'm very slow," she said.

"I'll wait for you," said Elizabeth, turning her glass in her fingers. She was so obviously planning *just* to wait, not doing anything else, that Natalie quickly drank down the last of her cocktail, catching the olive in her mouth and holding out her glass with her mouth still full.

When Elizabeth came back with the drinks, she said, "Try to keep up with me," as she set Natalie's glass down on the table.

"Yes," she went on, taking up her conversation where she had left it, "I never realized what I was getting into, marrying my English teacher." She sat down on the couch and regarded Natalie gloomily. "Sometimes I could *cry*," she said.

Natalie, who was unused to drinking at best, and certainly unused to two fast cocktails after a confusing afternoon, was beginning to feel delightfully at home, and friendly, and strong, and sympathetic. She could see clearly by now that Elizabeth was a wonderfully beautiful woman; it no longer seemed strange that a student in college should marry, but only strange that any unhappiness should approach this perfect creature.

"I wish I could help you," Natalie said. She was almost certain that there were tears in her eyes.

"Be my friend," said Elizabeth. She looked at Natalie earnestly. "Be my *friend*," she said. "Don't ever tell anyone."

"Don't ever tell anyone what?"

Elizabeth, who had risen at that moment with her empty glass in her hand, stopped, turning slightly toward the door to listen. When there was no sound in the room they could hear voices from outside, calling to one another and laughing. After a minute Elizabeth relaxed, and made a perfunctory movement toward Natalie's glass.

"No," said Natalie, "oh, no, thank you."

Without comment Elizabeth turned and went to the kitchen, and came back in a moment with her full glass. "Don't ever tell anyone," she said. "No one thinks I'm unhappy, no one even *dreams* I'm unhappy, and you know once you let them know you're unhappy then they start wondering why, and then they look at you and they think you're getting old or something. They were all so jealous *any*way. I'm still as pretty as I ever was." She turned her head proudly on her neck, and Natalie, feeling herself more than ever thin and unformed, nodded admiringly. "You see," Elizabeth went on, spreading her empty hands in front of her and looking at the fingers, "all the students think I'm friends with the faculty wives and all the faculty wives think I'm friends with the students or with the *other* faculty wives and all the other faculty wives think I'm friends with the other faculty wives and all the other—" She stopped, her eyes wide. There was a definite step outside the door, then it opened and Arthur Langdon came in.

He was handsome and tired, and looked, in his worn sports jacket with the elbows patched in chamois, rather as though his mental picture of himself was somewhat more refined than the actual sight of him to others. When he came in through the door his eyes took in, swiftly, his wife, Natalie, and their empty cocktail glasses. Without speaking he set his brief case down just inside the door, and came slowly into the room. After one quick, inclusive glance again at Natalie, he regarded his wife.

"My dear," he said cordially, and smiled over his shoulder at Natalie.

"I only had one," Elizabeth said. "This girl will tell you, I only had one."

"Of course you did," he said to her, and turned and smiled largely at Natalie. "My wife seems to be reluctant to introduce us," he said. "I'm Arthur Langdon."

Who did he think I *thought* he was? Natalie wondered. "I'm Natalie Waite," she said, and, to establish her position immediately (so that he might throw her out if he chose?), she added, "I'm in your freshman English class."

"I thought you were," he said. "Think I could join you in one of those?"

He took Natalie's nearly empty glass from her, passed his wife without apparently seeing her glass, and went into the kitchen. After a minute he came back, looked once at his wife, and handed Natalie her full glass. "Here's luck," he said, and he and Natalie drank, Natalie very cautiously, and noting that he had taken the one cocktail glass for his drink. "Well," he said, and sat down on a chair near Natalie, "what do you think of it here?"

"I like it very much," Natalie said. "It's a little strange still, of course."

"It will be strange for quite a while," he said. "It's taken *me* four years to get used to it, I know."

"I've been enjoying your class," Natalie said, thinking, My father taught me to be more intelligent than this; but Arthur Langdon perplexed her. He was subtly familiar to her, as though his words were meaningful on more than one level, as though there were an established communication between them in the course of five minutes, as though, actually, he were clearly aware that she *could* talk more intelligently than this, and was waiting indulgently for the strangeness of the environment to wear off before any conversation began. I wonder if he makes everyone feel like this, Natalie thought. The horror of feeling a reaction everyone else might feel led her to say, stumbling, "You reminded me of my father this morning in class."

He smiled. "All first-year students find sooner or later that some professor reminds them of their fathers."

"Now you remind me of him again," Natalie said. "*He* talks like that."

Arthur Langdon raised his eyebrows incredulously.

"He's a writer," Natalie said weakly; it crossed her mind that she would not have so much trouble bringing out the words if her father had been a plumber, or even a policeman; unless he asks me who my father is, she thought, I will have to come right out and tell him and then suppose he doesn't know who I'm talking about and what *can* I say? "Arnold Waite," she said.

"Really?" Arthur Langdon nodded; for a minute Natalie was sure that he had never heard of her father and that she might—with discomfort, with confusion and perhaps even apologies—have to explain, and then Arthur Langdon nodded again and said, "Like to meet him sometime."

"I hope you will," Natalie said politely.

Elizabeth Langdon, who had been leaning forward with her long hair falling about her face and her empty glass cupped in both hands, staring brightly from her husband to Natalie as each one spoke, now said with an appearance of alert interest, "Isn't he the writer?"

Her husband and Natalie both looked at her silently. "I mean," she said, moving her glass in illustration, "isn't he Arnold Waite, the writer?"

"I suppose so," said Natalie lamely, "although he's only really written one *book*."

"I was *sure* he was a writer," said Elizabeth Langdon with satisfaction. "You remember," she said nudgingly to her husband, "you gave me some article of his to read in some magazine, and I read it and I thought it was very good."

Arthur Langdon said to Natalie, "I hope when your father comes to see you we'll be able to get together. And when you write him," he added with a modest laugh, "tell him I'm using some of his stuff in my advanced classes."

"I certainly will," said Natalie thankfully.

"By the way," said Arthur Langdon, turning directly to his wife to show that he was speaking to her, "a couple of the girls are going to drop over sometime before dinner."

There was a short silence. And then, "Who?" asked Elizabeth Langdon.

"A couple of my students," said Arthur Langdon.

"It must be almost five," said Natalie quickly. "I'd better be getting back."

She rose, and Arthur Langdon said, "Don't go, unless you really have something important to do. You might enjoy meeting these girls."

"Well," said Natalie hesitantly, not knowing to what extent these people might be trusted to want her for her father's sake,

or her own. "I *would* like to stay," sh.
never-never land of no precedents.

"*Please* stay," said Elizabeth Langdon.

This, at any rate, could not be insincere. N
and sat down again.

Once she had definitely indicated her conti
Arthur Langdon seemed to feel free to speak t(
though Natalie were now enough a member of the f<
hear anything he said. Her seniority as guest allowe(
talk of the new guests expected, and even to hope, perh<
Natalie might share in their arrangements for entertain.
perhaps carrying glasses, or emptying ashtrays, or simply
paring herself with a stock of small talk to be used direc
they entered.

"They won't drink any more than two cocktails apiece,"
said Arthur Langdon to his wife. "Do you have any pretzels or
anything?"

"What's all the fuss over *them*?" Elizabeth asked, not moving.

"I like things to be nicely arranged when my students come
to see me," he said.

"It looks all right to *them* if they get a free drink and a few
words of wisdom from you," Elizabeth said.

"Nevertheless," he said emphatically, "I want my students
treated as well as possible."

Elizabeth addressed Natalie, "You and I don't need anything fancy, do we? Pretzels? Imported caviar? Breast of guinea
hen?"

Natalie opened her mouth to speak, Arthur Langdon opened
his mouth to speak, and the doorbell rang. "I'll get it," Arthur
said quickly. His wife watched him without expression as he
hurried to the door.

"Can't wait, can he?" she said unpleasantly to Natalie.

Natalie, uncomfortable and wishing she had left, and yet at
the same time enjoying immensely a series of events which she
could watch without being really implicated, stood up uncertainly as Arthur opened the door.

"Can I get the pretzels or anything for you?" she asked Elizabeth.

Arthur will get them," she said. "Wa...
...ttle host."

...k into the room, followed by two girls. Nat-
...em with a frank stare possible only because
...ooking at Arthur and for the moment ignoring
...nd Elizabeth, saw with the irritation she was
... know as jealousy that they were both lovely, in
...at Elizabeth Langdon was lovely: the rounded, color-
...beauty of girls who have been pretty babies and pretty
...rls and pretty boarding school girls and who have, at
...n college, reached a fulfillment of prettiness because they
...finally nubile; that their loveliness would be deadened as
...zabeth's had been deadened was not more than a small consolation to Natalie; that this loveliness built and recharged itself
with an awareness of loveliness, and almost certainly masked
vacant stupidity, was no consolation at all. The further thought
that, premising the loveliness of young women as nature's
infallible way of insuring them husbands, these two could at best
marry no more than a few of the men in the world, was less than
no consolation at all.

Vicki, one of them was named, and the other was Anne.
Vicki had great, long-lashed dark eyes which she disguised, as
though it were a joke between herself and the beholder, with
heavy-rimmed glasses; these glasses, to enhance the joke, she
played with constantly, taking them off and putting them on
with a mock-efficient gesture, using them to wave with, to
hold in her hands, but very rarely keeping them over her face.
With or without the glasses, she gave an additional impression
of seeing clearly everything that went on around her, and of
enjoying it without pity.

Anne—had these girls become friends on purpose?—was
sweet and subdued; like something out of *Little Women*, Natalie thought with scorn, thinking almost at the same minute that
she would not be wise to underestimate Anne, who smiled
shyly and almost curtseyed, who looked sweetly at Natalie and
at Elizabeth and at Vicki and at Arthur Langdon, as though in
this pretty world it was incredible that everyone should be so

kind to shy Anne; who would never, it was perfectly clear, give away an inch of anything she had once gotten hold of.

"How do you do, Mrs. Langdon?" said Anne softly to Elizabeth. "*How* are you?"

"Very well, thank you, Anne," Elizabeth said, not moving from the couch.

"Mrs. Langdon," said Vicki, coming over to Elizabeth with her hand out, "it's been so long since we've seen you."

Are these old friends of hers? Natalie wondered; perhaps some of the girls she knew as students? She turned as she heard her name. "Natalie Waite," Arthur was saying.

"How do you do?" said Natalie politely, and felt for a long minute the two pair of eyes regarding her, disdaining her perhaps, estimating her.

"I think I've seen you in the dining room or somewhere," Vicki said, as one to whom the dining room was a lesser estate, belonging to her general inheritance, but rarely visited, perhaps because of its barrenness, or the provincial nature of its inhabitants.

"You're new, aren't you?" added Anne.

And that, Natalie thought, is the extent of my impact upon the college so far; she signified that she was very new indeed, and somehow managed, unwillingly, to imply that she was now in the presence of the first four people she had spoken to as formal acquaintances since she had reached the college. All four of them smiled upon her, for the only time united, in their mutual superiority at having been in this place longer than Natalie had. Perhaps, too, at that moment, something vague solidified within Natalie, in the face of the three lovely girls in the room, so that she became less of a meek and submissive personality and was without warning as good a soul as the rest of them; from within the strongholds of her own possessive pride in herself it became now apparent to her that there were weaknesses of defense in other fortresses. She might, she thought in this minute, choose to pursue an acquaintance with these two girls; it was obvious that both Elizabeth and Arthur Langdon had perceived that, of the vast unidentified face of the new student body, Natalie had become an individual, with a father, and recognizable. Was it—and again this thought had never in these words troubled Natalie before—worthwhile bothering with any of them?

At any rate, acquaintances or not, it was first necessary for all of them to find a place to sit down, and for Arthur to get everyone drinks, and for Elizabeth, never moving from the couch, where she was now half-reclining, to say some few words, somehow—as it seemed—managing to choke out the barest civilities, in a manner both indifferent and insulting. Natalie looked into her glass with embarrassment, not so much for Elizabeth as for the fact that she had suddenly discovered that in the confusion attending the entrance of Vicki and Anne, she had consumed without knowing it the rest of the cocktail, making, with the new one Arthur handed to her, four strong cocktails for Natalie. She wondered, and thought she had wondered before, that this intoxicant should be liquid, why was it that a substance so indulged in should not be a solid, like candy, or a smoke, like tobacco, or even merely a scent? The oddness of having to *drink* alcohol (surely she could not have consumed so much water in the late afternoon) perplexed Natalie, and she wanted to speak of this unique perspective but could not find phrases; then she became aware that Arthur Langdon was speaking.

"—And so I thought that we might work from that angle for a while. You ought to read that book," he was telling Anne.

Anne looked at him for a long minute before answering; it had the double effect of keeping everyone's eyes fixed on her while they waited for her to speak, and of convincing everyone, apparently, that she was serious, and timid about voicing her opinions, and also led one to believe that when she did speak it would be with a slight, charming lisp. Natalie unwisely thought that this method must be ineffective with anyone of sense, after the first time. "Will you lend it to me?" Anne asked Arthur finally.

What a *fool* she is, Natalie thought, and looked at Elizabeth to see if Elizabeth too thought that Anne was a fool, but Elizabeth was staring again at her own hands and her empty glass.

"How do you like it here?" Vicki asked Natalie. "Still pretty strange?"

"Not at all," Natalie said politely. "Everyone has been so kind."

"Anne and I live on the floor below you," Vicki said. "Did you know it?"

"In the same house?" Natalie said, surprised.

"The same house," Vicki agreed, making it sound like a bordello. "They always put a few reliable upperclassmen in with the new students. To make them feel at home," she added, and grinned.

"I haven't seen you," Natalie said.

"We were in your room the other day while you were out," Vicki said carelessly. Natalie stared at her and she laughed. "We knew you wouldn't mind," she said. "We were curious about you because you looked more interesting than most. There's a red-headed character—" She shuddered theatrically. "Anyway, we thought we'd find out what you were like, so we wandered in one day when we knew you were out."

Anne had given over her conversation with Arthur to listen to Vicki, and now she laughed prettily. "We practically *sneaked* in," she told Natalie.

"Can't trust this pair," Arthur Langdon added with something that might have been pride. "They'll do *anything*."

"I don't understand," Natalie said uncertainly, meaning that she did not understand her own feelings at the moment; the thought of anyone, and particularly these two girls, coming unbidden into her room was abhorrent to her. On the other hand, they seemed to think nothing of it, but looked at her now with calm, guiltless, amused eyes; they premised their visit on what must be a complimentary opinion of Natalie, they criticized the red-haired girl, and they had Arthur Langdon's blessing upon them, although Elizabeth looked at them now with incurious contempt.

She shook her head; should she accept this and gamble upon the value these two girls might possibly hold for her; should she show anger and demonstrate to Arthur Langdon that she was not to be tampered with, that even Vicki and Anne might not tangle safely with Natalie Waite? Elizabeth was at best a dubious ally, Natalie's journal was always locked and the key always with her, she had as yet incriminated herself in no way with her room. She smiled quickly and said, "But how did you get in? I always lock the door."

Anne and Vicki laughed, and even Arthur laughed with them. Then Anne said very meekly, "All the corresponding rooms on each floor use the same lock. Your room is 27, so the keys to 17 and 37 and 7 all unlock it."

"Didn't you ever know we'd been there?" Vicki asked Natalie. "We sat on your bed and read some of your books."

And my letters, Natalie thought, and judged my clothes and commented on the dirty laundry under the bed and opened my dresser drawers and observed the view from my window and tried my lipstick and sampled my perfume and tested . . . "And what did you find out about me?" she asked.

"I thought," said Anne in her innocence, "that you must be an awfully interesting person to know." She just avoided saying "awf'ly int'resting." "All those *books*," she added.

"Except for your bedspread," Vicki said impolitely. "Who *did* pick that out?" She edged the remark over into a faint compliment by hesitating just long enough, and then saying, "Not *you*, of course."

Resolving not to be rid of the bedspread until it was worn to shreds, Natalie said, "My mother. She also chooses my clothes." She hoped she had implied that she was too mad a creature to concern herself with clothes and bedspreads, perhaps even the despair of her mother's heart for her giddy impracticality. "My father chooses my books," she told Arthur Langdon, and he nodded, impressed.

"Don't you make up your own mind about anything?" Anne asked sweetly.

"*My* mother," Vicki said ruefully, "doesn't care *what* I wear. Once just to prove it I put on black nail polish—this was when I was about fifteen," she added hastily, looking from Natalie to Arthur Langdon, "—and when I came to the dinner table and waved my hands around frantically trying to make her notice, she finally said to me, 'Victoria dear, I wish you'd eat more vegetables; you seem so nervous.'"

Natalie laughed; she had committed herself now to amiability, and she was determined to make the knowledge of her these girls had acquired legitimate; she thought, I will have to see the bedspreads in their rooms before I can sleep privately in mine again.

"Another drink?" said Arthur Langdon. He made a large gesture with his hand of sweeping all the glasses together.

"Thank you so much," said Anne, and Vicki held out her glass with a smile. Natalie discovered with horror that she had finished another drink, but her small protest was overwhelmed by Arthur Langdon. As before, he passed his wife without offering to take her empty glass, and Vicki and Anne glanced at each other, and then, bewilderingly, at Natalie, and they all smiled.

"Did you have a pleasant summer?" Elizabeth asked abruptly.

Anne shrugged perfectly, and Vicki said, "About the same as usual, I guess. Sort of dull."

"You were together, of course?" said Elizabeth, this time addressing Anne, the polite hostess speaking first to one guest and then to the other.

"Of course," Anne said, and laughed deprecatingly. "I guess we always are," she said.

"We were on the island, most of the time," Vicki said.

"This island," Elizabeth said deliberately to Natalie, it being perhaps Natalie's turn to be spoken to, "about which Vicki is so modest, is a little hideout of approximately four hundred square miles that belongs to Vicki's family. It's named something like Bide-A-Wee or Dew Drop Inn or Joe's Place."

"Shangri-La," said Vicki coolly. "*I* didn't name it."

"It's lovely there, though; so *private*," Anne said, looking at the wall between Elizabeth and Natalie.

Elizabeth said to Natalie, as though wanting this clearly defined, as though it were necessary now to emphasize these facts, "Anne's mother, by the way, designs evening gowns neither you nor I can afford."

First of all, Natalie thought, How does she know I can't afford . . . ? and then she understood that she was an as yet untried but possibly very strong ally, and if Elizabeth could use a heavy social parody to set Anne and Vicki into a different world and locate her sensitive, impoverished army securely behind their pride . . . thinking this far, Natalie thought, She must know I hate their going into my room, and said, "My mother chooses my evening gowns." Evening gowns, she thought, evening gowns for Natalie Waite, that debutante.

"*My* brother sells insurance in New Jersey," Elizabeth said, playing it just a shade too heavy.

Natalie laughed, and Vicki and Anne turned to look at her together, speculatively.

"She's making fun of us, you know," Anne said to Natalie.

In my own country I was accounted quite a killer, Natalie thought; next time she'll stay where she belongs. "I'm sure she *must* be," Natalie said sweetly.

Elizabeth leaned over the edge of the couch and set her glass firmly on the floor. Natalie and Vicki and Anne watched her silently, and then Elizabeth lifted her head and looked at Anne.

She is sure I'm with her, Natalie thought; what is she going to do?"

"You still chasing after my husband?" Elizabeth said suddenly to Anne. "Doing any better this year?"

"Everybody about given me up?" Arthur Langdon came back into the room carrying a tray on which were four full glasses and a bowl of pretzels. As he set the tray down upon the coffee table and began handing around the glasses, he said, "Sorry to keep you all waiting. I had to mix more cocktails." He looked for a long minute at his wife, who stared back solemnly at him. "They were all gone," Arthur said. "Pretzel?" he added politely to Anne.

"Dear," said Elizabeth softly, "Anne and Vicki have just been telling us all about what they did this summer. They had the *most* interesting time."

"Really?" Arthur said to Vicki; his voice was faintly wistful.

"The usual thing," Vicki said, and Elizabeth laughed loudly. Natalie was now far too happy to think of leaving. She thought she would like to be in Vicki's place, perhaps, in this scene, or even in Anne's; her feeling of pity for Elizabeth, which had been momentary at best, was now a sort of curious wonder; what further could this madwoman do? How could she expose herself as so weak before these two girls, before Natalie, whom she knew so slightly?

"Tell me about your father," Arthur Langdon said to Natalie. Natalie retraced his thought. (Vicki's family, money, fame, Natalie's father) and said, "I'm sure he'd love to meet you. I'll have to write him all about you, you know."

He looked at her inquiringly, and she said, "I write him almost everything that happens, and particularly," she said, thinking, Why not throw him a fish? "all about any interesting people I meet." She smiled with an excellent imitation of Anne's shy smile.

"He's certainly an interesting person," Anne said immediately.

"Your father will—" Vicki began.

"Interesting like a potato bug," Elizabeth said from the couch.

We are all a little drunk, Natalie told herself wisely.

When the phone rang it was perfectly clear to everyone in the room that Elizabeth was not going to attempt getting off the couch to answer it, and everyone except Arthur Langdon waited tensely for him to leave the room again.

As his voice came distantly from another room saying, "Hello?" Vicki said quickly to Elizabeth, "I don't think you ought to talk to Anne the way you did, Mrs. Langdon. After all, Anne has never—"

"I'll *bet* Anne hasn't never," Elizabeth said.

Vicki gestured helplessly at Natalie. "These women always suspect—" she said directly to Natalie.

Natalie thought of saying, "I understand," sympathetically, but decided not to. Further irony would not materially improve this situation, and she was still not irrevocably committed to Elizabeth.

"Suppose you come to my office," Arthur Langdon said from the other room.

Anne glanced briefly at the door beyond which Arthur was somewhere talking into the phone, and said with just the right amount of confused indignation, "After all, Mrs. Langdon, Arthur and I are only—"

"Mr. Langdon," said Elizabeth.

"Mr. Langdon," said Anne obediently. "We're only studying together. I mean, since I'm one of his students it's only natural that we should—" She hesitated admirably. "—Study together," she said.

"And remember," Vicki said, "*you* were one of his students once, Mrs. Langdon. You must remember what an interest he takes in—"

"Goodbye," Arthur Langdon said from the other room, and everyone was silent and did not speak again until he came back. He sat down in his chair again and said to Natalie, "You were telling me about your father."

"We *must* go," Vicki said. Anne nodded, and rose. Natalie, who had opened her mouth to speak of her father, closed her mouth again and started uncertainly to get out of her chair.

Vicki looked at her. "Come along with us," she said finally.

"We can go to dinner together," Anne said.

"I'd love to," Natalie said, thinking, I'm not an ally, I'm a mercenary. "Thanks very much," she said to Elizabeth, and to Arthur, "I've enjoyed myself immensely."

"Come in any time," Arthur Langdon said, seeming actually to mean it.

"It was terribly nice of you to have us," Vicki said to Elizabeth. She did not go over to the couch to say it, but stood near the door, as though she realized perfectly that she had better not get close enough to Elizabeth to let Elizabeth reach her. "Perhaps you'll be able to come over for a drink with us some day soon?"

"Thanks," Elizabeth said.

"Mrs. Langdon," Anne said. "Thank you very much." She and Vicki turned to the door, with Natalie following, and Anne said to Arthur, intimately but somehow very clearly, "Arthur it was *so* nice."

Arthur Langdon looked nervously at his wife, and said, "I hope you'll come again soon."

"We'd love to," Vicki said.

They got out the door, the three of them, with Arthur Langdon waving to them as they started down the path. When he had finally closed the door behind them, Vicki laughed, and then was quiet for a minute, she and Anne walking on either side of Natalie and both of them, Natalie felt, observing her and amused. Then Vicki said finally, as though to no one in particular, "How much did she put away before we got there?"

"I'm not sure," Natalie said. Should she carry tales? "Three or four drinks."

"Someone ought to slap her pretty face for her," Vicki said. "I wish Arthur had guts enough to do it."

Anne stuffed her hands into the pockets of her jacket and did a little dance step along the path. "*I* wish I could be there now," she said, "to hear them fight."

Natalie, my child,

No, indeed, I do not read Shakespeare any more; I have passed the age when such things are felt to be essential, and have reached the age when half a dozen esoteric quotations are all I ever need—those, that is, and a Concordance for any unexpected crisis. I feel very strongly the pull of the middle-aged personality, when a ball game and the evening paper are the food of love.

Which reminds me that your mother has had a cold and I must (see, here is a quotation, but, I fear, a rather usual one) I must trouble you, I say, once more for congratulations. Some odd little magazine has done me an odd little honor—my own modest way of rephrasing a particular request from them for a series of articles, so you may, if your mother permits, have a new coat this winter.

I admire your Mr. Langdon. Arthur Langdon, did you say? His name is familiar; ask him if he has ever published. I seem to recollect a series of poems in an arty journal, but perhaps, now that he is an associate professor, he would prefer to forget them? You do not say much about Mrs. Langdon, except that she used

to be one of his students—is that the only unusual fact about
her? Walk not in the sun, my Natalie, nor reproach your father
hereafter for his unlearning. Forgive also the fact that this letter
is so short. I am taking time from my writing to keep in touch
with you; your letters are, believe me, a very bright center in my
life. I sent you to college to enjoy yourself, not to get an education, but, my dear, please hereafter *do* try not to split infinitives.
("To enthusiastically admire Mr. Langdon" indeed! We neither
of us thank you!)

Your mother insists that I inquire about your health. I tell her
that it is no longer our affair, but she feels that maternal interest
is evidenced by a scrupulous investigation of your internal
workings. Do you have any trouble with your eyes, she wants to
know? Your chest? Your feet? Be sure, she says, to keep handy a
bottle of cough medicine in the event of that nasty cough you
used to have at night . . . when you were three.

Love,
Dad

Somewhere in the world trees were growing, Natalie thought
as she walked down the hall of the house where she now lived;
her feet on the linoleum floor made a flat sound, as of one
walking upon dead earth. And perhaps there were still flowers
in the garden at home and her father, glancing from his study
window—perhaps her father thought, I wish Natalie were here.
On either side of Natalie as she walked toward her own room
were doors: perhaps behind one door a girl was studying,
behind another a girl was crying, behind a third a girl was
turning uneasily in her sleep. Behind a certain definite door
downstairs Anne and Vicki sat, laughing and speaking in loud
voices whatever they chose to say; behind other doors girls
lifted their heads at Natalie's footsteps, turned, wondered, and
went back to their work. I wish I were the only person in all the
world, Natalie thought, with a poignant longing, thinking then
that perhaps she was, after all. She reached her own door, and
wondered again—Is this possible, my *own* door? Can it be that
after so short a time I can recognize one door among many,
and call it "my own"? Or is it only from here, in the hall, that

it looks so extraordinary—after all, I can only go *out* one door from my room; it's coming in that is so confusing.

Inside, her room was expectant and without interest in her, as though her final decision upon one door was a matter of small concern to the room itself, and she might as well have walked into limbo, or into a well of fire, for all the room cared. The book she had put down over an hour ago had not consumed any more of its own pages, the typewriter had not turned out any literature, the window had not seen any interesting sights since she left. She dropped her books tiredly on the bed and went with method to hang her jacket in the closet before she sat down at the desk. A vague ambition touched her briefly: should she put a sheet of paper into the typewriter, and perhaps even write on it? Should she read, dress, eat her mother's cookies, sleep? She was staring uncertainly at the window (she might jump out?) when there was a knock at the door.

"Come in," she said, thinking as always, Was it really my door they wanted? It was Rosalind, which made it certainly Natalie's door, above all others, that she wanted.

"Listen," Rosalind said without greeting as she came through the door and half-closed it softly behind her, "listen, Nat, want to see something?"

"What?"

"Come *on*, then," Rosalind said urgently. "Come *on*."

Natalie rose and followed Rosalind through the door again, and back down the hall. They reached a door halfway down toward the stairway—it belonged to someone Natalie knew vaguely; perhaps the girl with bangs whose name might have been Winnie Williams or a girl they called Sandy—and Rosalind stopped in front of the door and said very softly, "Wait, I'll open it, then you'll see."

"Listen—" Natalie began.

Finger on her lips, Rosalind took hold of the doorknob and turned it, opening the door with a sudden push. She craned her head around and said, "Look, look."

Natalie, embarrassed, looked over her shoulder, phrasing apologies ("Sorry, thought it was the john") in her mind, but there was no one inside.

"They've gone," Rosalind said, disappointed. "You should have seen them."

"Who?"

Rosalind laughed, and shrugged. "Next time," she said. "See you later." She went off down the hall and Natalie, going the other way, went back to her own room.

It was that night that the talk of theft was first openly in evidence. In the basement room where the girls played bridge, where there was a stone floor and one dismal ashtray and a broken couch, and where Natalie sat cautiously in a corner, hoping that someone would notice her, and comment, perhaps, on her professional manner of smoking, the girls gathered noisily, the two or three who always heard news before anyone else raising their voices and insisting.

"*Honestly*," Peggy Spencer said honestly, "I wouldn't have said a *word* unless I *knew*. They are *really* going to search *every*body."

"Me?" said Natalie, raising her voice for the first time in that room.

"*Honestly*," Peggy Spencer said, addressing herself for the first time to Natalie across the room. "See, there's been so much stuff missing . . ."

Natalie did not know. Because she did not, had not heard, she found that all at once everyone was talking to her as though they knew her, even though one girl did persistently call her Helen and another thought that she lived on the fourth floor (it was here a comfort of sorts to Natalie to know that she had not been so universally observed as she thought), they all spoke directly to her.

"I lost this evening dress," one said, her voice riding over the others. "That was really the *first*. You see, I went out of my room for a minute and the dress was hanging . . ."

"Someone on the second floor lost forty dollars," said someone else.

"It's been going on for *ages*," Peggy Spencer said. "Everyone's been missing things for about a month, and no one said anything because . . ." She hesitated, searching for a reason

why no one had said anything. "Anyway," she went on, "it
finally got so bad that Old Nick heard about it, and then of
course when she started asking questions . . ." Peggy shrugged.
"Why, *then*," she said, "it turned out that nearly everyone had
lost something or other. I don't think," she added thoughtfully, turning her red head around to look at everyone in the
room, "I don't *really* think that all those things were *really*
stolen."

"My *dress* is gone—I know I didn't send it to the cleaners
that day because I remember thinking especially—"

"—and this little cigarette lighter I got from this boy—"

"—and imagine a pair of *shoes*. Who could wear anyone
else's *shoes?*"

"—and lots of money. There was this girl lost forty dollars,
and lots of other people had money that just—"

"—and someone said a girl on the first floor lost some letters and a lot of jewelry."

"A slip, too. Real lace."

Natalie, smoking professionally, was checking desperately
over her belongings; if she had lost any clothes or jewelry she
would hardly have known it, since she had worn the same
sweater and skirt for a week, and except for the formality of
hanging her jacket on the hook just inside her closet door had
not opened her closet since she took out the skirt she was now
wearing, but the persistent thoughts rode her mind side by side:
first, it would not look well if she had not lost anything, and,
second, was she not an obvious thief? She felt her cheek red-
dening, and turned her head down to watch her foot scuffing
out the cigarette; if I *had* stolen anything, she thought (And
had she perhaps not? She was suddenly aware of the excitement
of going silently into someone's room, looking smilingly over
someone else's possessions, reading letters, scrutinizing pictures, fondling jewelry, discarding whatever did not meet her
fancy, and then—the most dangerous part; up until this
moment her carefully planned excuses would let her off—
slipping the roll of bills into her pocket, stuffing the book into
the front of her sweater, flinging the real lace over her arm as
though it belonged to her, and coming softly out of someone

else's room, closing the door gently, walking boldly down the hall, counting over her new dear ownings behind the tightly locked door of her own room), and she thought that all of them were looking at her, unexpectedly quiet, all thinking at once, Why, it was *that* girl, of course; I remember now, I saw her coming out of my room, I always *said* she was . . .

"Have *you* lost anything?" Peggy Spencer asked Natalie directly.

In the small brief silence Natalie said, thinking, "Only some change that I left on my dresser. I put it there when I came in and then I went to take a shower and when I came back it was gone." All the faces were turned to her now. "I didn't want to say anything," she explained, "because then I didn't know that anything else was missing and I didn't want to make any trouble for anyone."

"That's the way *we* all felt," someone said approvingly.

"And yet," Peggy Spencer said earnestly, "if no one ever *said* anything, whoever it is would just be getting away with it all the *time*."

"That's true," Natalie said. "I mean, now that I know about it, I feel differently about it." Why am I talking, she wondered in shame; who am I convicting, whose soul am I selling, what murder am I helping to commit; why am I here, she thought sadly, pretending that someone else has stolen from *me?*

After the special trip Natalie had made back to her room to freshen her lipstick and comb her hair, it seemed almost callous of Arthur Langdon not to turn and smile at her when she stood timidly in the doorway of his office, not daring to knock for fear he had already seen her, not daring to enter for fear he had not already seen her; she thought of trying a slight cough, or of saying softly, "Mr. Langdon?" or of going away a step and walking heavily up to the door again, but all these devices were of course only endless vicious circles around the central point, which was that for some reason Mr. Almighty Langdon thought he need not, if he chose not, notice Miss Natalie Waite, and really thought he could keep her waiting uncertainly, endlessly, in the doorway to his office. As she was wondering, then, if a sort of dignified march back down the stairs might not prove that she was something more than this, he looked up at her, blankly for a minute, as one who thinks deeply, and then recognized her with a nod of companionship that said she was to enter but not speak. She moved respectfully into the room, thinking that she was the kind of woman who knows when to keep quiet, and sat docilely in the chair beside the desk, her hands folded, and her eyes discreetly turned away from him, to show that she was not in the least interested in what he was doing. She could see, however, from the corners of her eyes, that he looked tired as he bent his head over the papers on the desk; he's been fighting with Elizabeth, she thought with new knowledge, and hoped he would notice her quiet sympathy.

"I wish I were an insurance salesman," he said abruptly, shoving the papers back on his desk.

Natalie lost her moment, in the split second during which she realized that *he* had been hoping that *she* would notice; she held with herself a seemingly endless debate over what to say and do ("Stop acting like a child, my dear," her hand gently on his?), and by the time she had finally decided that his remark was to be treated as a joke, he had swung around in his chair to face her and was saying, "Well, Natalie?"

She smiled, and the moment became unexpectedly one of excruciating embarrassment. Natalie heard the back of her mind gibbering obscenities, and thought for a mad moment that she might be saying them aloud and not realizing; perhaps, she thought, I am undressing, or in the bathroom, or looking at myself in the mirror, and only pretending that I am here alone with Arthur Langdon; perhaps I am here with Arthur Langdon and pretending that I am dressing and talking really to myself; perhaps I will say something frightful and never know whether I have really said it or not, because of course he would pretend I never said it but he would always remember—a thousand years from now, Arthur Langdon telling Elizabeth for the hundredth time about the girl (Natalie? Helen? Joan?) who had said the shocking thing to him, and Natalie laughed suddenly, bringing herself immediately back to the present in Arthur Langdon's office, where she certainly *was* at the moment, and he was saying curiously, "What *were* you thinking about?"

"I was thinking about when I would be dead," Natalie said.

"Dead?" he said, surprised. "Are we going to die, you and I?"

"I only worry about *how*," Natalie said soberly; unlike most of the things she found herself saying to Arthur Langdon, this was true. "I keep thinking that of course it's *got* to happen, and even to me, but then I always think that somehow and someday this interesting person of mine will . . ." She searched for a word. "Subside," she said finally. "I mean, I will be very suddenly aware of an ending, and that there is not going to be any more for *me*, and that I am not going to be with myself any longer. And all of that's all right," she said, going on quickly as he opened his mouth to speak. "I'm only afraid of being caught unaware, of that terrible fast panic that comes when you're very very frightened, and of being *afraid* when it happens. So then, of course, I always think I'll kill myself before it *can* happen."

She stopped, and Arthur Langdon said, "You have a very original mind, Natalie."

"That's what I mean," she said, thinking, Oh, the fool, "can you imagine having a mind like mine and losing it when you die?" Had she, she wondered, had she *the* original mind?

He waved his hand at the papers on the desk. "There are almost two hundred papers there," he said. "I have to read every one of them. And I always watch for yours."

(Joan? Helen? Anne?) "I find your criticisms very helpful," Natalie said demurely. "My father discusses my work with me very much as you do." She thought of her father with sudden sadness; he was so far away and so much without her, and here she was speaking to a stranger.

"Does your father think your work shows talent?"

"My father does not praise anyone."

"Do you plan to be a writer?"

A what? Natalie thought; a writer, a plumber, a doctor, a merchant, a chief; the best-laid plans of; a writer the way I might plan to be a corpse? "A writer?" she repeated, as though she had never heard the word before.

He was staring at her with his mouth half-open; she must have delayed her idiotic answer beyond any reasonable time for thought. "Do you plan to be a writer?" he asked again.

He *did* mean it, then. "Look," Natalie said, "why does everyone say they're going to be writers? When they're not? I mean, why do you and my father and everybody say 'to be a writer' as though it were something different? Not like anything else? Is there something special about writers?"

Her delay had not helped him any. "It's because writing itself," he began, hesitating, and then, "I suppose it's because writing—well, it's something important, I suppose."

"Well, then, *what* am I going to write?"

"Well . . ." he said. He looked at her and then irritably at the papers on his desk. "Stories," he said. "Poems. Articles. Novels. Plays." He shook his head and then said, "Anything—well, creative."

"But why is it so important, this creating?" Natalie was positive at the moment that she was asking him something very important, and that he could answer it, and she leaned forward eagerly; she needed only one answer, only one, she thought, and then she knew that he would not tell her, because he shook his head and said, "Natalie, this is metaphysical nonsense. Questioning one's own soul is not something at which I am particularly good at any time, and certainly it is not a subject which ought to be indulged in broad daylight. Some other time," he laughed, "we can sit in the darkness under an oak tree and tell one another vast truths."

It was precisely as Natalie's father would have rebuked her; she sat back in her chair and thought, I will never ask him this again, and then thought, What a silly person I am, and now he *does* think I am a fool.

"Tell me," he said, leaning forward. "You were giving me your ideas about death."

———

"But the *best* thing they did," Anne said, laughing before she had even begun to describe it, "was the time they wrote to someone's boy friend and told him not to come to the dance."

"They sent him a telegram," Vicki said. "And the girl waited and waited and of course he never showed up."

"But everyone knew except *her*," Anne said. "That was the joke of it."

"Didn't she ever find out?" Natalie asked.

"*That* was the best part," Anne said. "Of course she found out later, and of course it was *awful* for her, but she had to be a good sport about it, *naturally*. It was only a joke, after all, and she waited and waited all dressed up for the dance."

"And remember the time they called up and pretended to be some guy's mother and had this girl almost in hysterics?"

"And that old car and they ran it right across anyone's lawn or anything or anywhere they pleased, and they weren't afraid of *any*one; and the time they poured iodine all over someone's fur coat?"

"*She* was sore," Vicki said with satisfaction.

"I should think so," said Natalie.

"But of course she had to be a good *sport*," Vicki said.

"And the time," said Anne, giggling, "that they sent invitations to all the faculty, inviting them to a party, and on the bottom of the invitation it said in big letters 'Your wife is NOT invited'?"

Vicki laughed. "There was trouble *then*," she said.

"Nothing's the same since they graduated," Anne said wistfully. "No one can think of anything to *do*, any more."

Natalie, my dear,
Needless to say, your letters amuse and delight me, although, as I have often told you (how humorless I sound!) your style leaves much to be desired; how *very* often, my dear Natalie, have we, you and I, spent our morning hours puzzling out the intricate filigree of the subordinate clause, and yet I find, in your last letter but one, the following (please forgive my quoting you, my dear; it is the only way, you know, to improve you. I have a

notion you would hardly read a bare, invented example): "I like college very much, but am still a little confused. I don't think I'll ever learn French. I like philosophy, though. Is there any chance of your coming down soon?"

Ignoring the sense of the quotation (except to mention, in passing, that it is not possible to "learn" French; as I believe someone else has said, one either is or is not born with the kind of personality to which French is a mother-tongue), let me only say that two self-evident remarks connected with "but" do not constitute an English style. Nor do a series of short sentences, unless they are building into something very clear and definite, which in your case seems to be "with love to all, Natalie"—a desirable sentiment, and one your mother could hardly do without, but surely not an adequate consummation—almost, in fact, an anticlimax.

Enough for your letter; you are presumably studying English composition and we may expect to see an improvement soon. Your mother and I are better able to avoid one another without you and your brother cluttering up the house. Your mother remarks nostalgically that the dinner table seems unusually deserted, which of course is true, although it persuades me finally that your mother has from the beginning counted her children only by the places set at table, and has marked your growth from one chop to two with pride and appreciation—soon her little girl will be quite grown up, and able to manipulate her own knife and fork. You may, however, suppose that we miss you.

Has your Mr. Langdon seen my piece in the last *Passionate Review*? If not, you may use its arguments as your own, and confound him.

> Obediently,
> Dad

Natalie's journal; middle October:
I suppose you have been wondering for a long time, my darling Natalie, what I can find to be thinking about. I suppose you have even noticed—Natalie seems so strange lately, she seems so withdrawn and distant and quiet, I wonder if Natalie is coming along all right, or if there is something troubling her. Perhaps you have been thinking, dearest, that Natalie had something she

wanted to say to you. Perhaps, you thought, Natalie is frightened and perhaps she even thinks sometimes about a certain
long ago bad thing that she promised me never to think about
again. Well, that's why I'm writing this now. I could tell, my
darling, that you were worried about me. I could feel you being
apprehensive, and I knew that what you were always thinking
about was you and me. And I even knew that you thought I was
worried about that terrible thing, but of course—I promise you
this, I really do—I don't think about it at all, ever, because both
of us know that it never happened, did it? And it was some horrible dream that caught up with us both. We don't have to worry
about things like that, you remember we decided we didn't have
to worry.

No, what I have been thinking about is something entirely
different. I have been thinking—and it is very very hard to say
this, so be patient with me—about the beautiful wonderful
exciting things that are happening. That does not quite describe
it. Look. Let me say it like this: when I came here to college I
was all alone and that bad thing had just happened and I had no
friends and no one to think about and I was always frightened.
Now all of a sudden I find that I am walking around in a world
very full of other people, and because they are all frightened too
I can afford to be frightened, and then once I *know* I am frightened then I can go ahead and forget about it and start looking
around at other things. And of course now I know that it isn't
important about other people, and only the people who don't
dare be all alone need friends. I don't suppose I will need any
friends or anything for the rest of my life, now that I am not
frightened.

But of course I think sometimes (thank heaven no one will
ever read this but you and me, my dear) about being in love,
which is something I hardly expect ever to happen to me, but I
think I have just a slight idea, from the way I feel about other
things, what it would be like. I think, for instance, that no one
can really love a person who is not superior in every way. For
instance, I know from how I feel about people who are superior
to me in some things just exactly how I would feel about some-

one who was superior to me in everything, which of course would be the only kind of person I could really love.

I wanted to tell my father about this, and I wanted to tell Arthur too, but of course it is not really possible to go up to some man and say that you could never really love any person who was not superior to you in everything and let them see clearly that they are *not* that.

I wish I knew why I am so excited all the time. I keep thinking something is going to happen. I keep thinking I am right on the point of telling someone all about myself.

I wonder what I would say to a psychoanalyst. I wonder where people find words for all the funny things inside their heads. I keep turning around in circles and finding how well things fit together, but nothing is ever complete. I think if I could tell some-one everything, every single thing, inside my head, then *I* would be gone, and not existing any more, and I would sink away into that lovely nothing-space where you don't have to worry any more and no one ever hears you or cares and you can say any-thing but of course you wouldn't *be* any more at all and you couldn't really *do* anything so it wouldn't *matter* what you did.

Of course I realize that the first thing to do if you wanted someone to tell you everything would be to make your minds go along together, so that if for instance a psychoanalyst wanted me to tell him everything in my head, he would have to be very close to me so that our minds were running exactly together, coincid-ing, and what I told him would not be told, really, but only an echo of the way both our minds were going, and would sort of cancel out. And there, you see, is what I mean by superior, because after all this he would have to have enough left over after he had taken all my mind, so that he could keep on think-ing by himself, after I was nothing. But of course I don't believe anybody really exists like that and that all these people like Elizabeth who talk about going to psychoanalyst don't want this at all, or perhaps their minds are so little and move on such a small amount of energy or space that a psychoanalyst could use just a little bit of himself to capture them and have plenty of mind left over, so as not to be absorbed in them at all particularly. And that, I suppose is why these people find it so easy to get along with the idea of having their minds taken away from them, because their minds were never very useful to them in the first place. Although I do not have to worry about being modest here, it is certainly not necessary to point out to *you* that Elizabeth is not as wise as I am.

I want somebody who will fight about it, too. Suppose there is a person, somewhere very near me, right now, who is thinking about me and who watches me and knows everything I think about and who is just waiting for me to recognize

Odd things, these days, came back into Natalie's mind. For instance, she remembered a scene that happened when she was about six years old; it recurred to her often, and mostly during classes when her mind relaxed and she drew strange little patterns in her notebook, and, with her eyes fixed earnestly upon the front of the room, wandered away by herself. The scene she remembered so clearly was of herself, small vague Natalie in a pair of shorts and sneakers, looking honestly and with the eyes of pure truth up at her mother, who bent down over her and listened with concern. "I found a wishing stone," little Natalie was telling her mother. "I knew it was a wishing stone because when I dug it up it *looked* like a wishing stone, so I held it tight in my hand and closed my eyes and wished for a bicycle, and then nothing happened at all and so I threw the stone away." Natalie could still, this many years later, see her mother's stricken eyes. She remembered that her father had laughed, and that her mother had begged for the bicycle for Natalie; these cynical later days, Natalie suspected that her mother had been right. It was less important, Natalie thought, to allow her father's humor to be transmitted to his children than to keep alive her mother's faith in magic. Too, Natalie saw now that if she had kept the wishing stone until the right time came, she could have used it to wish for a bicycle on that Christmas Eve when a bicycle was so obviously awaiting her under the Christmas tree. Then, magic would have been sustained, and cause and effect not violated for that first, irrecoverable time.

Behind Natalie a girl said aloud, puzzled, "Well, *I* think that if Romeo wanted her so much all he had to do was *take* her. I mean, why all that bother with secret marriages and stuff when they could just walk off together?"

Mustn't violate the sacred rules of magic, Natalie thought sleepily. Never wish for anything until it's ready for you. Never try to make anything happen until it's on its way. The formal way is best, after all; no short cuts allowed in this passage.

"Seems to *me*," said someone on the far side of the room, "that if the ending was happier it would be a better play."

She was a minute or two late and was trying to phrase apologies in her mind when she knocked softly on the door of the Langdon's house. It was a perfectly legitimate delay, but it was difficult to tell Elizabeth Langdon that one was late for tea with her because her husband had stood in the center of the path, refusing to recognize any hints about appointments, asking endless questions, making well-turned compliments . . . she knocked again, a little more emphatically. The door was not latched, and slipped back and open under her hand. For a minute she stood there and then, thinking that she was expected and telling herself she would do the same anywhere, she pushed the door a little farther and stepped in. For a minute she saw nothing and then, all at once, she saw Elizabeth Langdon asleep with her head on the arm of the couch, and the thick line of smoke rising from the upholstery near her head. Moving quickly and crying out, "Elizabeth," before she thought to say, "Mrs. Langdon," Natalie went to the couch and pushed Elizabeth's head aside, and began to slap at the burning couch.

"Oh my God," said Elizabeth from somewhere behind Natalie. She too began to slap at the chair, hitting Natalie's hand, and then she said, "Wait, wait," and ran down the hall and into the kitchen. The cigarette that had fallen from Elizabeth's hand had burned itself out of sight in the couch, and the smoke coming from some horrible secret inner part choked Natalie as she leaned over it. Elizabeth came back behind her with a shakerful of cocktails and said with a giggle, "Couldn't wait to fill a pitcher with water. Got to remember to save two drinks." Natalie knocked her arm away so that the cocktails

poured on the floor, and said, "That stuff burns! Get *water!*"
Elizabeth stared vacantly, and Natalie, thinking, I am acting
in an emergency, ran into the kitchen and filled a saucepan
with water and hurried back, spilling water on the hall floor as
she ran, and poured the water carefully and accurately into the
burning hole on the couch.

As the smoke died away Natalie realized that Elizabeth was
laughing, and she began to laugh too. The hole became a sod-
den ugly spot, the smoke stopped, and the room suddenly
smelled most violently of gin. Elizabeth lifted the shaker and
peered into it. "Terrible waste," she said.

"I'll never be able to drink it," Natalie protested, laughing
because it was over and she felt that she had been perhaps a
little impulsively heroic. "I thought *you* were on fire," she
explained with embarrassment.

"I nearly *was*," Elizabeth said, wide-eyed. "Thanks," she
said.

"I'm sorry I shouted at you," Natalie said. They stared at
one another uncomfortably for a minute. Then Elizabeth said,
"Saved some cocktails, anyway."

"Spilled water on the hall floor," Natalie said.

"*That's* all right," Elizabeth said largely. "That's the third
time I've done it, you know. Fires, I mean."

"The *third* time?" Natalie said, unbelieving.

Elizabeth nodded. "Third time this year," she said. "Once
the fat in the frying pan caught fire because I wasn't watching
it, and before I could put it out the kitchen curtains caught,
and then if Arthur hadn't been there my dress would have
caught but he pulled me out of the way and put the fire out. He
was so frightened he couldn't talk. I could have been killed."

"That's terrible," said Natalie earnestly.

"And the second time was when I accidentally dropped a
lighted match into the wastebasket in Arthur's study, and the
wastebasket flamed right up and that time my skirt *did* catch
fire, but I picked up the wastebasket and ran into the bathroom
and turned on the shower and threw the wastebasket under it
and got under myself. So *that* time was all right."

"I'll bet he was frightened then," Natalie said.

"He was when I told him. He wanted me to stop smoking. He said—" Elizabeth looked at Natalie queerly "—he said I was trying to kill myself."

"Are you?" Natalie asked in spite of herself.

Elizabeth shook her head. "I don't know," she said mournfully. "I really don't know. Sometimes, though, I think I have cause." She stopped, thinking, and there was a silence. Natalie stirred uneasily, and Elizabeth said, "Serve him right, too."

"That's no way to die, though," Natalie said.

"It certainly is *not*," said Elizabeth, and shuddered. "My God, I was scared," she said.

"Me, too."

"Well," Elizabeth said, as though done with the subject. "How about we finish off the cocktails?" she asked.

Natalie made a face. "I don't know if I can stand it," she said, and gestured at the room at large. "Seems like it's into everything."

"You won't notice it after you've had a drink," Elizabeth said. The shaker sat on the table where she had put it down, and she picked it up and looked into it again. "There's really *quite* a lot left," she said, and carried it with her out into the kitchen to get glasses. While she was gone Natalie opened the window and stood looking out onto the college campus. Somehow, inside this room, in the house, she was removed from those girls in their bright sweaters who walked easily across the grass, under the colored trees, ignoring the paths and putting their clean brown-and-white shoes down as though their tuition had bought them a permanent share in this very land. They understood the functioning of the college, these girls outside, talking to one another as they walked, and knowing the places to which they were bound; they were intimate and sympathetic with this college, and never saw it as the spot where Arthur Langdon taught, or where one was held apart from home and kindness by the dubious good intentions of strangers. Inside here, Natalie thought, turning abruptly to look into the room and at the furniture and books and even the burned couch, inside this room is the only place except my own home where everybody knows my name.

"At least two drinks apiece," Elizabeth said gaily, "and probably more."

"Hadn't we better save some?" Natalie said prudently.

Elizabeth's face turned sullen. "At least this time," she said, "he won't be able to say I drank them. *This* time he can't blame *me*." She looked at the couch. "He can't even be angry at *that*, very well."

"I don't think it's badly burned," Natalie said.

Elizabeth shrugged. "Oh, well," she said, and sat down on the couch; because her favorite corner was burned she was forced to go to the other end, and she sat there uncomfortably, resting on her wrong elbow. "I was reading," she said, looking irritably at the burned spot. "That's what happened, I was reading."

"Next time put out your cigarette before you fall asleep."

"That's what I get for reading," Elizabeth said. She pointed with her toe to the book on the table. "Psychology," she said. "*I* can't understand it."

"Then why do you do it?" Natalie asked, wondering at the vast freedom of one who could learn if she chose and could, if she chose, flatly refuse to understand.

"We *all* do it," Elizabeth said. "All of us, the faculty wives. Got to do something, you know. And besides, it feels good to sit next to those kids in class and look at them frowning and trying to make something out of it, and you sit there thinking how much more you know than they do, and they have to call you Mrs. Langdon."

"At least you don't have any trouble passing."

Elizabeth made a face. "I never finish up the courses," she said. "Those poor kids, they have to come rain or shine, and answer when they're asked questions—me, I can just say, 'Go to hell professor,' and walk out if I'm bored."

"How about your husband's class?" Natalie asked.

"I *took* that class," Elizabeth said, and laughed. "I got through the whole thing—and I passed, too—before I ever married Arthur. He used to give me back my papers with notes written on them. I'd laugh out loud, sometimes, in class when he gave me my papers back with those notes on them. And he'd read things like speeches from *Antony and Cleopatra*, and some of the kids would be blushing and some of them would be just looking at him like lovesick chickens, and I'd think of how anytime I wanted I could get him to read the same things to me all alone and I'd look around that class and think how pathetic those kids were and I'd want to laugh in their faces."

A great envious excitement filled Natalie; she promised herself quickly that she would somehow, later, examine how it would feel to sit in class with such special secret knowledge, with such delicious sense of possession.

Elizabeth sighed. "I *liked* that class," she said. She was smiling reminiscently still as she rose to fill Natalie's glass. "And sometimes," she said, "I'd meet people like Mr. and Mrs. Watson—he was biology teacher then—and I'd say, 'How do you do, Mrs. Watson, Mr. Watson,' so politely, and all the time I'd be thinking of how when Arthur and I were married I could call them Carl and Laura. And about sitting with the faculty at trustee dinners or college movies. And running into Arthur's office whenever I pleased, and not caring *who* saw me. And staying out all night if I felt like it, and laughing in anyone's face the next morning. And faculty parties," she said, "and pouring at teas. And getting the best of everything." She sighed again, her head on her arm and her long hair falling against her face. "I thought it was all going to be so wonderful," she said.

Suddenly, again, Natalie felt the small chill of dismay when Arthur Langdon's footsteps sounded outside the door and, with the opening of the door, the same familiar shock of finding him slightly smaller than she had remembered him.

"Hello?" he said, blinking after the bright sunlight outside, and then, his voice hard, "Smells like a brewery in here."

Elizabeth stood up quickly and hurried across the room to him. "Arthur," she said, and her face showed alarm but her voice was rich, "Arthur, listen, I tried to kill myself again this afternoon—"

It was on a Thursday evening early in November that the peculiar events in the dormitory where Natalie slept began to attract attention. On that Thursday evening (there was a full moon, which several people insisted hysterically had certainly something to do with it) the girl who lived alone in the room almost directly under Natalie's arose from her bed asleep and unlocked her door and moved slowly and with seeming purpose down the hall. Where she could, she opened doors and went in to awaken all sleepers. At each bed, the story went, she bent over gently and smoothed the pillow, before giving the girl asleep a quick slap to awaken her. "No sleep tonight," she told each of them pleasantly, and left the room. By the time she had reached the end of the hall a group of girls had gathered, half-asleep and frightened and talking among themselves in whispers. One girl who found herself more competent than the rest separated herself at last from the group, and, approaching the sleepwalker, threw a blanket around her; then half a dozen girls of great courage half-carried the sleepwalker—now walking awake—and shut her into the closet of her own room with the door locked, where she stayed all night, crying and promising to behave if they let her out.

The next night—that would be Friday, with the sleepwalker safely in the infirmary—word of thievery again spread through the house. Natalie, who had not been awakened the night before, was tonight on the outskirts of the group that gathered swiftly in the hall—almost as though everyone had been waiting for some new excitement—when one of the girls announced that she had caught another girl coming out of her room with a blouse in her hand. Miss Nicholas was quickly brought from her bed—she too had missed the excitement the night before, although she had been notified in time to let the girl out of the closet before breakfast—and, with judicious attention to all those who had something to tell her about things stolen, and with sober announcements about being *sure* before any charge was brought, searched thoroughly the room of the girl accused, assisted by the accuser and several friends. Although none of them were able to uncover any of the stolen articles, it was said and echoed that the girl could have sold the clothes and spent the money. One or two most subtle minds, who volunteered to help the girl tidy up her room after the searching party had finished, reported later in the smoking room that she had said nothing which might be construed as incriminating.

On Sunday afternoon, while most of the girls and Miss Nicholas were at Sunday dinner, one of the girls on the top floor, who had stayed away from dinner because she had to lose two pounds by the next weekend in order to fit into the dress she was wearing to a houseparty dance, walked out of her room and saw a man running down the stairs. It was decided that he was a Peeping Tom, and several of the girls recalled having seen someone in what must have been that same brown coat hanging around outside the dormitory, as though he were a janitor, or something. One of the girls, who had been severely surprised when she was eleven years old by a man who exposed himself before her as she passed him on the street, explained that this was a kind of neurosis some men had. Many people recalled having heard that such things happened frequently around women's colleges, and one girl left school because she wrote her mother some of the things she heard around the smoking room.

A senior girl, questioned in the smoking room, said that such things always came in waves. It was a college season, she explained. She told some of the things that had happened during comparable seasons when she was younger, and added that she believed it had something to do with the fact that the Thanksgiving and Christmas vacations were due soon. "Some people have trouble adjusting between college and home," she explained.

The girl who had been accused of stealing left college, and almost immediately afterward a girl who lived on the second floor reported that her allowance check was missing from her room. It turned out during the next day or so that several people were losing things; one girl went to look for an angora sweater she had put away in her bottom drawer and it was gone; shortly after that, two cartons of cigarettes disappeared from another room, and everyone in the house who smoked that particular brand changed abruptly.

A very brief enthusiasm sprang up for bringing tiny bottles of rum into the dining room and adding the rum to the dinner coffee. This was replaced by an inexplicable and childish two-day enthusiasm for pig-latin. Also in the dining room one evening, an entire tableful of girls rose and walked out in the middle of the meal because they were refused more bread. A girl on the third floor who was seen crying was reported faithfully as suffering from a venereal disease, and a petition was sent to Miss Nicholas to require the girl to use the basement lavatory. Miss Nicholas was reported to be secretly married, and the Peeping Tom identified as her husband, looking for her on the top floor. Two girls in another house tried to kill themselves with double doses of the infirmary sleeping medicine. An unnamed girl, also in another house, was said to have died of an abortion, and several people knew the name of the baby's father, who was reliably identified as a local man who worked as a lifeguard summers and in the gas station winters. It was generally believed that it was completely possible to become pregnant by using the same bathtub as one's brother, although not necessarily at the same time.

November 12—Nov. 13

Natalie, my dear,
It is late at night, and I have just come home from a rather ribald gathering, and nothing, it seems to me at the moment, would delight me more than a note of paternal warning to my only daughter. May I—and through how many faulty media—*may* I, then, issue one note of paternal warning? And over again I reflect on the faulty media—mine own words, the United States mails, the extreme long chance that this letter will reach you at all, that your benevolent housemother (Old Nick, did you say?) should not read this herself and destroy it, that your house should not burn down and this letter with it, that the stamp should not fall off nor the address be erased by some postal cataclysm— suppose, indeed, daughter, it should be one of those letters we read about in the daily newspapers, lost for twenty years, but faithfully found and delivered at the end of that time—how will you feel, twenty years from now, reading a lost letter from your father, with advice well meant and long useless—faulty media? I begin to perceive that it is impossible for this letter to reach you at all.

Let me, then, warn you direfully against false friends. And against those for whose friendship toward you you can find no material motive. And against all fawners, all liars, all nodders. Believe me, girl, without a motive no friendship can be, and without a motive no friendship can last, and whether it be father to daughter or lover to wife, no friendship can come to birth without it have a motive and an end in view.* And further, daughter, I charge you: do not trust entirely to your own knowledge for these things. One person inaccurate upon his own behavior may nevertheless be accurate upon yours. Consult, therefore, the blind and honest; they can do you no harm, and one, at least, wishes you none.

Later

Natalie, I wrote this much last night and would not for the world deprive you of my paternal effusions, particularly since I can see that in spite of my heavy manner, very much, I believe, in the style of an Old-Testament God, I was trying to say something very real, which I must have supposed last night you were old enough to hear. What worries me is, I think, the fact that in your letters you show yourself as not entirely happy. I have been sure for a long time that things were difficult for you, but please remember, my dear, that they would have been difficult anywhere. I chose this college for you because I knew that it was a fairly exclusive, expensive place and, while I pretend to no less snobbishness than any man, it seemed to me additionally valuable in that you *will*, snobbishness or not, find intelligence and culture accompanying persons of a certain social class. There is no doubt but what the class of girls you have as friends is not a representative one, but my plans for you never did include a broad education; an extremely narrow one, rather—one half, from the college, in people and surroundings; the other half, from me, in information. My ambitions for you are slowly being realized, and, even though you are unhappy, console yourself

*Here I perceive imperfectly my own meaning, and apologize if you understand, but if you do not, I—being this morning more sober—charge you to keep it in mind until you do. Do you get any other letters with footnotes?

with the thought that it was part of my plan for you to be unhappy for a while. The fact that you associate intimately with girls who do not care for the things you do should strengthen your own artistic integrity and fortify you against the world; remember, Natalie, your enemies will always come from the same place your friends do. So try to bear with these girls, try not to let their occasional silliness upset you, try not to let them cultivate you for mental values rather than social values—briefly, try to do what I advised last night: scrutinize carefully anyone aspiring to be your friend, examine her conduct for motives, and deny your friendship if your estimate of her motives shows them ignoble. I should, if I were you, be extremely cautious with Arthur Langdon; I have been re-reading his poems. He is a spiritual man, and one to whom things of the spirit are meaningful. Past a certain point this sort of person is not trustworthy; he will expect more of your compliance than you should be ready to give; your humor will offend his mysticism. Do not under any circumstances allow Arthur Langdon to convert you to any philosophical viewpoint until you have first consulted me.

As the person who knows you most dearly, and who loves you always the best, I am equally the one most capable of telling you these things. It has been *my* plan, Natalie, all of it, and when you approach despair remember that even your despair is part of my plan. Remember, too, that without you I could not exist: there can be no father without a daughter. You have thus a double responsibility, for my existence and your own. If you abandon me, you lose yourself.

Your devoted,
Dad

Being assistant hostess to Vicki and Anne at cocktails was not in any way similar to standing up with Mrs. Arnold Waite to receive guests. For one thing, Mrs. Arnold Waite had been supplied, beyond all else, with the material for bribing people to like her house. On the other hand, since the college had once been progressive, and retained privileges where it had lost principles, students were allowed to own and serve liquor and a minimal amount of food (food, after all, was served in the dining room, but there was no bar on campus) without the conviction, which Mrs. Arnold Waite had to perfection, that it was in any way possible to live differently. Ice might be readily procured at the college store, and carried dripping from a newspaper the length of the campus lawn. Toothbrush glasses might be freely confiscated from the common bathrooms, rinsed inadequately, and dried on other people's bath towels. There were, of course, girls who brought their own sets of glasses to college, and kept them on the bookcases in their rooms, but these were mostly upperclassmen, or girls who realized that their lives were unendurable without the tradition of dressing for dinner.

At the entertainment proffered by Vicki, Anne, and Natalie, the glasses used to serve cocktails to Arthur and Elizabeth Langdon had been borrowed up and down the hall, so that on the front of the tray, with Vicki's good vermouth and Anne's gin, bought that morning in town, were two unchipped and matched cocktail glasses, property of someone on the first floor who lent them with the information that if it hadn't been for Arthur Langdon she would have declined and that, furthermore, Arthur Langdon or not, she would have the hide off anyone who broke them; they had fine gold edges and looked really quite professional. Farther back on the tray, and hidden carelessly behind the gin bottle, were a chipped wineglass, a fruit juice glass stolen from the college dining room, and a plastic bathroom glass; these were for Vicki and Anne and Natalie. On the bookcase next to the tray were a plate, also stolen from the dining room, a jar of cheese spread, and a box of crackers. The cheese was to be spread on the crackers with the wrong end of a nail file.

"You see, the trouble with *us*," Vicki said sardonically, surveying their preparations, "is that we try as hard as we can to live up to the standards of the Langdons. We try to make it look as though—"

"If you'd like to take them into town to a restaurant," Anne said, "you go right ahead. It's your twenty bucks."

Natalie, who had supplied the crackers and cheese and felt a maternal obligation toward them, was trying to spread the cheese on the crackers with the nail file; the crackers shattered into crumbs in her hands. "We should have gotten pretzels," Natalie said. She was still very polite and tentative with Vicki and Anne, sternly repressing in herself the constant question as to why they bothered with her at all. She could have understood their kindness in including her often on occasions such as this, inviting her to the movies, accompanying her to meals, if they had been—say—bored with one another, or needing someone to run errands for them, or amused by her, or respectful of her learning, but none of these estimates seemed reasonable—they were almost too careful of her, so complete in themselves that they needed no one and yet including her with courtesy and insistence, smiling only at her jokes, waiting for her to finish speaking before they began, indifferent to her quotations and yet seeking her company. If they liked her, then, it was for no reason. She had not found yet in them anything to excuse.

"*Any*way," Anne said, "you give Lizzie a drink, and she doesn't care if you spread the cheese with the bottom of your shoe."

"Look," Vicki said, turning from Anne to Natalie. "What *about* Lizzie drinking? Shall we make her take it easy?"

"I really think she'll behave herself since she's not in her own house," Natalie said.

Vicki laughed. "If she's within reaching distance of a bottle? 'They're all so jealous of my catching Arthur,'" she said in a high whining voice. " 'No one understands that I *only* want everyone to *love* me.'"

"I don't think it's any of our business," Anne said in her sweet voice. "After all, *we* can't presume to judge her behavior."

"Well, if Arthur doesn't care, *I* don't," Vicki said. "Listen, there's the doorbell."

She ran out of the door and down the stairs. They were entertaining in what might be called Vicki's room, which made her nominal chief hostess; Vicki's room and Anne's were on a corner of the second floor of the house, and were prized by all students as the most desirable location on campus. Vicki and Anne had kept the corner rooms for two years; they had lived here together through two years when these rooms must have been more intimately home to them than the island Elizabeth Langdon despised, or the other homes they knew where the rooms were larger and the service better. The room which was listed as Vicki's in the college offices had been made into a study, and Anne's room a bedroom; they entertained, naturally, in the study. This room proudly held less of the college furniture than any other room on the campus; the bookcases were recognizably institutional furniture, but then, as Anne had told Natalie reluctantly, bookcases that size were so difficult to transport, and the wastebasket was an undeniable college wastebasket. There were, besides, a studio couch, and a coffee table, and a modern lamp. The pictures on the wall had been painted by Vicki in her second-year art class, and were beautifully framed; the books in the bookcases showed precisely which classes Vicki and Anne had attended during their college years, and gave an occasional sense of their having sampled all the possible courses given at the college in order to learn the names of the textbooks. The blockprint on the curtains had been especially designed for a whimsical sort of person by someone who could afford to do so, the rug was softer than most college beds. How this room could exist not more than one floor and half a dozen doors from her own bare small room on the third floor was a matter of continual surprise to Natalie, and it seemed to her frequently that Vicki and Anne had moved in here, and stayed here, only as some kind of a concession which they made with their usual courtesy to the college authorities.

Possessed tonight of a part-interest in the room, by right of the crackers and cheese she had supplied, Natalie rose with dignity from the studio couch and came to stand in the doorway with Anne, careful not to come too close. They could hear Vicki greeting the Langdons downstairs. "So glad you came," Vicki was saying, and "Come on upstairs, Nat and Anne are waiting."

They could hear the Langdons coming up the stairs before they could see them rounding the turn halfway. "I wish . . ."

Anne said, and then was silent. What would she have said if I had been Vicki? Natalie wondered, and felt Anne sigh and saw Elizabeth Langdon coming up the last part of the stairs. She was dressed up, perhaps more than the occasion demanded. She was wearing a dark-blue dress, very tight at the waist and full in the skirt, with a low-cut neck and much heavy jewelry; it was a dress more fitting for a student than for a faculty wife, with its pretty cut more suitable for a date with a college boy than a cocktail with three college girls. Perhaps Elizabeth had felt this when she dressed, because she had added to her costume a most mature hat, with a caught-up veil and a frill of small feathers, not at all the sort of hat which might be worn by anyone who described herself as a "pretty girl" rather than "an attractive woman." She looked, altogether, very handsome, and would have looked far handsomer if Anne had not been wearing a soft rose wool dress which touched up the highlights in her blonde hair. Natalie had spent some little time over her own clothes and felt more gaunt and ungraceful than ever, standing in a small circle with Elizabeth and Vicki and Anne; but, she thought to console herself, no one is looking at me anyway.

For a minute they hesitated in the doorway, Anne's excessive good manners not adequate to induce Elizabeth to forgo an entrance and come into the room normally. At last, by judicious edging backward by Natalie and Anne, and tactful urging from behind by Vicki, Elizabeth was subtly introduced into the room and seated in an armchair; she tried to go to the couch to sit in what was most closely approximate to her own spot at home, but was forestalled by Vicki, who insisted upon the armchair. Elizabeth sat, then, uneasily, with the two bookcases meeting behind her back and the open windows across from her. Anne sat on the couch next to Arthur Langdon, who had entered the room last, and quietly, as though he had only come along unwillingly with his wife, and Vicki and Natalie hovered uncomfortably over the small table at the side of the room, the one over the tray of liquor and glasses, the other over her cheese.

"You've changed things around," Arthur said to Anne, thus

committing with a grand unconsciousness his first magnificent blunder of the afternoon.

"Only the couch and table," Anne said sweetly. "How do you think it looks, Mrs. Langdon? We find it maddening to make these college rooms look civilized."

"If you used the college furniture you wouldn't have so much trouble," Elizabeth said, moving in her chair. "It looks nice, though."

"Like a warehouse, actually," Anne said. "You know, everything piled up together. If we only had some space."

"Very pleasant place to work," Arthur said.

"Writing papers for Langdon's class," Anne said. Everyone laughed gaily.

"I may think I'm making something here," Vicki said, over their laughter, "but actually it's more mudpies than anything else—heaven only knows what I'll have when I'm through."

"May I help you?" said Arthur immediately.

"I'd be ashamed," Vicki said. She lifted the vase they had decided looked just enough like a cocktail shaker to pass if no one examined it too closely, sniffed at it, shook her head dubiously, and said, "Well, how wrong can you *go*, with just gin and vermouth?"

Arthur closed his eyes in pain, and Anne said to him, "*You'd* better make the next round." Vicki began to pour the cocktails carefully into the two good glasses, and Anne said politely to Elizabeth, "You look so well, Mrs. Langdon; that dress is so becoming."

"You look well, too, Anne." She has promised Arthur to be civil, Natalie thought with sudden pity; she is pretending to be Old Nick being gracious.

"You look as though you'd been out in the sun all day," Anne said to Elizabeth.

Elizabeth smiled deprecatingly. "I've been doing housework."

"I sometime think," said Anne, who was perhaps imagining that *she* was Old Nick being gracious, "that housework must be really the *most* satisfying work of all." Elizabeth stared at her incredulously, and Anne smiled shyly at her and added to Arthur, "It must be *wonderful* to see—well, *order* out of *chaos*, you know that you've done it yourself."

"I suppose you've never scrubbed a floor?" Elizabeth asked. She was still sitting very stiffly in her chair, her hands folded in her lap over her suede pocketbook and her gloves. She turned her head to watch whomever was speaking, and when Vicki brought her a cocktail in the first good glass, she accepted it with an unsmiling bow of thanks, and sat holding it poised in her hand. Arthur got the second good glass, of course, and sipped at it immediately in order to nod to Vicki and say, "Very good indeed," with a faint air of surprise.

"Is it really?" Vicki said. She nodded her head proudly. "I always *knew* I could do it if I tried."

Natalie had achieved several unbroken crackers with cheese on them, and she passed the plate to Elizabeth. As Elizabeth took a cracker she looked up without expression and said to Natalie, "And how are *you*, my dear? Studying hard?"

"Not hard enough, I'm afraid," Natalie said. You ought to meet my mother, she was thinking.

"What accomplished hostesses you all are," Arthur said, when she passed the plate to him.

"There's a real art to getting cheese on crackers," Natalie said.

"It's a talent every young girl should have, making and serving a good cocktail," Arthur said.

"I'll have to take lessons, then," Anne said.

There was a small silence, and then Elizabeth said, "Arthur dear, do you realize that these girls have gone to a vast amount of trouble and expense just to entertain *us?*"

"I think it extremely kind of them," Arthur said gallantly.

"You were very kind to come," Anne said, and Vicki said, "It's a pleasure to us, too," and Natalie said, "Yes, indeed."

"I am sure we were both delighted to come," Elizabeth said. She sipped daintily from her glass and said, "Quite a good cocktail, Vicki."

"Thank you, Mrs. Langdon," Vicki said.

"What do you hear from your father?" Arthur asked Natalie.

Natalie laughed. "He said if you hadn't read his piece in the latest *Passionate Review*, I could use its arguments to confound you."

Arthur was delighted. He laughed, and drank deeply from his glass, and put the glass down, and laughed again. "Splendid," he said largely. "As a matter of fact, I haven't gotten to it yet, so you would have a real advantage over me."

"I haven't read it either," Natalie confessed, and this further delighted Arthur.

"I don't think Natalie ever reads Daddy's articles," Anne said in her soft voice. "Vicki and I got the *Passionate Review* from the library and frankly I—" she smiled, managing an unexpected dimple "—couldn't understand a *word* of it. I could no more manage to confound anyone . . ." She moved her hands helplessly. "Nat is so *smart*," she said.

"We've been *dying* to meet him," Vicki told Arthur, "but Nat is ashamed we'll disgrace her by looking like fools."

"Which we *would*," Anne said. "Can you imagine me telling Daddy I couldn't understand a word he *wrote?*"

Natalie, who could precisely imagine Anne telling her father she could not understand a word he wrote, said with amusement, "I think he'd be flattered."

Anne said to Elizabeth, "We're all afraid of Nat anyway; do you know she writes the most *wicked* descriptions of all of us to her father? I positively *dream* sometimes of what Nat is telling Daddy about me."

"Is that so?" Arthur asked with interest. "*I* never saw any of this."

"What sort of thing do you write, for instance?" Elizabeth asked with sudden real curiosity. "All about everyone you know?"

"That's not a fair question to ask *any*one, my dear," Arthur cut in smoothly. "Natalie and I have discussed her writing very conscientiously," he added, and Natalie, remembering their conscientious discussion of her writing, was tempted to describe it to Elizabeth. "And," he continued, "believe me, I have the *greatest* faith in Natalie's talent."

Elizabeth turned her eyes from her husband to regard Natalie for a long minute. Then she said, "I suppose that sort of thing is all right to do until you're married."

"And *after* you're married," Anne said lightly, "you're too busy doing housework."

"May I pour anyone another drink?" Vicki said. There was a silence while they all consulted the contents of their glasses. "Thank you," said Arthur, and, "*I'd* like one," from Anne.

"Mrs. Langdon?" said Vicki. Everyone avoided looking while Elizabeth glanced down at her glass, barely touched. She shook her head, turning slightly to her husband. "No, thank you, my dear," Elizabeth said.

Everyone had another cocktail except Elizabeth and Natalie, who was beginning to feel that she had seen more drinks than books in her first few months of college. In one of her letters to her father she had told him, "I am beginning to think that the symbol of college, at least for me, has been a kind of drink I never remember seeing much before. Martini. What do you suppose the name means? I know the names of most drinks have no sense to them anyway, but this one sounds like it had been named after someone; do you suppose he could have been a college president?"

Her father had written back: "A martini is a sort of cocktail (which I do not, myself, regard with great enjoyment) served exclusively and drunk exclusively by a clearly defined type of person. As far as my experience makes it possible for me to judge, this person is usually volatile, high-strung, and excitable. All of these are qualities shared by good vermouth, which is one of the ingredients of a martini. Another ingredient is gin, which is feminine and appears more harmless than it is: another characteristic of your martini-drinker. The third ingredient of the martini is bitters, and I need labor my metaphor no further, I hope. I will add that the drink is served ice-cold, that some people prefer to have the ingredients shaken, some prefer them stirred, that it is possible to refine one's position with regard to the martini by discarding the traditional olive, and passing along further stages of refinement through the black olive, the twist of lemon peel, to the final, most effete, pearl onion. It is thus possible, you will perceive, to express the most exquisite shadings of personality—but I believe I have made myself more than clear. From this you should be able to believe without taxing your forming critical mind that by definition the martini is a natural college cocktail."

"We have to be at the Clarks' at six," Elizabeth was reminding Arthur.

Arthur nodded. "Plenty of time," he said.

"I'm so sorry," Anne said to Arthur. "We hoped you'd go into town later and have dinner with us."

"Our engagement for tonight is of several weeks' standing," Elizabeth said grandly, sipping then at her drink with her eyes on Anne. "Naturally we can't disappoint the Clarks, but I told Arthur you girls would be so unhappy if we didn't come here first, even for just a few minutes; I really had to persuade him to come."

"So glad you did," Vicki said. "Another drink?"

Elizabeth looked again into her glass, and again at Arthur.

"I thought I'd *never* stop laughing, this morning in class," Anne said to Arthur at that moment.

Vicki said quickly to Elizabeth, "They're terribly weak."

"Weak?" Elizabeth said. "Weak. They *are* weak." She made the word sound comic, and she handed over her glass. Vicki filled it quickly and brought it back, and then sat down next to Elizabeth, on the floor with her legs crossed. Natalie, who was sitting on the floor with her legs crossed on the other side of Elizabeth's chair, moved to sit at precisely the angle Vicki adopted, and Vicki clearly and deliberately nodded at her, as though to say: We're doing beautifully; good work.

"I *love* that pin," Vicki said to Elizabeth lavishly.

"Thank you," Elizabeth said coldly; it was to be clearly understood that she did not like Vicki and she did not court flattery.

"Will you *look* at the colors in that pin?" Vicki said to Natalie. "Have you ever seen anything so *lovely?*"

"Beautiful," said Natalie. "Enamel, isn't it?"

"I believe it is," Elizabeth said to Natalie. It was to be clearly understood that while she did very likely regard Natalie with some favor, she was not prepared to commit herself until she found out exactly how far Natalie was in turn committed to Vicki.

"I wish I could make you understand how much we all admire you," Vicki said to Elizabeth. "All the things you do— taking care of your husband and your house, and keeping up with classes, and still somehow managing to look so lovely all the time, and everything."

Natalie, thinking, She surely cannot accept this seriously, heard with surprise Elizabeth saying with modesty, "Well, of course, I don't really . . ." and Vicki interrupting smoothly, saying, "Another drink?"

At six-thirty, then, Elizabeth sat up suddenly in her chair and said, "Arthur, what time is it? We have to go to the Clarks'."

"Plenty of time," Arthur said.

"We have to go the Clarks' for dinner," Elizabeth explained to Vicki and Natalie. "They must be expecting us because they're expecting us for dinner."

"It's very early," Vicki said.

"Plenty of time," Natalie said.

"Have another drink," Anne said, and giggled.

Natalie was reciting to herself, softly, "Around the campus and double quick, Have a drink with Annie and Vick; Vick's the butcher, Anne's the thief, And Langdon the boy who buys the beef." She thought she had better not copy this out to send to her father; she was not, at this point precisely sure of the metre. It seemed to her that she had spent too long sitting in one position, and she got up and stretched lazily.

"Where *you* going?" Elizabeth demanded immediately. "*We've* got to go to the Clarks'. Arthur?"

He turned. "Plenty of time," he said.

"No," Elizabeth said insistently. "What time *is* it? Anyone know what time it is? Because we've *got* to go to the *Clarks'*."

"I know," Arthur said. "We've got to go to the Clarks'. But we can be a little bit late, can't we?"

"Are we *late?*" Elizabeth said. She appealed to Natalie, "Are we late for the Clarks'?"

"Not at all," said Vicki. "You have plenty of time."

"Time for another drink, anyway," Arthur said. "Only across campus, after all," he told Natalie.

"You've had too much to drink now," Elizabeth said. "You can't go to the Clarks' drunk, Arthur darling. You know," she said to Natalie, "we shouldn't have come here at all. I wanted to call you and say we couldn't *possibly* make it, but he told me, 'Elizabeth,' he said, 'they've gone to great trouble and expense just for us,' he said. And so we came here first, but now we've really got to be getting along to the Clarks'."

"Suppose I call them and say you'll be a minute or so late?" Vicki asked brightly. "That way they surely wouldn't mind."

Elizabeth looked at Vicki and then uncertainly at Arthur. "Will we be late?" she asked. "Because the Clarks have gone to great trouble and—"

"Only a minute or so late," Vicki said.

"Time for one for the road," Arthur said.

At about eight-thirty it became pressingly necessary to dispose of Elizabeth. Arthur Langdon, who seemed to notice only suddenly, got up from the couch and crossed the room to where Elizabeth had been sitting ever since she first came in, and, looking down at her without expression, said, "Why in God's name does she *always* have to do this? Can't we ever go *any-where?*"

"She's probably just tired," Anne said tenderly. "Should we take her home?"

"Nothing else *to* do," Arthur said. His voice had become a little bit shrill, and Natalie, watching him as he stood between Vicki and Anne, wondered how she could ever have admired him, or thought of him together with her father. "*Why* does this *always* happen?" he demanded.

"We can see that she gets home," Vicki said. She glanced at Natalie and Natalie nodded, and said, "Certainly."

"*Would* you?" Arthur said, relieved. "Because I'm really *too* angry with her to care."

"I'm sure she'd go with Nat," Vicki said. "She's very fond of Nat."

"Who isn't?" Anne said fondly. "Nat, see if you can get her to stand up."

With the infinite superiority and tolerance that comes to a moderately sober person addressing a very drunken one, Natalie said to Elizabeth, "Elizabeth, are you ready to go home?"

It is really an instinct, the knack of dealing with irrational people, Natalie was thinking; I suppose that any mind like mine, which is so close, actually, to the irrational and so tempted by it, is able easily to pass the dividing line between rational and irrational and communicate with someone drunk, or insane, or asleep. "Elizabeth," she said severely, "wake up, Elizabeth."

"Why does she *always* have to do this?" Arthur said. He appealed to Anne. "Why?" he insisted.

"I think she just has no head for liquor," Vicki said wisely. "It affects some people that way, of course."

"But *always*," Arthur said, looking as though he were about to cry. "I *never* have a good time because she's always doing *some*thing like this."

"Elizabeth, wake *up*." (. . . and, bending over the maniac, writhing in his bonds, Natalie spoke softly, only a word or two, and he, ceasing at that moment his struggles, opened his eyes and looked lucidly and gratefully up into her face . . .) "Elizabeth, *wake* up."

"Golly," said Anne. "She could sleep here. I mean, she could have my bed, and I could take the couch."

"She doesn't *deserve* a bed," Arthur said. "She ought to be in a gutter somewhere."

"Arthur!" Anne said reproachfully. "Please don't be so bitter; remember who she is and—"

"Let's be sensible," said Vicki quickly. "If we can't wake her or get her home, she's got to sleep here, that's only common sense. But I really think we can wake her and I know she'll go home with Natalie because she's really *terribly* fond of Natalie."

"I don't remember ever seeing her do *this* before, after all," Anne said.

"Elizabeth," Natalie said, and Vicki said, "Elizabeth," and Arthur, his voice at its firmest, repeated, "Elizabeth."

Finally, stirring, Elizabeth muttered, and moved, and opened her eyes. "Arthur?" she said.

"Listen," Arthur said, leaning down to speak more forcefully. With his face close to hers, he said, "Elizabeth, we're going to take you home. Now wake up and behave yourself, because we're going to take you home."

"I'm awake," Elizabeth said crossly. "What's the matter?"

"You're going home," Arthur said.

"All right," Elizabeth said contentedly. She held up her arms to him, and he stepped aside and let Natalie take her. At the touch of Elizabeth's full, fumbling hands on her arms Natalie recoiled for a minute, but Arthur gave her an ungentlemanly push, and she took Elizabeth around the shoulders and with Vicki's help hoisted her out of the armchair in which she had sat all evening. Elizabeth stood, speaking incoherently, and reaching her hands toward Arthur. Vicki took one of Elizabeth's arms and swung it over her shoulder; Elizabeth's whole weight fell against Natalie, and Natalie, shivering under the pressure of Elizabeth's legs against her, began half to pull, half to carry Elizabeth.

"I'd help you," Arthur said nervously, "if I didn't think she'd make a scene when she woke up and saw I was here."

With Arthur and Anne helping from behind, where they were sure they would not be seen, Vicki and Natalie got Elizabeth out the door and down the stairs. How inglorious, Natalie thought, going down the stairs with the heavy weight of Elizabeth against her, how perfectly abominable it is to be the receiver of such a thing, how dreadful and horrifying it is to have no choice at all about the swinging arms and legs that enwrap you, how sickening to be aware and to know that the unconscious one does not even see that it is you she is embracing, how horrid, how nauseating, how weak . . . Could I let go of her now? Natalie wondered, rounding the curve in the stairs, could I let her fall and kill herself, die perhaps, because I could not bear the holding of her? What obligation do I have toward her, what call has she upon me, that she should be leaning intimately against me, and never knowing it? How does she think I can bear it? Will I ever lean so upon her? Would she care, then, or let me fall?

"*There* we are," Arthur said, at the foot of the stairs. Elizabeth was draped, half-conscious, over the stairpost. "Can you get her home?" he asked Natalie. "I know how fond of you she is."

"I'm sure I can," Natalie said. "She seems to recognize my voice."

"She heard Nat when she didn't even move for the rest of us," Anne added.

It was suddenly apparent to Natalie that she was, alone, to get Elizabeth home. "Listen," she said anxiously, "I'm not sure I can do it without—"

"She'll listen to *you*," said Vicki over her shoulder; she did not smile, but she was following Anne and Arthur up the stairs. "She *likes* you," Vicki said, and disappeared around the turn in the staircase.

It was obviously impossible to leave Elizabeth. Even as Natalie turned in dismay to look at her, Elizabeth sagged, and began to slip gracefully to the floor. "Elizabeth," Natalie said, wanting to cry, "oh, *damn* it." She remembered, or tried hard to remember clearly, how Elizabeth had been the first person to speak to her kindly on this campus, and how it would be impossible in any case to leave Elizabeth here and join the others, because they would surely ask where Elizabeth had gotten to; and how Elizabeth had told her unmentionable, or almost unmentionable, secrets alone in her house in the afternoons, and how everyone owed it to Vicki and Anne to get Elizabeth home and out of their way, because Vicki and Anne were friends too, and it would be hardly kind of Natalie to ignore such an obligation they had left her, and if she left Elizabeth here it would mean possibly never seeing Vicki and Anne again, and surely not going back to them tonight, and so she might go alone to her own room if she chose, and, after all, she told herself, everyone was mortal and everyone was faulty and everyone was all together in one great world where only one life was vouchsafed to any of us, and there was never enough time to reflect on whether to do a thing or not to do a thing, because when you looked at someone it was someone no more or no less than another mortal, and, after all, who could deny another mortal some small solace in a life on this world, and, in the last analysis, Elizabeth . . .

"Arthur?" Elizabeth said.

"It's me, Natalie," Natalie said, thinking at last how she should describe this to her father and tell him not to tell her mother.

"Natalie?" said Elizabeth. She moved a little away, and said again, "Natalie?"

"Elizabeth," Natalie said gently. She put her arms around Elizabeth, and Elizabeth's head fell against her shoulder and Elizabeth said, "Natalie," softly, and Natalie was jubilantly glad that she had not said, "Arthur," again.

"Natalie, I want to die," Elizabeth said.

"We're going home," Natalie said.

"I want to die," Elizabeth said.

"I know you do," Natalie said tenderly. "Come along home."

"Home?" said Elizabeth.

She was able to walk by herself, although Natalie had to guide her. As they went through the doorway out onto the campus Natalie was thinking, for some reason she never knew, of the trees ahead, of how she and Elizabeth could go from tree to tree across the campus, holding onto each one until they recovered themselves. Once out in the open air, however, Elizabeth recovered amazingly and walked alone, without even help from Natalie.

"I want to die," she said once.

"Don't be silly," Natalie. said, and added, "we all want to die, I suppose, from the minute that we're born."

"No," said Elizabeth, "*I* want to *die*."

It was difficult for Natalie to think clearly, walking across the dark campus under the trees with Elizabeth. For one thing, it had suddenly come to Natalie that when people were sober they repudiated everything they had done when they were drunk, and when they were drunk they repudiated everything they had done when they were sober. Natalie felt this to be very profound, and she worried over it, thinking, How silly I was to be frightened before, talking to Arthur, and what I should have said was . . .

"I want to die," Elizabeth said. "I wish I were Anne."

"I wish *I* were Anne," Natalie said, and thought, *That*, I hope, is not true—except that she *did* wish that she were Anne, and the recollection of Anne bent over, listening intimately to Arthur Langdon speaking, had everything to do with the desire.

"You know," said Elizabeth wanderingly, stopping under a tree to point at Natalie, "Anne is a bitch and I used to be a bitch and now I'm not any more." She began to cry; Natalie could hear her, although it was too dark to see. "Goddam little bitch," Elizabeth said.

The Langdons had left a light on in the foyer of their apartment. Natalie could see it and recognize it from halfway across the campus, and she blushed in the darkness to think of how often she had gone past the apartment and thought that Arthur lived there. "Six proud walkers," she said obscurely.

"Bed," Elizabeth said.

"Bed," Natalie said. As they approached the apartment Elizabeth began to sag again, and Natalie had to put an arm around her to support her. Suppose I were Arthur, she thought, unwillingly, and suppose I *wanted* to do this . . .

"Dark," Elizabeth said.

And suppose she were one of my students and I wanted badly to marry her, and suppose we were walking in the darkness just like this and I thought *now, no,* and suppose just the touch of her shoulder under my arm, so strong and firm across the weak flesh, suppose just that touch and that feeling, and suppose in the darkness she turned slightly toward me so that . . .

"Natalie?" sid Elizabeth. "Are we nearly in bed?"

"Nearly," Natalie said. "Only a little way now."

And suppose, suppose, only suppose, that in the darkness and in the night and all alone and under the trees, suppose that here, together, without anyone ever to know, without even so much as a warning, suppose in the darkness under the trees . . .

"I want to die," Elizabeth said.

Natalie did not, mercifully, have to undress her. Once in her own home where she had gone staggering to bed alone so often, Elizabeth seemed to know by a molelike instinct what to do, and while Natalie worried in the brightly lighted kitchen over coffee and which burner to use on the stove, Elizabeth disappeared silently into the bedroom and took off her clothes. "Natalie?" she called at last, and Natalie came running, to find Elizabeth, in her own nightgown, in her own bed.

It was the first time Natalie had ever visited the Langdons' bedroom, and, while she had never been shocked at the twin beds in the bedroom of her mother and father, she was at this time grieved over the understanding that Arthur Langdon insisted upon—so young, so pretty—maintaining at night a space of floor between himself and Elizabeth.

"Are you comfortable?" Natalie asked. "Is there anything I can do for you?"

"Good night," Elizabeth said, and held up her face for Natalie to kiss her.

Hesitantly, Natalie moved around the foot of Arthur Langdon's bed and to the side of his wife's bed and femininely kissed Elizabeth upon the forehead.

"Good night," Natalie said. "Sleep well."

"Good night, darling," Elizabeth said.

"Good night, darling," Natalie said. She tiptoed around the foot of Arthur's bed and stood for a minute looking at Elizabeth already asleep in her bed before she turned out the light.

On her way back across the campus she did not find anything particular in her mind to identify this evening beyond others marked in other ways. There was a strong feeling of triumph and an odd feeling of vengeance, and once when she stopped under a tree and leaned her head against its firm rough trunk she whispered softly, "I know, I know." But that was all; beyond that she seemed to have nothing to say to herself. Without question she left the tree, satiated with the night and the stars indistinctly seen, and went on to the house where she lived, without ever troubling herself to look back at the light from the foyer of the Langdons' apartment, which she had left on, after some thought, for Arthur to find his way home again.

She went back into her own house, and quietly up the stairs, realizing with a shock from the sounds of voices in other rooms that it was still very early, perhaps not more than ten o'clock. She went immediately to the rooms which Vicki and Anne shared and found—as she had known without question, coming up the stairs—that they were dark.

She went on up the stairs to her own dark room with its locked door, the room which she had left, carefully dressed, at some time in the late afternoon, her own safe dear room, where she might sit by herself without interruption, and, as she entered with her key in her hand, she saw even in the darkness the white paper of the note on the desk.

"Thanks very much," it said. "How was Lizzie? V."

                                                            Tuesday
My dear captive princess,
It is as much as any knight can do, these days, to keep in touch with his captive princesses, let alone rescue them. For one thing, I find my armor much too tight; it has rusted since I last wore it in combat, and I cannot for the life of me remember where I last saw my sword. I think of you, princess, languishing in your tower, peering anxiously forth from the narrow windows, wringing your long white hands and pacing the floor in your long white gown, looking constantly out at the long winding road below, out to where it disappears among the mountains far beyond your tower . . . I keep thinking of you looking, and waiting, with no knight coming. And of course I *shall* come eventually, with or without armor; perhaps I can find me a reputable tinsmith (although the tinsmiths themselves are not at all what they used to be) who will fashion for me some snow-white armor and a helmet to which I can attach some small insignia of yours—your old hockey stick, perhaps, with which I can also defend myself if need be. Or half a dozen pages from a learned quarterly, which might not prove so fine a means of defense, but would certainly mark me unerringly as a knight errant. (This last is a joke depending entirely upon your knowledge of

word roots. I have wasted too many jokes on you to let them pass now without identification.) I am not quite sure, moreover, how to attack the dragon which guards your towers; does he ever sleep? Can he be bribed? Drugged? Enticed away? Or must I fight him, after all? Or, worse still, *is* there a dragon? You are surely not confined only by magic? I positively will *not* battle a sorcerer.

Your mother insists that I include in this letter the statement that she has sent you a black evening dress with, I believe she said, off-the-shoulder-sleeves. She remarks sadly that that was what *she* always used to want, and I truly believe that it was an entirely goodhearted and unselfish gesture, that your mother honestly has sent you a black evening dress with off-the-shoulder-sleeves because, considering more than she usually does, she thought it the most wonderful gift a mother could possibly send her daughter.

You have probably found easier ways of evading enchantments than I shall ever learn. It has always been my opinion, you know, that princesses are confined in towers only because they choose to stay confined, and the only dragon required to keep them there was their own desire to be kept. And I further believe, now, that if you erect a tower, princesses will flock to it demanding to be locked up therein. So why do you not gratify your mother and myself, and, I believe, even your brother, by spending a weekend with us soon? If you let me know when you choose to escape the dragon's ceaseless vigilance, I shall send you train fare, operating upon your mother's theory that it would be the nicest thing anyone could send *me*.

Your devoted,
Dad

Saturday

Dear Sir Knight,

It was not you, then, caroling lustily under my window these three nights past? Nor one of your emissaries? I fear me that the enchantment surrounding my tower is too strong for you, and that my rescue will not be effected for a thousand years—by which time, I wot, I shall be somewhat older and grayer than I am now. At any rate, if it is not a dragon guarding me, it is something very like, something called a Maiden Lady (and, her name being Miss Nicholas, she is of course also yclept Old Nick) which, breathing fire, stamps around at the end of its own chain restraining more adventurous damsels from the straying.

I mean, I can't come home for a while yet. If there is any enchanter it is Arthur Langdon, who confidently expects that I will write him a thousand words about Milton by next Wednesday. What is there to say about Milton? I thought of comparing him with King Lear but it looked too hard.

There is a very strange character around here who would interest you very much. She is always off by herself somewhere, and when I asked someone about her they laughed and said, "Oh, that's that girl Tony Something." I keep seeing her around and I think I would like to meet her.

Tell Mother I got the dress and it's beautiful. Don't tell her I have no place to wear it. I didn't get invited to the Tech Dance, which is Friday night, but then neither did most of the girls I've met around here. Apparently you have to know people here before you come, so that you don't start out fresh making friends. Anyway, I feel sort of crestfallen about it, but when I watch the other girls who were not invited, and listen to them talking, I feel better because at least I haven't managed to think of an *excuse*. They all say things like well, they didn't *want* to go anyway, and they were *asked*, of *course*, but the boy was such an awful dancer they turned him down . . . and so on. I don't have any excuse except I wasn't asked. Anyway, tell Mother thanks very very much for the dress; I tried it on and it was lovely. Everyone said it was very becoming to me.

Speaking of magic, I figure that now I have once mentioned that I would like to meet that girl Tony, I will certainly meet her soon. I have discovered that all you have to do is notice a thing like that concretely enough to say it, as in a letter like this, for it to happen. I suppose once I meet her I will be disappointed.

As soon as I can write a thousand words of counter-enchantment, I will come home for a day or so. The sorcerer has a way of casting further spells on young women who ignore his simple ones. And I don't really *like* Milton—do you? Write and tell me what is good about him.

Lots of love to you and Mother,
Natalie

It had the feeling of middle-of-the-night when Natalie was awakened, and she thought for a minute, not coherently, that perhaps she was never to get a full night's sleep again, and wasn't it fine that she didn't mind being awakened if it was exciting, and then she opened her eyes into actuality and heard the urgent soft voice in her ear. "Wake up," it said, "oh, please, wake up." It was a whisper and without personality and, saying over and over again, "Please, please wake up," it was terrifying.

"What?" said Natalie, hearing her own voice loud in the room.

"Wake up, please, and be quiet—and *hurry*."

"I'm awake," Natalie said. It was unusually dark and the figure beside her bed was unidentifiable; this then is the time, Natalie thought, the time is upon us, this is the occasion I have been living until, when crisis and danger and terror are upon us all, and we are awakened in fear and run for safety; who has been thoughtful enough to remember me in the general flight? Fire? she wondered as she had before, and, War?

"What is it?" she whispered.

"*Hurry.*"

"I'm *hurrying*," Natalie said, reaching in the darkness for her bathrobe, feeling with her feet for slippers; then, suddenly, she heard through the darkness the soft giggle and with it felt the first cold actual fear. War, at least, and fire, were possibilities. This, the giggle, was here in her own room.

"What is it?" Natalie said again.

"Come *on*. And *hurry*." Again the giggle. "You don't need your *bath*robe, come *any* old way. I'm naked—but hurry."

"Listen," Natalie said, fumbling her hand for the light cord, but her hand was taken in another hand and she was pulled firmly, and the vague figure and the faint enduring giggle led her to the door. Natalie was without her slippers and without her bathrobe and in the cotton pajamas her mother had chosen for her, and on the pajamas was a pattern of black-and-red scotty dogs, and the door into the hall showed further darkness instead of the usual night lights from the stairways and the bathrooms.

"I turned them out, the lights," said the voice ahead. "But *hurry*."

"What for?" said Natalie, following down the dark hall.

Again the quiet giggle. "*You* needn't think you're the only one," she said. "Wait till I show you what *I've* got." They were passing rooms in the darkness, Natalie knew, where girls slept peacefully, with their eyes closed and their hands relaxed against the pillows; why, she thought almost hysterically, why don't I just *scream?* and knew with humor that she did not know how; screaming was in itself an act perfected by few, a sort of coloratura not given to the many; screaming was not something the Natalies might do unprepared. If I were really very frightened, Natalie thought, following barefoot the naked figure ahead, I might yell, or shout, but never deliver a telling scream; then I am not really very frightened, she thought, since I am not able to make any kind of a sound at all, but only follow blind and dry through these black spaces and of course I am dreaming, of course, of course; how profoundly interested I am in all this, she thought. "And," the voice was going on ahead, "you can lie very still and not move and not say anything and you can hear everything and even though they think you're there they don't know who you are and they go right ahead. And even when they come right into my room I just look at them and I say, 'Go ahead with what you were saying because *I* certainly don't care,' and then they go away because of course when they are right in my room they certainly can't, can they? And there's this little girl and she came into my room and she said, 'May I please sleep with you tonight?' and I said, 'Of course you may only I have to get up early in the morning but it's four hours before I have to get up so you go right to sleep,' and she got into my bed and she fell right asleep and she had these lovely little animals with her, like birds, or squirrels, only they had no tails, and she set them in a row at the foot of the bed and there were six of them all in a row and she made the most beautiful pictures on the wall, this *little* girl, and wait till you see them and when you hear them you'll know what I mean." Down the stairs, in the darkness, feeling barefoot for one step after another, and the voice ahead continuing, "And of course her mother and father are leaning up against the window and they're listening too and they can't hear a thing because we talk so softly and they try and try to listen and we only whisper and you know this is the same little girl who came before and who comes all the time and she sleeps in my bed."

After they had gone down the stairs and turned, a door ahead of them showed light in the small space of its opening; it was very late, because there was no other light from any room along the hall, and the hall and bathroom lights were turned out down here as well as upstairs. Natalie thought without wishing to at all of the cautious giggling thing that had gone soundlessly from one light to another, turning off each, for whatever dark reason, before coming unerringly in the dark to Natalie's bed. "Here now," the voice said, still with that flat giggling undertone, "now we can all listen together, and sit tight next to the wall and then we can hear what they are saying, only be very careful when you laugh to put your hands over your mouth. Little girl? Little girl?" It was a loving call and Natalie, waiting and held outside the lighted doorway, wanted to call too, "Little girl?" Then, "She's fallen asleep again, they're always like that. Leave them for a minute and they're gone asleep. Little girl? Come on, we've got to *hurry*."

She pulled Natalie violently in through the open doorway into the lighted room, and then closed the door very carefully behind them. "Little girl?" she said lovingly. The bed was rumpled and she went over, still calling, "Little girl?" and giggling, and turned the blankets back, lifted the pillow and looked under it, and then, giggling, looked under the bed. "Little girl?" she asked. "Little girl?" Then, saying, "Come *on*, please hurry, we'll never be able to hear a *thing*," she looked quickly into the closet and then into the dresser drawers, pulling out the angora sweater, the real lace slip, and cartons of cigarettes and unassorted shoes, the money carelessly thrown inside. "Little girl?" She turned to Natalie and said helplessly, "She was here a minute ago. I can't imagine where she went— I told her to *wait* for me. Look, she left her coat." Natalie, staring at the jacket that had been reported stolen a week or so before, was still not able to speak. "Little girl? Where do you suppose she went? Little *girl*."

Natalie opened her mouth, still not knowing what she was going to say.

"Well, come *on*, then, *any*way, it will serve her right if we start without her, only remember they're listening and don't make a *sound*. Hold your hands over your mouth when you laugh and don't run around the floor because they're right out-side, and they hear *every*thing. Little girl? Come on over here, right down on the floor next to the wall and do what I do— anyone could *tell* you've never been here before but we'll excuse you this time and whatever you hear don't make a sound because then *they*'ll hear *you*. Listen to her . . . she's singing."

Very quietly, in acute fear, Natalie was backing to the door. When she felt the panels behind her back, she opened it with-out a perceptible sound, her hand behind her, and opening it still behind her, backed farther into the hall and closed the door in front of her face, shutting out all the light in the hall but feeling more at ease in the darkness; she was on the first floor of the house, she knew, and up two flights of stairs—oh, interminable!—was her own room again and a safe light she might turn on.

Backing away from the doorway, she stumbled over nothing and almost fell against the opposite wall. I must be very calm, she told herself; it is only, after all, a question of finding my own room in the dark, and if on the way I can find a light switch for anywhere, the halls, the stairs, the bathrooms, so much the better, and if I do not get frightened and try to run I will not fall on the stairs, and if I do not fall on the stairs she will never hear that I have gone, and why doesn't anyone wake up and come and help me?

Then, of course, she heard again, "Little girl?" and the door

opened and the light came out into the hall, and Natalie, turning to run in any direction, realized too late that she had come
the wrong way and in the darkness was pursued by sly brushing footsteps not on the way to the stairs and her own room
but on the way to the front door. In the darkness, the light
from the room left far behind her, she heard the soft giggle
and felt almost the seeking hand brush her face and heard very
close, and softly, "Little girl?"

And then mercifully she found the latch to the front door and
it opened more easily than she had even prayed it would, and as
it swung before her she thought, This will set off the burglar
alarm, and almost laughed as she slammed it tight behind her.

It was incredible and of course still a dream to be running
freely and in her pajamas with the shameful black-and-red
scotties on them, barefoot first over the gravel of the walk, and
then primitively over the wet grass, and to be under the trees
with everything dark around her. She thought then, I will go
back when the sun is out and they are all awake and I can tell
them about it, and then she thought she heard wailing from
the house behind her, "Little girl?" and knew a sudden horrible shock when, going across the grass under the trees she saw
in the moonlight a figure coming toward her.

Standing helplessly, thinking, Now, I cannot run, this is the
time, she said, "Who?"

"Is there something wrong?" asked the girl Tony.

Wednesday

Madam:

Unless you comply with the following conditions, and without
fail, I shall have a black vengeance to wreak upon you:

1. Enclosed find check for twenty-five dollars. (That is a con-
dition I deem it not overdifficult to meet.)

2. Cash this check. (Any rich acquaintance will do.)

3. With the money thus secured, buy yourself a round-trip
ticket to this place. (Try the bus station for this.)

4. Pack a toothbrush, whatever books you need, a pencil and
paper, and two chocolate bars in a small valise, put on your coat
and hat, and go directly to the place where buses congregate.

(This is the most complicated of all, but if you do these things one after another, in the order in which I have stated them, you should have little or no trouble; I recommend, however, that you do them in *strict* order; it would be most unorthodox for you to go first to the place of buses, for instance, and *then* try to pack your bag.)

5. Get on the first bus that will bring you here. (Ask the driver, if you are puzzled, or, better still, pin a label on the lapel of your coat and he will see that you are delivered.)

Meet these small conditions, sign my book in blood, and I shall turn over to you my key to all the treasures of this world, including, very possibly, some small amount of information of John Milton (1608–74) and a cordial invitation to escort you, in person, to any and all future dances. Fail, as I say, to meet these my conditions, and upon you shall fall the wrath of one who has never yet feared to make his presence known. Did I remember to put in the check? Yes. Good.

Dad

Sir:
I hear and obey. Arrive Saturday afternoon 2:30. Thanks for the check.

Love,
Natalie

Tomorrow morning was Friday and biology lab, and it was past eleven now; anyone desiring to get up at seven and yet have eight hours' sleep should be at least ready for bed: teeth brushed, hair done, clothes for the morrow set out. And, leaning forward, her face terribly bright and alert and terribly terribly interested in what Arthur Langdon was saying, Natalie sought hopefully for a state of frozen unconsciousness, perhaps drunken, perhaps only the little swift precious moment that slipped her from a dull world into a bright one; she nodded intelligently at what Arthur was saying, and thought, People have had heart attacks and died without realizing anything more than what is probably that brightly flashing second of knowing you are dead. People have managed to do it.

"I'm not at all sure what I really do believe," Arthur was

saying, and, "When you consider that art itself is a process of . . ."

"Dearest," said Elizabeth Langdon, who had almost overnight, it seemed, adopted a dogged persistence of displayed affection, and a hearty, throaty-voiced sort of intelligence, in order, it seemed, to give the impression that she and Arthur were still newlyweds and insanely in love, "dearest, couldn't it be said, actually, that with reference to—oh dear, I sound so stupid—but *any*way . . ."

I could slip right away, Natalie thought. I could die here, with my eyes wide open and my mouth parted admiringly, and my glass poised in stunned admiration halfway to the chair arm; I could die right here. Or I could pretend I was going to be sick and sneak off home to bed. Or I could even speak, say something so very unkind that they would all listen, and nod at me the way I nod at them.

"Although, actually . . ." Arthur said. He frowned, weighing his glass as well as his words, while his wife leaned forward breathlessly, and Natalie, embarrassed at having been thinking while other people were talking, closed her eyes briefly and said, "Someday someday someday," to herself.

"I have never been able to come round to the way of thinking that would . . ."

Is something going to happen? Natalie wondered. Has he gone too far, and will someone be witty at his expense? Oh dear, she thought, I wish I'd been listening and watching, instead of closing my eyes; something has led to something else, and I've missed the beginning and shall have to smile vacantly; is something going to happen?

She thought sadly of how empty lives must be where something was not going to happen. No one seemed to be particularly witty at Arthur's expense, and so whatever was going to happen was apparently still on its way, choosing its own moment, building for its own effect, so that it should be neither too soon nor too late, neither an anticlimax nor a cause.

Is it just that something is going to happen to *me?* Natalie wondered. She closed her eyes again experimentally; was she falling asleep while Arthur Langdon was talking and while the

Langdons' guests, students and faculty members sitting together as though in social pleasure, listened with civility? I shall walk out onto the porch, Natalie thought. As a penance for closing my eyes twice, I have been directed to stand up in my chair, dislodging the ashtray that sits on the arm, I have been directed to move, trying to be unobtrusive but watched with gratitude by everyone in the room, I shall go to the door and someone will say, "Natalie?" and I will turn around and smile vaguely and pass quietly through the doorway and out onto the porch. Later I shall find that I have to come back, and again, the only large movement in the room, I shall find everyone watching me while Arthur pauses in his sentence, regarding me thoughtfully and testing, in a fraction of a second, ways of using me as an example. "Take Natalie, now; she has been gone, and come back, and did anyone . . . ?" "If Natalie had not entered the room at that minute, then, would the thought of her . . . ?" "Natalie is wearing light blue; now, if we assume that the color we believe to be light blue . . ."

Now, she thought. I shall move now, but she did not. No one looked at her at the moment, and the thought of the strength required to draw every eye in the room to her direction wearied her for a moment, so that the order to her muscles to arise, counteracted halfway, brought her convulsively out of her chair in an abrupt movement that spilled the ashtray onto the floor. Then, while Arthur waited patiently in mid-paragraph, she collected the cigarette butts and the burnt matches, thinking as she did so, Ungainly, awkward, clumsy—and she left the ashes. Elizabeth Langdon watched her without expression; she needs some more positive explanation of what I am doing, Natalie decided, before she estimates it and decides on a reaction, particularly in this new personality of hers, which still does not fit her very well. Perhaps she wants to be angry at someone and is trying to see if I am the one; I could so easily be a good person for Elizabeth to hate, and also I am the only person now standing in this room, and Elizabeth is usually angry at the largest moving target; Arthur cannot mention me now because the course of his argument is planned out for the next paragraph and it does not include me; he is probably, however, going ahead with the other parts of his mind to construct a new paragraph for use when I come back.

She set the ashtray back on the arm of the chair where she would be sure to knock it off again when she sat down after coming back, and threaded her way tactfully and gracelessly through the people sitting on the floor, excusing herself to those in chairs as though they were a higher order of being; she avoided spilling a drink that sat on the floor, and stepped in an ashtray. Someone took advantage of her movement to begin a paragraph of his own. "On the other hand," his voice began from another part of the room, "while this is all very true, you can hardly call it a complete picture of the problem. Take Kafka, for instance—I think you mentioned him as an example, and—"

There were never any real silences in this conversation, except for the involuntary secret moment of dismay everyone felt at seeing Natalie move; these people—although there seemed to be so many of them, there were only nine or ten— all carried with them, seemingly, arguments of their own, arguments against the invisible, always-defeated antagonist who mocked ineffectually from the darkness of the bedroom at night, the bathroom wall, the window beyond the typewriter. They all carried their arguments well, and spoke when they could, and laughed occasionally, and sometimes found themselves in agreement with one another, although always the mocking antagonist needed to be conquered again, and, conquered, returned, in the face in the mirror, the logs in the fire, with his ceaseless nagging.

"I was just about to explain that point," Arthur Langdon said, his voice overriding the other. "When, for example, we consider the whole question as one purely of . . ."

Natalie sighed as she reached the small foyer, and found the door ahead, and the porch beyond, and the cool night air awaiting her; with the door shut it was not possible to hear Arthur's voice.

The porch was actually only a miserable excuse for a place to sit; it was no more than a step up or a step down, so that sitting on the porch steps at the Langdons' house meant the knees under the chin and the feet awkwardly placed and the back twisted, but the same trees were outside, living in the ground without curiosity about the insides of houses, and growing toward death as surely as Natalie. When one tree demonstrated that it was not rooted and perhaps not completely indifferent by disengaging itself from the others and coming toward Natalie where she sat on the porch step, she was not surprised—it was an odd night, anyway, and the day after tomorrow she should be going home for a while—and said only, with some crossness, "I don't want to talk."

"All right."

It was almost companionable, and Natalie without intention moved over on the narrow step to leave room. "It's so cool out here," she said.

"Then you *do* want to talk?" said the girl Tony.

"They're all talking, inside," Natalie said.

The girl Tony had not been invited within, Natalie knew wisely, and thought, She doesn't care whether she sits on the steps of people who don't invite her or whether she stands around with trees or whether she talks to me or not. She knew she ought not to talk because she had said she was not going to and because she knew this calm girl Tony calmly expected her to do what she said she was going to, but she said anyway, "You weren't invited?"

"No."

"Would you go if you were invited?" Natalie asked.

"That depends," said Tony carefully, "on where I was invited to go."

"This damn place," Natalie said, "it always turns out not to have the things I want, after all. I get up inside and I knock over an ashtray and everyone looks at me and here I come rushing outdoors because I think it's where I want to be, and then when I get out here it turns out to be the same old place I passed coming in."

"That's because you came out the same door," suggested Tony.

She stood up, and Natalie thought quickly, She's bored with me, and said, "You going away?"

"I'll see you again," Tony said. "Good night."

It was not pleasant sitting on the porch after Tony had gone; a spot where two people have been talking, however briefly, is not after that a spot for one person to sit alone. Natalie got awkwardly to her feet and turned to go inside.

In the brief foyer she met Elizabeth Langdon; the space was so small that they almost touched standing together, and Natalie crushed herself back against the door.

"I came to look for you," Elizabeth said. "I wanted to make sure you were all right."

How she would love to help her fallen sisters, Natalie thought. "I was all right," she said.

"I saw you with someone," Elizabeth said.

For a minute Natalie was surprised at Elizabeth's tone; does she think I made an appointment with the girl Tony to meet her during Elizabeth's party? Natalie wondered; does she think I intended to invite her inside? or does she think we meet outside in the darkness, as though we had been outlawed from meeting in the light? For a minute Natalie wanted poignantly to ask Elizabeth what she thought she had seen through the eyes which for Elizabeth registered what Elizabeth's brain recorded, and then she said instead, "Let's go back inside."

Arthur seemed hardly to have stopped for breath, although his glass had been refilled, and he was saying, "It is not impossible to imagine a situation in which . . ."

Saturday morning

Dear Dad,

I'm terribly sorry that I can't come home, and I'm sorry too that this letter won't reach you in time. I would have called you except I didn't know until a little while ago that I couldn't make it. You see, Arthur Langdon has given us this paper to do, and I've simply *got* to get it in by Monday, so of course I can't come home, because the paper has to be very long and detailed and I'll probably spend all weekend working on it. And even if I did come home, of course, I'd have to work all the time. So I'm really terribly sorry.

By the way, you remember Tony? The girl I wrote you about? Well, I finally met her and I like her a lot. She lives in a house on the other side of the campus and yesterday afternoon we walked about four miles through the country just beyond the campus. I think she's terribly interesting. Well, I'm sorry about not being able to come home. I'll keep enough money from the check for my train fare home at Thanksgiving. I'm sure I can make it then. Hope Mother's not disappointed. Give her my love.

Natalie.

Perhaps—and this was her most persistent thought, the thought that stayed with her and came suddenly to trouble her at odd moments, and to comfort her—suppose, actually, she were *not* Natalie Waite, college girl, daughter to Arnold Waite, a creature of deep lovely destiny; suppose she were someone else?

Suppose, for instance, that all of this, from the day she could first remember (running through the grass, calling, "Daddy? Daddy?"), suppose it had all been no more than a split second of time, as in a dream, perhaps under an anesthetic; suppose that after this split second when her wandering mind fancied she was someone named Natalie Waite, that then she should wake up, bemused at first, and speaking thickly, and not really quite sure of her surroundings and the nurse bending over her and the voices saying, "There now, it wasn't so bad, was it?" and suppose, waking, she should turn out to be someone else, someone real as Natalie was not? An old woman, perhaps, with a year or so to live, or a child having its tonsils removed, or a woman with twelve children having a charity operation, or a man. And, waking, looking around the white room and at the clean nurse, she could say, "I had the funniest dream all this time; I dreamed I was Waitalie Nat"—the dream already fading, and not complete—and the nurse could easily say, "*Everyone* has dreams under ether," moving capably forward with a thermometer.

Or even suppose, imagine, could it be true? that she was confined, locked away, pounding wildly against the bars on the window, attacking the keepers, biting at the doctors, screaming down the corridors that she was someone named Watalie Naite . . . suppose, during the time she thought she was eating in the dining room and going unwillingly to classes and sitting in her room reading . . . suppose these things were not real? Could it be that some sudden lucid horrible moment (a new treatment, perhaps? An inevitable return to actuality?) should show her brutally that the dining room and the professors were not at all there, but existed far away in her mind, provoked into life only by her mania? "I'm not prepared today," she could be saying to her music professor, and the doctor, turning back her eyelid to look at her cornea, would murmur, "How long has she been in this particular stage?"

But then, perhaps she was not dreaming, not mad, but alive and sound—living in this caught second of life only in the musing mind of some salesgirl or waitress or prostitute or some drab creature to whom the life of a girl in college named Naitalie Wat seemed romantic; suppose somewhere a murderess slept lightly, dreaming for a minute that she was young again and had a life to live; suppose that some minute, any minute, she should suddenly turn, move her head, speak strangely, and find herself not at all real?

It was this that made her write her name crazily on everything, knowing and yet forgetting that her books and her clothes and her written sheets of paper would be gone with Natalie Waite, were only part of a larger dream; it was this which gave her the sudden sense, in conversation perhaps, that this particular portion of her dream might be condensed, only a fleeting shorthand scrap of words to be remembered later as a whole conversation; it was this which brought her abruptly to a perception that if she were dreaming her room and her words, she might well be dreaming her world, and so when she awoke she might say, amused, to the nurse, to the girl in the room next door, to the police, "Listen to what I dreamed; I dreamed there was a war; I dreamed there was a thing called television; I dreamed—listen to this—that there was something called an atom bomb. An *atom* bomb—*I* don't know; I tell you I *dreamed* it."

Beyond this sense, however, of swift transient passage, was

the worse, the frightful, conviction, of perhaps being in reality no more than Natalie Waite, college girl, daughter to Arnold, and unable to brush away the solidity of this world but forced to deal with it as actual and dreary. Yet then—why, if this were true, the sudden sharp sympathetic picture of the white walls and the nurse coming closer? Why the graphically remembered room with the iron bedstead, the sure knowledge of the moment to slip the poison into the cup, the remembered pain? Why, above all, the constant unusual shock of the sound of her own name said aloud?

It must be assumed that at one point, to be known as *there*, was the college, dark and drowsy under Natalie's absence, and that at another point, known as *here*, was the home where her mother and father and brother lived, and to which she had been brought during a passage of time that in retrospect seemed nothing, so that her transition from there to here seemed no more than a fading in of one place upon another, a travel between points in time rather than in space.

When her father met her at the bus stop late on Wednesday night Natalie was embarrassed, thinking of the seventy-five days, the ten and a half weeks, the two and a third months, since she had seen him or her mother or her brother or her home; he did not look different in that he still as always resembled the various pictures of him in so many different places, but before he had a chance to speak to her, Natalie said quickly, "I've got to go back on Friday—" before he had a chance, that is, to spoil everything by expecting too much of her, and he, after a long and surprised look, nodded and said, "It's nice to see you again."

Once in the car, she asked, "How is Mother?"

"Fine," he said.

"And Bud?"

"Fine."

"*You* look well."

"I am, thanks, quite well."

Natalie thought then, He expects some embarrassment; he expects to even it off when we can sit and talk as usual. "How is everything?" she asked.

"Much the same."

"I'm sorry I couldn't come home before."

This was such an extraordinary statement that he obviously felt it impossible to answer. It was strange being close to him again in the car, just as they had been many times before, when for so long (seventy-five days, for instance) he had been a signature on a letter, a name she had used speaking to people, no more than the absent father of Natalie Waite.

"Have you been well?" she asked to console him.

"Very well, thank you," he said.

On the bus, in the hour and a half it took her to reach the bus stop where he met her, Natalie had conscientiously tried to plan out a suitable greeting for him. A theatrical "Daddy!" shouted while throwing herself into his arms was probably undesirable, considering that Mr. Waite could most likely not be counted on to stand agreeably and catch daughters hurling themselves at his head; no more could she consider seriously a brief handshake and a meaningful look, a caught breath, and a murmured "Father"; her favorite greeting, which she saw vaguely as taking up and carrying on a conversation as though they had just left it off, was impossible because she could not think how to start a conversation which might not have been finished; not, at least, a conversation with her father, who might leave many things undone but never a word unsaid. Because she had not quite made up her mind by the time she alighted from the bus, what had happened was what she had never stopped to consider, which is that her father—perhaps phrasing impossible greetings in his own plan of action and had with wisdom apparently decided to pass over the whole question of greeting as a useless civility and one only to be regretted later, and had decided to do his real receiving of Natalie at some more appropriate time. When Natalie stepped down from the bus and recognized her father, with an unfilial shock of dismay, she stood and he stood, and then she said, not at all truthfully until she heard herself saying it, "I have to go back on Friday."

"I'm sorry I have to go back on Friday," she said again in the car.

"Your mother will be disappointed," he said dryly.

"How *is* Mother?"

"Very well, thank you."

The driveway to her own house came as a surprise, and for a minute she was comfortable in recognizing, with a satisfactory feeling of difference, the old landmarks, and looking with the pride of new places on the stay-at-home grass and trees and flowers, and regarding with contempt the former narrow boundaries of her world.

"It's good to be home," she said inadequately; *unbelievable* would perhaps have been a better word, or *stupefying.*

Greeting her mother was no problem at all; for a minute the air was so full of Natalie's appearance, her probable health, her shocking clothes, that there was no need for anyone to answer until her mother, accustomed again to Natalie after three minutes, subsided into her usual civil silence; Natalie and her brother greeted one another with false cordiality and endeavored heartily not to speak again to one another past necessity.

It was by then ten o'clock in the evening, and all four of them realized at once that they had from then on an evening of sorts to get through; they traditionally stayed up late, and tonight was a kind of gala evening, since everyone had been persuaded to give up other plans because Natalie was coming home, and Natalie herself had avoided appointments in order to come, and then, once Natalie had come and had turned out to be very little more entertaining or novel than the Natalie who had left seventy-five days before, there was nothing left to do except carry on the sort of formal conversation suited to the formal sort of guest Natalie had become. Seventy-five days before not one of them would have thought it necessary to address her unless they wanted to, but now it was almost obligatory to assure her warmly of the fact that she was always welcome in her own home—always welcome, with the clear implication that she was thus always a visitor there.

As a result Mrs. Waite exerted herself to say, "I have a twenty-pound turkey for tomorrow, Natalie." All such remarks as this were, too, directed pointedly and almost accusingly at Natalie by the addition of her name. "Biggest turkey I could get."

"Fine," Natalie said, with an enthusiasm she had not ever before shown toward turkeys. "It's been a long time since I've had a good meal."

"How *are* the college meals?" Mrs. Waite asked eagerly.

"Terrible," Natalie said, trying to remember the college meals.

"How do you like it there?" her brother asked, making a supreme effort.

"Fine," Natalie assured him earnestly. "I think it's fine. How is *your* school?"

"Oh, fine," he said. "Fine."

"Well," Mrs. Waite said fondly, and sighed, surveying her family circle. "All home again at last, and all together."

"Studying hard?" Natalie asked her brother hastily.

"No harder than I have to," he said, and everyone smiled.

"And Arthur Langdon?" asked Mr. Waite, who was not immune to the general convulsive emotional quality of the hour. "How is he?"

Natalie, who had been full of things to tell her father about Arthur Langdon, said, "Well, I haven't seen much of him lately."

"Been working pretty hard, I guess," her father said. Too late, because she was out of practice, Natalie found the irony in his voice, but she had already answered too carefully, "Well, not as hard as I *should*."

"*How* about we all have some coffee and cake?" Mrs. Waite asked, looking brightly around at all of them.

"Thank you," Natalie said politely.

They filed out into the kitchen, using their tenuous family relationship as an excuse for not having cake brought to them in the living room, but each one waiting civilly for the others to go through doors first.

"It is *so* good to have my little girl back home again," Mrs. Waite whispered when she said good night to Natalie.

At the college on Thanksgiving Day they had turkey and cranberry sauce and mashed potatoes and peas and mince pie and small candies in paper baskets; at the Waites' on Thanksgiving Day they had turkey and cranberry sauce and mashed potatoes and peas and mince pie and small candies in Mrs. Waite's best silver candy dishes. Except for the fact that if she had been at the college she would not have eaten at all, Natalie found being at home not much better. The Thanksgiving dinner was one prepared solely and lovingly by Mrs. Waite, tended and planned and rich in delicate touches, and was eaten by her family in ill humor and weariness; as though, in fact, it were an ordinary meal. It was served at three on Thursday afternoon, a time when no one was ordinarily hungry, and was preceded by cocktails, a ceremony which made Natalie and her brother stare at one another, since neither of them was quite prepared for the immoral spectacle of the other's drinking in the bosom of the family.

"Taken up liquor in your old age, Nat?" Bud asked Natalie, and she answered him childishly, "What about you? Keep a bottle under your pillow?"

Mr. Waite glanced away, and Mrs. Waite beamed at them, pleased to see her two children talking together as though, she seemed to think, they were not brother and sister at all. The two children, suddenly aware of this, fell immediately silent, and Mrs. Waite said brightly, "Well, all together again. We must drink a toast to our own little family."

Mr. Waite regarded his wife without expression for a minute, and then lifted his glass and said solemnly, "To our own little family."

Looking around, at her tall daughter and her masculine son, at her husband, at her full dinner table, Mrs. Waite said meltingly, "Where will we all be next year?"

"Dead, perhaps?" Mr. Waite suggested helpfully.

"Don't *say* that," Mrs. Waite told him, "I don't even like to *talk* about it."

"Let us flatter ourselves," Mr. Waite said into his glass, "that *I* may be the survivor."

On Friday morning Natalie came to her father, as usual; not knowing until the last minute that he awaited her in the study, she was only reminded of it by her mother's fearful grimaces and gestures. As a result, when she knocked at the door and heard him say, pleased, "Come in," she felt that she had an unworthy advantage of him in that he would be humiliated if he knew that she had forgotten when he remembered. She grinned at him when she closed the door behind her and said, "*This* is what I've been waiting for."

"Natalie, my dear," he said, and smiled back at her across the desk. This was his real greeting; neither the encounter at the bus nor the toast before the Thanksgiving dinner were communications to Natalie from her father; it was when he looked at her across his desk and saw the door shut behind her that he recognized her at last.

"Well," she said, and sat down.

"Well, Natalie," he said.

They sat without speaking for a minute, her father looking down at his hands on the desk, and Natalie knowing with pleasure the feeling of the study, of the books, of her father, and hearing faintly an echo which made her almost smile ("What if I told you that you were seen?"); after a minute she said, "Did I write you about Arthur Langdon?"

"No," he said, his voice quiet so as not to disturb her possible revelations, "what about him?"

"I keep thinking of the time I went to see him in his office and it reminded me of coming in here to talk to you, and he made such a fool of himself."

"And I?"

Natalie laughed. "I'm really glad to be back," she said. "It's hard to say it, though."

"Is everything going well?"

"No," Natalie said, considering. "Not at all well, I guess. I'm doing very badly."

"How?"

"In everything."

"Anything you need from me?"

"No, not right now. Later, perhaps."

"Can you tell me about it?"

This is not going right, Natalie thought; how much he wants to know, and what shall I tell him? Daddy dear, I am a failure, I hate college and I hate everybody? Or is that just what he expects? Does he have an answer for that, even?

"I'll tell you when I can," she said.

"Right," he said. "Working?"

Funny, Natalie thought, when anyone else says, "Working?" it means are you getting anything done, really—are you going to classes, passing your exams, finishing your biology notebook, have you got a job, is the plumbing business picking up any, is there a spot for you in a new Broadway production, are you earning any money? When my father and Arthur Langdon say, "Working?" they mean is anything happening inside you that might possibly interest them, like yeast working in bread. "Sure," she said.

There was a short pause, and then her father said gracefully, "I am not so great a fool myself, Natalie, but what I can recognize foolishness in others. I can still remember the almost irresistible impulses toward melodrama which strike one at your age. Please forgive me if I say that I never expected you to be immune to ordinary impulses, although I expect equally that you will be receptive to extraordinary ones. I do, however, feel that you might reserve your sardonic impulses for your mother, perhaps, or for your friends at college, without trying them out on me. I have—please understand me, my dear—too much trouble with my own adolescent hangovers, to feel *yours* very deeply. This attitude of yours is one requiring only a slight, although basic, change in viewpoint to become a valuable and constructive state of mind, and the sooner you adopt this change in viewpoint, the sooner you may become a profitable member of society. There is—and *please* believe me—no vital change in personality involved. There is, as a matter of fact, not even any pain. You have only to shift perhaps a quarter turn to the northeast, and your problems are gone. Perhaps nothing more is required than one clear view of your situation and your present actions; it is very possible, you know, to be doing the right things and thinking the perfect thoughts for one's position, and yet seem entirely wrong because that one faint shading of understanding is missing; perhaps you feel that you are doing badly these days because you do not perceive that you are, in fact, doing very well indeed, and only lack the perception of your own worth to know exactly how well. Perhaps, Natalie, if I remind you what a very worthwhile person you *are*, it will give you the quarter turn you need."

"Nothing will help," Natalie said; even after her father's mention of melodrama, she could not help saying it, although she did not look at him as she spoke.

"Well," he said, after a minute, "I had not intended saying these things to you so soon, certainly not on your first visit home. It is of course necessary to achieve a certain solidity in one's way before taking a shift in perspective to see it clearly. I daresay that by the time I see you again—since, as you say so emphatically, you *must* go back today—you may be readier to listen to me. I should hate to deprive you prematurely of the glories of the suicidal frame of mind, since I am fairly certain that depriving yourself of the ability to feel this way would be more cruel than any sort of physical torture you might inflict upon yourself, so that I can use 'suicidal' as a descriptive adjective without really feeling that it implies any action."

"You're trying to make me say that I want to kill myself," Natalie said.

"You need hardly say anything quite so meaningless," he said tartly, "and I would vastly prefer that you confine your statements to pure descriptions of fact. I think better of your vanity, Natalie, than to believe that two months out of seventeen years could destroy you."

She was almost irresistibly tempted to tell him all about herself, to justify somehow the facts of herself that he did not seem to understand, and which, so horribly acute to her, seemed to him only to point up a statement about general personalities; she wanted to pound on the desk before him and shout, "What do *you* know?" walk wildly up and down the room, pulling words from the very air to tell him about herself, and she wanted to shout, and to stamp, and to cry, and yet before she had time to do any of these things she heard ahead of her his calm voice saying, when she had done, "Precisely, my dear Natalie, precisely what I was . . ." And so instead she said, "No one likes me."

"I hardly blame them," he said briefly.

When she saw that he was laughing she laughed too, and as he stood up to show her it was time to go, that he had no more, really, to say to her, he added, "I think we understand one another, Natalie, you and I."

She had come home on Wednesday night, bringing with her a certain sense of romance, as one who could bring heartbreaking stories of haunted lands, who had seen and heard and touched and known the improbable, the unbelievable ("and in that country I saw as well an image, made of a virgin pearl, and its eyes were diamonds and its hair was beaten gold, and it was set on a block of marble and no one might worship it face to face . . .") and brought back perhaps small odd things, dug from the bottom of a trunk and mused over, held in two hands lovingly . . . ("*This* I found at the bottom of a well, and they said it would bring death to any who touched it . . . and *this*, there's a story goes with *this* one—I was lost, and wandering in the jungle, and it had been three days since I had eaten, and six weeks since I had seen a human being, and when I awakened, raging with fever, I saw bending over me . . . and, then, look at *this*, observe the intricate carving the cipher scratched on the handle—I bought it from an old . . .") . . . who had seen and heard and touched and known more than might ever be found at home. Who had seen, perhaps, beasts walking like men and jewels shining like stars, and who smiled at certain remembered scenes a million miles away, and stared bewildered at old familiar sights and found the faces of mother and father and brother more strange than the face on a carving made in pearl.

Natalie had not been at home for more than twenty-four hours before she felt that her visit was complete and her purposes served; she had slept once more in the bed politely called hers, she had kissed her mother and father and been mildly surprised by the actuality of her brother, she had tried out the familiar things and found that she remembered them well enough, then it was time for her to be off again. It had rained steadily since she first set out for the bus stop at college, and the damp unkind weather filled the rooms at home with gray cold; she had worn her raincoat home from college and although she had not gone out of the house since, the raincoat still lay across a chair in the back hall crumpled and wet, the floor beneath it muddy where it had dripped all night.

Two days before the living-room fire had dried Natalie out, but even the memory of the rain to be waded through, like a dark impenetrable barrier, before she could be again at college, would not dampen her urgent excitement or soothe her. "So you're not staying for dinner tonight?" her mother asked her softly on Friday afternoon, and the question was a statement about Natalie's unquiet eyes, her spot before the fire, her hands moving beside her on the rug. And the question was as well a continuation of her mother's welcome to Natalie on Wednesday evening, meaningless and full of incoherent dread; if her mother had said, "Will you stay on, then, for dinner tonight?" Natalie would have turned quickly and perhaps answered without the constant fearful check she had been keeping upon herself at home, would perhaps have answered, an answer being required, with the sublime impatience which had possessed her while she was with her family these days. If her mother had asked her any question at all, anything to make Natalie speak, the whole quiet forward movement of the day could easily have been impeded, the extra moments consumed might have made Natalie later at the college, and so in some way deprived of something, her mother might have had her answer and not have been the better for it.

Stirring uneasily before the fire, Natalie said, as softly as her mother had spoken, "I'd better get on back." She knew that behind her, her mother had set her needle down soundlessly in the cloth and was resting her hands on the arms of the chair, staring over Natalie's head into the fire; Natalie felt rather than heard her mother draw breath to speak, and then resign it. No point in speaking, no reasonable thing to say. It had all been debated endlessly in the second between her mother's drawn-in breath and Natalie's involuntary movement that checked it. Her mother had almost said, "Natalie, are you happy?" and Natalie had almost said, "No"; her mother had almost said, "Everything seems somehow to go badly," and Natalie had almost said, "I know it and I can't help it"; her mother had almost said, "Let me help you," and Natalie had almost said, "What can *you* do?" and that had been the nervous movement of her head that her mother had recognized and which had silenced her before she ever spoke.

After a while, at work with her needle again, Mrs. Waite said, as though they had been discussing lesser matters all the afternoon, "Dear, are you trying to settle down to work?"

"Sure," said Natalie, because this kind of spoken conversation could be carried on easily without thinking, or truth.

"I've told you this before," her mother said, and her voice added, *so many, many times,* "I've said it before, Natalie, and you know I hate to keep dwelling on it—but you *do* know that the money sending you to college is really more than your father can afford. We have deprived ourselves of many things."

Natalie perceived that she was supposed to come to her mother in gratitude, as she had been invited to do many times before, so that between them they might make many false promises, and sketch out brilliant unreal futures, and console one another with imperfect emotions; in all her travels Natalie had not learned how to come to her mother in gratitude, and so she merely turned her head and said, "I know it, and I do remember it. I'll try to keep out of trouble."

"Not *trouble*," her mother said, as though trouble were murder or robbery or arson, something she could understand and possibly find among her own temptations, "not trouble, Natalie; just try to do better with your studies and with the other girls and even with your professors."

Strange, Natalie thought, in all his wisdom my father never found from my letters that I get along badly with people; I suppose it's the first thing my mother fears, just as she is afraid that I have been visited with all her sorrows, because those she is better able to heal in me than she could in herself. It seemed that perhaps her father was trying to cure his failures in Natalie, and her mother was perhaps trying to avoid, through Natalie, doing over again those things she now believed to have been mistaken.

"Everything's really fine," Natalie said to her mother. "I'm really doing very well. Everyone says so." She decided that this last statement smacked too much of eagerness, and turned her head back abruptly to stare again into the fire.

"I haven't told your father," her mother said surprisingly.

"You haven't?" It was the weak, the completely wrong and unnecessary thing to say, but for the moment Natalie was not able to think of any right thing. Her mother was silent for a minute, perhaps to give Natalie a chance to say something intelligent, and then with a little rustling sound she folded up her sewing. The small sounds of her mother's breathing nearly put Natalie, suspended in the silence her mother did not seem inclined to break, to sleep before the fire, but the realization that her father and brother would soon be home prevented her from relaxing completely. Before they came back she must have her coat ready and her mind made up and be standing near the door, ready for farewells; she hoped that her father would not want to drive her to the bus stop, and was resigned at the same time to the fact that he would not possibly allow her to take a taxi, or, better still, to walk.

"Natalie?" her mother said helplessly, looking at the back of Natalie's head, and as if her mother had been warning her, Natalie rose effortlessly, proud of the swift movements of her own long body. "You're getting so big," her mother murmured. "I can hardly recognize my little girl."

"Better get ready to go," Natalie said hastily, moving toward the door and twisting involuntarily as she went past her mother, as though to avoid clutching hands. "Bus leaves at four."

Her mother started to speak again, but Natalie hurried, and could safely pretend not to hear by the time her mother was ready to say anything. The wet raincoat smell was exciting, carrying with it remotely the institutional smells of the college, a faint echo of a cologne Natalie had never worn in her life;

near the pocket was a cigarette burn she had not made; the raincoat was in itself a symbol of going and coming, of wishing and fearing, or, precisely, the going out of a warm, firelit house into the heartbreaking cold.

She tied a scarf over her head and thought that now she would not be able to hear her mother's last admonitions; when she went back to the fire her mother had risen and was standing where Natalie had been lying, and her father stood next to her mother by the fire. I didn't hear him come in, Natalie thought, and thought again, I suppose by now I'm out of practice on his coming and going; he and her brother had been to call on people she did not even know, and although they had asked her to go along, she had been able to decline without minding very much; her new acquaintances were all at college and a new acquaintance at home was, after all, so much time wasted.

An uncomfortable thing happened: her father spoke and for a minute Natalie thought it was her mother. "Well, my dear," he said and again the conversation between him and her mother while Natalie was getting her raincoat became suddenly explicit; he had not believed that his wife was letting Natalie go, had perhaps been surprised at the exertion necessary to keep Natalie, had wondered over and abandoned as unworthy the notion of himself asking her to stay, had been then incredulous that his wife should ever have expected Natalie *not* to go.

"Did you have a nice time?" asked Natalie formally.

Her father bowed ironically. "No better than I expected," he said, "I believe we keep better company at home."

"We have been very quiet here," Natalie said. She went over and put her arms around her mother; a little of this affection was surely not out of place at leave-taking, and did not commit Natalie to any certain course of action except going. Until this moment her going had been no more than a wanton impulse, but of course saluting her mother made it definite, and her father stirred, moving the car keys in his pocket.

"Bus at four?" he asked.

"Better get going," Natalie said, disengaging herself easily from her mother and stepping back to nod at her brother, who nodded back and said, "See you sometime."

Natalie and her mother and father stood then uncertainly together in the middle of the room, each of them with something to say to the others ("Will it always be the same?" "Will we any of us change by the next time?" "Has it always been like this?"), and involved themselves in a sort of dance, maneuvering one another into the most favorable position for a gesture whose extreme simplicity, that of departure, had become a sudden awkward thing. Natalie, finally, moved first. She found that as she went toward the door she was saying, "Goodbye, goodbye," as though to confirm her going, and that her father, following her, was still rattling the car keys in his pocket. "Goodbye," Natalie said at last, actually hesitating again in the doorway, looking beyond the solid coated figure of her father, past the expectant figure of her mother, to her own spot by the fire, untenanted and probably of no interest to anyone save herself, to remain empty of her until the next time, still optimistic, that she came home. "Goodbye," she said again, directly to her mother, and went outside into the rain.

Once in the car with her father, but out in the rain nevertheless, she looked with interest on the street light at the corner, ornate and suburban, belonging undeniably to the home where her mother and father lived, and she saw with satisfaction the rain slanting brightly against the light; it was already dark on this rainy afternoon and this was the last outpost belonging to her father. Beyond here the people she might see were less familiar, less the exclusive property of her father, more the potential shining world of her own.

"Seems like I hardly had a chance to say hello," she said politely to her father, her voice warm with the excitement of leaving.

"I expect you'll be home again," her father said. "In any case we have heard you say hello in the past."

"Has Mother really been well?" Natalie asked.

"Very well, thank you. Very well indeed."

Once in the bus, cradled in the deep heavy seat, her father

waved away through the thick window, the movement of great wheels under her, her family behind and the college ahead, Natalie leaned back comfortably; there was no time now for remorse over the perfunctory way she had treated her loving mother and father and even her brother—what was important at this moment was the quick control of muscles all up and down her leg, bent now, but potentially straight, the narrow solidity of her fingers, bare and still wet with the rain, the unity that began with her eyes and forehead and tied to her back and into her legs again, all of it bound together into a provocative whole that could be only barely contained within the skin and sense of Natalie Waite, individual.

She wanted to sing and did so, soundlessly, her mouth against the fogged window of the bus, thinking as she sang, And when I first saw Natalie Waite, the most incredible personality of our time, the unbelievably talented, vivid, almost girlish creature—when I first saw her, she was sitting in a bus, exactly as I or you might be, and for a minute I noticed nothing of her richness . . . and then she turned and smiled at me. Now, knowing her for what she is, the most vividly talented actress (murderess? courtesan? dancer?) of our time or perhaps any time, I can see more clearly the enchanting contradictions within her—her humor, her vicious flashing temper, so easily aroused and so quickly controlled by her iron will; her world-weary cynicism (she has, after all, suffered more than perhaps any other from the stings and arrows of outrageous fortune), her magnificent mind, so full of information, of deep pockets never explored wherein lie glowing thoughts like jewels never seen . . .

She thought too of worlds that lay ahead for Natalie Waite, and tried to estimate them by a secret formula of her own: one hundred, for instance—one hundred years, one hundred dollars—was a summit which had achieved and passed unachievable and unpassable reaches like fifty-nines and seventy-fours; seventy-four is, after all, a point so vastly beyond one, or two, and even beyond three; the month of May (reflecting further, Natalie thought that she had never in her life lived through the month of May; it was a fable, a month non-existing, a month for maying and greenswarding, not an ordinary month full of weeks and days and probably Tuesdays and Sundays like any other month) was something that might or might not happen long after the unthinkable barriers of January and March and Valentine's Day and Lincoln's Birthday had been gotten past somehow. Before her, then, lay a hundred years, each one glee-fully passing without hesitation seventy-four and February, and perhaps a hundred Mays, each one to be welcomed and duly decked. A vague and voiceless yearning filled her, to take these days and force them to solid rich tangible form, to ham-mer at this foolishness of time and make it into . . . into . . . She fell asleep here, and slept until the bus stop before the col-lege stop, when complimenting herself upon her unerring accuracy and supernatural sense of time, she awoke and rec-ognized where she was.

In the regular and offensively straight line of windows across the third floor of the house where she lived at college, Natalie found the one dark one which was her own, and a little thrill of anticipation followed her up the absolutely even walk to the door; inside the dark window was her own sure place, and she had been away from it. She lingered going up the walk, pro-longing the last few minutes before she entered.

When she opened the door of the house and came into the hallway where the mail pigeon-holes dominated the graceful lines copied approximately from an eighteenth-century town house, the peculiar atmosphere she had somehow forgotten in two days swept down on her and left her almost breathless for a minute. First, and overpoweringly, there was the smell of the cheap dark wood used for the furniture, and the smell of the noon's soup from the kitchen—it was a student joke that the furniture polish and the soup were made from the same basic substance—and then, strongly reminiscent of the furni-ture polish and a little of the soup, was the scent Old Nick, who had rooms on the first floor of the house, used on herself, her room, and her clothes. This scent swept up the hall from Old Nick's apartment halfway to the dining room, trailing up the stairs and through the halls even of the third floor, identifying the transoms where Old Nick listened, clinging to the doorknobs she touched, a stronger and more pervasive influence than any of Old Nick's advisory remarks.

From where she stood in the eighteenth-century foyer Natalie could see, on her right, the hall that led to the dining room, past the half-open door to Old Nick's rooms—this doorway, by the way, was subject, due to its nearness to the kitchen fires and the fact that it was inhabited by Old Nick and the additional fact that it was on the bottom floor, to a series of student jokes Old Nick had undoubtedly heard and probably fostered—and the long row of slim doorways on the eighteenth-century wallpaper, opening onto nothing. On Natalie's left were the stairs, curving up and over her head and going past the rooms on the second floor and going past the rooms on the third floor—on the third floor was Natalie's room, and it only took mounting the stairs to reach it. Beyond the stairs, farther down the hall to her left, lay the living room where she had been called upon to name herself her first night in college, a room she had entered perhaps twice since, although there were girls in the house who used it regularly, as though it were their own.

There was no one in sight, but from beyond the door to Old Nick's rooms came the sound of voices, in the tones of two old friends complimenting one another and drinking sherry before dinner. Natalie, her moccasins making no sound on the linoleum floor that duplicated the black-and-white tiles of an eighteenth-century entrance hall, went to her mailbox, but it was empty; without looking into any other, she turned abruptly and was about to start up the stairs when she was caught, helplessly and suddenly, by the sound of the dinner bell and the lunatic rush of the girls down the stairs. Rather than be trapped halfway up the stairs she retreated quickly, annoyed at herself for not having timed things better; she started down the hall but was cut off by the further opening of Old Nick's door and Old Nick's large voice urging her friend into the dining room. Natalie moved toward the front door and stood finally in the shadows under the stairs, listening to the pounding feet coming down over her head. Their voices were shrill and excited; you would have imagined, Natalie thought with disgust, that it was worthwhile getting to dinner, the way they ran. After a minute or so the footsteps began to slacken off, and the burden of the voices swelled from the dining room. There was a polite rattle of silverware and a constant urging questioning to the voices, as of three hundred girls together asking one another, "What's for dinner?"

When the last footsteps were gone from the stairs, Natalie came out of the shadows and went quickly past the open hall to the stairs. No one had noticed her, seemingly. The last time she had gone into the dining room she had been shy, and had come in alone and sat down at a table near the entrance; the three girls already sitting at the table had waited, watching her until she sat down, her napkin in her lap; then they had risen, all three, and had gone without gesture to another table. Dinner in itself was no temptation to Natalie—there was no food in the world could get her into that dining room again.

She went upstairs quickly, her wet feet soundless on the linoleum steps. She did not hesitate, but went directly upstairs and ran down the hall to her own room; she always carried the key with her instead of leaving it in her mailbox as as she had been told to do, in case Old Nick wanted to come into her room, and had lost her passkey and could not find the maid's and for some reason was not able to get one of the master keys from the main college office and could not locate any of the other girls—the ones who lived in seventeen, or thirty-seven, or seven—whose keys would open Natalie's door. Inside, the room was hot and airless. Without turning on the lights, she dropped her raincoat on the floor and went over to the bed, which was pushed hard against the window. She sat on the bed, opened the window and, dropping her head onto the windowsill, rested quietly with her eyes closed.

There were noises again in the hall before she felt refreshed and could lift her head; the girls were coming up from dinner and the dark night air had filled the room; she could see her desk and her typewriter in the dimness, the line of books all around the room next to the baseboard, the one straight chair next to the desk. One night, in a fury at not being able to turn freely in her own room, she had taken her clothes from the dresser and crushed them into the suitcases in her closet, and shoved and tugged the dresser out into the hall, along with the maple armchair and the bookcase the college provided. The college handy man had been petulant about the furniture in the hall, but eventually it had been taken away and now Natalie, with her bed under the window and her desk and chair crammed into a corner and her door eternally locked and—this was a month-old whim, which no longer surprised her by its convenience—her wastebasket hanging just outside the window by a string fastened to the head of the bed, was able to move about in her small square room undisturbed. It was necessary, of course, to keep the transom shut always, and the key securely in the keyhole while she was inside the room.

She was very lonely here. So much so, in fact, that tonight after a few minutes when the sounds in the hall had quieted down, she found a cigarette in the pocket of her raincoat and holding it in her hand unlocked the door cautiously and went out into the hall. There were voices coming from lighted rooms farther down the hall; several doors were open, giving a sense of girls running in and out, from one room to another, so that Natalie slipped softly to the stairs and down them to the first floor, and along the hall to a doorway where, standing as much as possible in the shadows, she knocked as though her knock were distinguishable from all others, and waited. After a moment spent crushed against the doorway, staring into the panels on the door and wondering at them, she thought she heard, "Come in," and she opened the door and slipped inside, shutting the door quickly behind her.

"Hello," she said.

"Yes?" said Rosalind. She was lying on her bed holding a movie magazine and she looked up in polite surprise. Natalie, looking at the bright-orange pajamas Rosalind was wearing, thought that these days Rosalind was gay in the center of a group, admired and appreciated, one of the girls whom other girls wanted to meet; so small a change, Natalie thought, so slight a variant; all she would ever remember someday of Rosalind, she knew, was the quick bright picture of Rosalind walking down a campus path with a girl on either side of her; "Yes?" said Rosalind.

"May I borrow a match from you?" Natalie asked; she kept her voice light, as though the request were trivial.

"Certainly," Rosalind said. She tossed over the book of matches that lay on the table next to the bed, and added, "Keep them, I have plenty." Without looking again at Natalie, she raised her magazine expectantly.

"Mind if I stay and talk for a minute?" Natalie asked, as though this request, too, were trivial. "You busy?" she asked. "I don't want to interrupt."

"Well, I *was* reading," Rosalind said, and glanced down at her magazine.

"Of course," Natalie said. She was thinking, I know, I know, I'm the only one who knows, and she isn't a bit afraid of me, and I could tell if I wanted to and she doesn't believe anyone would listen, but *I* know. She tumbled in her hurry to be out of the room.

With the door closed behind her, she thought soberly that it was two flights of stairs back to her room and so little space to cover before she was outside, and she knew where she was going even before—with a gesture of contempt she wished she had been able to do two minutes before—she tore Rosalind's matchbook in two and threw it on the floor outside Rosalind's door. The door of her room upstairs was locked, because she locked it even if she went ten paces out into the hall. She had cigarettes with her, and her own matches, although her raincoat was still in her room. Moving lightly, without sound, she ran swiftly down the stairs and out into the campus, stepping with gratitude onto the grass.

The rain had stopped, but every sign of continuing after a breathing spell. Drops of water slid off the trees onto Natalie's hair and although she wished she had brought her raincoat the thought of going after it, back into the lighted house, was untenable. Long before this hour late in November it was dark; Natalie knew by now how to find her way along the campus paths almost without looking, and the thought of the taut lighted square of her room behind her was disgusting, out here where she was able to take long steps and move as far as she wanted. Ahead of her she could see lights in the Langdons' home, and there were voices coming indistinguishably from the houses she passed, and somewhere a radio; although she could not have identified the tune it was playing, she could have narrowed the possibilities down to half a dozen tunes she heard girls whistling in the hall or singing in harmony in their rooms.

She was not the owner of this land, and as she turned to go along the narrow path that would take her behind the main lecture buildings and around again to the campus houses, she thought, I am walking around my country, I am telling its boundaries, describing its edges, enclosing it. The beautiful clarity of all marked outlines occurred to her—there would be a deep satisfaction in strengthening fences, for instance, going along on the inside of a strong fence enclosing a large land, leaning outward to push toward the extreme limit of property; too, what about the lovely definition of a sheet of white paper alone on her desk, oblong and complete, the tightness with which the sky fitted onto the earth at the horizon, the act of caressing the spine of a book? Irresistibly, she thought with a shiver of a razor-sharp edge slicing horizontally through her eyes, into her mouth, and then coming around the hard corner of a building, saw again the campus and its lights and heard its sounds. She stopped for a minute, surveying her country with interest and with tolerance; she was infinitely tall and these tiny buildings—although scaled to exact measurements: a tenth of an inch, perhaps, to a foot—had been set up by her own hands, furnished, and peopled with the small moveable dolls she had herself created, planning with care and perhaps not entirely wisely the numbers of their arms and legs and the location on their heads.

Perhaps tomorrow, she thought, when it is light, I shall consider moving all the trees together to make a real forest at one end of the campus. It might on the whole be better to take the houses out of two straight lines facing one another and put them at random, so that no homunculus coming out of the doorway of one house could find the doorway to another house. Perhaps I shall move the Langdon dolls to the steeple of the Commons building, and leave them there for a week, while they sob and beg to be released and I look down, so large they cannot see me, and laugh at them.

Perhaps tomorrow I shall pick up one of the houses, any one, and, holding it gently in one hand, pull it carefully apart with my other hand, with great delicacy taking the pieces of it off one after another: first the door and then, dislodging the slight nails with care, the right front corner of the house, board by board, and then, sweeping out the furniture inside, down the right wall of the house, removing it with care and not touching the second floor, which should remain intact even after the first floor is entirely gone. Then the stairs, step by step, and all this while the mannikins inside run screaming from each section of the house to a higher and a more concealed room, crushing one another and stumbling and pulling frantically, slamming doors behind them while my strong fingers pull each door softly off its hinges and pull the walls apart and lift out the windows intact and take out carefully the tiny beds and chairs; and finally they will be all together like seeds in a pomegranate, in one tiny room, hardly breathing, some of them fainting, some crying, and all wedged in together looking in the direction from which I am coming, and then, when I take the door off with sure careful fingers, there they all will be, packed inside and crushed back against the wall, and I shall eat the room in one mouthful, chewing ruthlessly on the boards and the small sweet bones.

And then, taking another house (the small unfortunates, looking up and not daring to wonder which house will be next, seeing the inevitable hovering hand hesitate over one house, choose perhaps another, or descend awfully and with decision upon the one where they hide), I might be amused by violating all the inhabitants; perhaps—and this might be the funniest of all—set fifty mannikins naked crammed into one room with Arthur Langdon in the center, and poke and prod at them and laugh when they sobbed and tried to move where they were packed in so tight. Or take the Old Nick doll and drag it by one foot up and down the campus paths, banging it gently against the door of every house and against the heads of any dolls who look out. Or, undressing one of the dolls with infinite care—although the dolls are so small it is almost impossible, surely, to undress one without tearing the tiny clothes and sometimes even snapping the thin arms—I might wind a long strip of cloth about it and stick the cloth to the doll with a pin in back and set the doll on a tiny chair on the roof of one of the houses and shout in my ringing voice from the heavens that this is a queen and they must all climb up to the roof and kiss the queen's toe.

Or take all the houses and stack them crazily one on top of another with the dolls inside and then on top of the teetering stack of houses set the Arthur Langdon doll and turn it on its head and then with one full laughing breath . . .

"Hello? Is that Natalie Waite?"

She stopped, wondering horribly if she had been speaking aloud and he had recognized her voice. But then he said, "I thought I recognized you even in this darkness; what are you doing wandering about on a night like this?"

"It was too stuffy inside."

"I thought so, too. Thought I'd just wander over to the library. You going that way?"

"No," said Natalie, although she had been going along the path that led to the library. "I'm going the other way."

He glanced down at the row of houses, as though knowing surely which one she would be wanting. "Have a nice time over the holiday?" he asked.

"Fine."

"How is your father?"

"Fine. Working hard."

"Hope to meet him one of these days."

"He says he'll be coming to see me here very soon."

"Hope to meet him. Well," he added vaguely, taking a step along the path toward the library. Then, as though just reminded of it, he turned back and said, "I suppose you've heard our news?"

"No," said Natalie.

He laughed embarrassedly. "We're having a baby," he said,

and since such a bare announcement obviously impressed him as lacking in some effective emotional quality, he went on to say weakly and without any note of conviction in his voice, "We're very happy about it."

"Congratulations," said Natalie, thinking, Elizabeth? "That's wonderful." There seemed to be very little else to add; when they actually had a baby it might be possible to say soberly that it was a pretty thing, or that it resembled Arthur, or that it was incredibly small, and look at its tiny hands, but at present she could only say again, "How wonderful for you both."

"We're very happy about it," he said. "Well, good night."

"Good night," Natalie said. She did not wait for him to leave—perhaps for fear that he should turn back with such another startling announcement—but went quickly on down the path, toward the house which Arthur Langdon had noted and to which she had known all along that she was going.

Once she started toward the house—it was diagonally across the campus from her own and she could have reached it much more easily by going directly to it, rather than wandering along the edges of the campus to reach it obliquely—she went quickly, almost running at last up the walk. This house was rococo where her own was classic, and its hallway was colorful and filigreed with gold. She went in silently, knowing exactly how to go, and up the stairs, putting her feet down lightly and barely brushing the bannister with the tips of her fingers, her most vital intention to move without noise and not to be noticed if possible. She met no one on the stairs, but when she reached the second floor, she stood hesitating, looking down the hall where lines of open, lighted doorways looked much like those in her own house. She would have to pass them all, and the question was whether to walk with dignity or make a run for it. There was a light, she could see, shining through the transom of the door at the end of the hall and she straightened her shoulders, almost laughed at herself, and then began to walk with quiet sure steps down the hall. She attracted no notice from the first open room; no one even looked up, but the second open room was filled with girls, lounging on the bed and the floor, and someone noticed her and called, "Hey, here she comes." Without turning her head, she was aware of the girls crowding to the doorway, and knew what their half-audible voices said and how their eyes looked, following her down the hall. The noise brought girls to the doorways all up and down the hall, and even ahead of her Natalie saw doors opening. She pretended to be trying not to smile and she walked without turning her head to the last door on the left. When she hesitated before the door, she heard the great mocking silence up and down the hall, and an echoing burst of laughter and jeering which almost obscured her knock. Then she lost her courage, feeling them all watching her, and, knowing that this door was rarely locked, she opened it without invitation and slipped inside. Standing then with the door safely shut behind her, she took a long breath and laughed; outside she could hear giggling and the sound of footsteps coming softly down almost to the door and then turning back—the sounds of many girls all together saying to each other hilarious things meant to be heard beyond the door.

Natalie said, "I'm sorry, I really am. I came to say I was really terribly sorry. I shouldn't have gone, and I'm sorry."

"I'm never *really* angry with you anyway," Tony said.

"It was horrible," Natalie said.

"Of course."

"I told you they would be. Did they hang on you?"

"They were all there. Even my brother."

"They fed me," Natalie said. "They didn't do anything else *except* feed me, I think. May I come in?"

"What are you afraid of?" Tony asked. "Me?" She was sitting cross-legged on the bed; she had not moved when Natalie opened the door and now she only lifted her head and smiled. She was playing solitaire with the ancient fortune-telling cards called the Tarot, cards old and large and lovely and richly gilt and red; Natalie, glanced down at them and could almost feel their remembered softness which from long use was so little like cardboard now, and almost, she thought, like parchment. Tony and Natalie believed that they were the only two people in the world who now loved Tarot cards, and used them—so reminiscent of antique, undreamed games—for games of their own, invented card games, and walking games, and a kind of affectionate fortune-telling which was always faithful to the meanings of the cards as recorded in the Tarot book, but which somehow always came out as meaning that Tony and Natalie were the finest and luckiest persons imaginable. Of all the suits, Tony most favored swords, and the card named Page of Swords was always her particular card; Natalie liked the card named the Magician, and thought that the face on the card resembled her own. Tony's solitaire with the great cards covered half the bed, and Natalie could see that the Magician had been moved out to fill a space, and the page of swords lay upon the queen of cups. "Come along," Tony said. "You're back now, at any rate."

Natalie came away from the door and stopped in the middle of the room to slip off her shoes. "Wet," she said.

"You come to me miserable and helpless and soaked and probably starving," Tony said pleasantly.

"I have fifteen dollars, though," Natalie said, remembering suddenly what had not seemed actual to her before. "My father gave it to me."

"Splendid," Tony said absently, regarding the cards on the bed, "now I shall have a stamp to write home for money." She stretched. "Seven of pentacles on eight," she said. "The trouble with these infernal cards is I never can tell whether my solitaire comes out or not."

Natalie, moving across the room, stopped suddenly to listen. "They get worse and worse outside," she said.

Tony lifted her head to listen for a minute. "Beasts," she said. "Have they fed?"

"A little while ago. I nearly got trampled to death on the stairs."

"*Do* you suppose," said Tony, marveling, "*do* you suppose they've got hold of a *man* out there?"

"Sounds like it, poor devil. Those cards are certainly not meant to give sensible answers—you can't make a solitaire come out with them."

"I suppose not." Tony swept the cards together and began

to shuffle them. "I like the way they feel, though. And ordinary cards are so dull and silly." With the cards still in her hand, she got up easily, and without seeming to have an objective went casually over to the door and opened it. "*Get* away," she said amiably.

The girls outside scattered shrieking, and Tony closed the door and went back over to sit on the bed again. "Someday I shall be allowed to torture them," she said. "I believe I shall take them one by one and peel them like apples." Idly she spread the cards out before her. "Tomorrow we can get a new deck if you like," she said. "One full of jacks and spades and diamonds, and I can play solitaire with *that* and leave the Tarot deck for you to read dubious futures in and my solitaire *still* won't come out."

"If you had a deck of cards with only one card in it . . ." Natalie said.

"Someday," Tony said vaguely.

"The Langdons are having a baby."

"Page of swords," Tony said. "Imagine breeding Elizabeth to Arthur. The American Kennel Club will of course have to destroy all the cubs."

Natalie realized happily that she was very sleepy; it was a feeling of warmth and comfort and security, and she said without thinking, "You said I'd be right back here."

"Did I?" Tony laughed. "Damned queen of pentacles." Again she lifted her head and stared for a long minute at Natalie. "You'd better sleep."

Sleepily Natalie stood up and came to the bed. "Move over," she said and without waiting squeezed onto the bed between Tony and the wall.

"Just as I got my cards set out," Tony said. She gathered the cards together and slid off the bed onto the floor. "Take the damn bed," she said. "There was a letter for you from the Student Committee, I picked it up at your house yesterday. They said you haven't been to any classes for two weeks."

"I haven't?"

"You're to go see them at ten tomorrow morning," Tony said. "I lost the letter somewhere."

"Too bad," Natalie said. Sleepily she pulled the blankets over her head. "Door," she said.

Tony again went almost silently to the door, opened it, and with a large and menacing gesture drove away the girls outside. When she came back into the room she sat quietly on the floor next to the bed, shoving the cards away.

"I'll read to you," she said. After a minute her voice began quietly, " ' . . . She screamed in genuine alarm as Alice came out of her room with only her shoes and stockings on, and her large matinee hat, a most coquettishly piquantly indecent object! Poor Fanny went red at the sight of her mistress and didn't know where to look as Alice came dancing along, her eyes noting with evident approval the position into which I had placed her maid.

" ' "*Mes compliments, mademoiselle!*" I said with a low bow as she came up.

" 'She smiled and blushed, but was too intent on Fanny to joke with me. "That's lovely, Jack!" she exclaimed after a careful inspection of her now trembling maid, "but surely she can get loose!"

" ' "No, no, Sir!" cried Fanny affrightedly; "Yes Jack do!" exclaimed Alice, her eyes gleaming. She evidently had thought out some fresh torture for Fanny, and with the closest attention, she watched me as I linked her maid's slender ankles together in spite of the poor girl's entreaties!' "

Effortlessly, Natalie found herself falling asleep, warm and happy. She was agreeably aware of the slow relaxations of her hands, her feet, her face, and felt the lines beside her mouth smooth out and her face fall into nothing more than a covering of bone; she thought vaguely that at this moment she must look as she would when dead, and heard then Tony rising to go once more to the door. "*Will* you leave us alone?" Tony said quietly.

A confused murmur outside, and then Tony said, "What would I expect of you, poor things? Go off to bed—there won't be another sound from *here*."

Much, much later, Natalie was sound asleep aware of Tony's slipping into the bed beside her. Side by side, like two big cats, they slept.

Opening her eyes in the morning Natalie saw first that it was barely light outside and then turned to see Tony's eyes regarding her.

"—Morning?" Natalie said.

"Come on, lazy," Tony said.

They got out of bed together, enjoying the quietness of the morning when everyone else was asleep, and enjoying, too, the feeling of being together without fear. They did not speak much, but moved as though speech were not necessary: first Tony, rolling out of bed, turned a somersault on the floor and rose laughing silently, then Natalie, stretching and turning to the window to see the rising sun, bent and touched her toes without bending her knees. Together, warning one another not to laugh, they went down the hall full of the sounds of sleep from rooms on either side, into the showers, where they bathed together, washing one another's backs and trying to splash without sound. Then, dry and shivering from a cold shower, they went back to Tony's room and dressed.

"I have to get the money from my room," Natalie whispered remembering when she saw her clothes.

"I'll get it," Tony said. "You finish dressing."

Natalie laughed helplessly and silently as Tony slipped out the door in a battered blue bathrobe. Although she could not see the campus and the path Tony must take from the window of the room, she set her elbows on the windowsill and contemplated the rising sun and wondered with amusement on Tony's probable progress across the sleeping campus to Natalie's room in an old blue bathrobe and the insolence of being awake before anyone else.

"Did you get it? Anyone see you?" she asked anxiously when Tony came back into the room. Tony tossed Natalie's raincoat onto the bed and shook her head.

"I could have danced up and down the paths," Tony said.

Dressing quickly, then, because although they were awake before anyone else, time went on without them, and they might yet be caught by some early riser, they combed each other's hair and slipped into coats and opened the door softly and went out into the hall. Natalie thought as she followed Tony down the hall how easy it would be to create some kind of sensation in this, or any other, house; how easy it would be to write some kind of message, probably obscene, or else menacing, and leave it under each door, and was proud and pleased with herself because she had not, and it was too late now.

They tiptoed down the stairs, afraid at this moment of waking some curious person who might ask them where they were going, and reached the front door in safety. Once Tony had opened the door they knew they were surely out, and they gave up trying to go quietly; Tony let the door slam behind them in a gesture calculated to awaken every sleeper within hearing, and, followed by Natalie, ran down the path—running not from fear, but because it was early morning and they were together and they had fifteen dollars and a world ahead of them and no one to know at any time where they were.

The college was located, with singular lack of imagination, on School Street, and was approximately a mile from the center of the town from which it derived its name. The college owned most of the land along School Street, and all the land behind School Street; where the college land ended, there were nothing but fields and trees. On the one side of the college, where School Street ended and Evergreen Street began, there was a quiet and slightly decayed residential section, inhabited largely by single professors and married students. On the other side of the college, where School Street ended and Bridge Street began, there was—with the odd literal quality that characterizes the inventors of towns—a river with a bridge across it. Bridge Street turned into Main Street when its function as a street over a river ended, and Main Street was, inevitably, the street which led into the center of the town. The stores at the Bridge Street end of Main Street had a bare, utterly straightforward look; they had intruded boldly into a section formerly devoted to small dirty shops with dubious wares, building and asserting themselves under the banners of "improvement" and "help our city grow," and they found themselves now, their banners still valiant and their cleanliness untarnished, unpaid for and unpatronized, since the people who shopped and longed for a cleaner city drove naturally to the center of town to the grimy stores they already knew. On one corner, here, was a new grocery, all chromium counters and great glass windows, with red and black and white signs shouting, "Veal chops, special," and, "Our coffee is the best in town," and, "Holiday bargains"—the holiday unspecified in case the sign should not be taken down before Christmas, or Easter, or Judgment Day. Nestled comfortably close to the shining grocery was a stained small hollow calling itself a "Coffee Shop," with a crude counter in front exhibiting candy bars and gum to the public, and, within, another counter supported by three stools, at which no doubt the weary shopper could sit and drink coffee made, at least by assumption, from the best coffee in town sold next door. Across the street was an antique shop, flaunting its dirt by rights of the unwritten law which requires that antique shops should soil the white gloves of matrons who drop in, laughing, to see if they can match the brasses on Grandmother's breakfront. Next to this, an empty showroom which had at one time exhibited pianos, had at another time housed an importer of fine woolens and which was now borrowed annually by the Girl Scouts for their White Elephant Sale, by the Campfire Girls for their Handiwork Show, by the P.T.A. for their home-cooked Food Sale, by the Crippled Children's League, by the D.A.R., by all the organizations who take in, and sell, one another's washing. Beyond this charitable center which was at this time—due no doubt to the impending holidays—empty of beggars, was a tiny one-column tailor shop, odorous and hardly large enough for a winter coat in need of repair. And next to the tailor, but possessing odors enough of its own from imported cheeses, was what called itself an "Epicure Shoppe" and dealt largely in elaborately packaged foreign foods; this shoppe was the only one in the neighborhood which had any kind of trade at all, since it was virtually impossible to find Norwegian herring in sour cream or authentic Turkish delight or *espresso* or English tinned biscuits anywhere else in town. Farther down the block was the town's one movie house which showed exclusively foreign films and dazzled the honest townfolk with *Blood of a Poet* seven times a year. The college students went to the large movie houses in the center of the town, and it was only such folk as lady librarians, traveling in packs, and ambitious interior decorators, coming from the newly adapted apartments in the city's older residential sections, and an occasional French faculty member, who ever went into the small unpolished theater to see *Blood of a Poet* or *The Cabinet of Doctor Caligari* or *M*.

This street hurried along, widening and becoming more populated, until it turned (with the large intersection where four department stores faced one another dourly, each stubbornly insisting that its bargains were more bargainful than the others', each featuring, in its own decor and color scheme, a Garden Restaurant, or a Spanish Tea Room, or a Black Watch Grill, or a Bayou Terrace) into the center of town, and became a busy, imperative, trafficked Main Street. Here one might find the better dress shops, here were a candy store and a bookstore—which also sold novelties and souvenirs—here were the restaurants with Men's Grills and Business Men's Lunches, and the jewelry store and the large hotel with afternoon Thé Dances. Here the buses congregated, and the radio station sent its antenna curiously, skyward. There were offices where secretaries (local girls who could not afford college) typed busily, and a radio store, and a toy store, and a bank.

If a child building with blocks had planned a city, saying, "This is the town, and here is where the people go to shop, and here is where the man lives, and here is where the lady takes her little boy to the dentist, and *here* is the school, and when you want to go to the park it is *here*, and then here is where the trains go, and the station with the station man is right here, and . . ."—if such a child, building on a rainy afternoon, had planned a city, he might have planned it to look like this one: square, respectable, carefully designed without criminal or foreign or unsubmissive elements, boasting of its college, fostering within itself a small and very decent community organization, a community playhouse, a health center, a fearless and extraordinarily biased newspaper, and all the other elements necessary in a city to keep its loyal inhabitants from becoming restless, or uncharitable, or content.

Down this street—turning from School Street to Bridge Street and from there onto Main Street, Natalie and Tony came, almost dancing; it was twenty minutes to eight.

"Three of wands," said Natalie, stopping in front of the antique shop and indicating the three-section candelabra.

Tony, who was required by the rules of the game to give the Tarot meaning of the card symbol Natalie had found, thought for a minute and then said, "Established strength. Trade, commerce, discovery. Ships crossing the sea. Reversed, the end of troubles."

"I saw three ships a-sailing," said Natalie meaninglessly, but they both laughed.

"Three of pentacles, then," said Tony, indicating a pawnbroker's sign which stood unobtrusively but emphatically just around the corner, as though hiding from preference rather than timidity.

"Nobility, aristocracy," said Natalie. "Reversed, pettiness."

"I wonder what the rest of them do with their time?" Tony said absently. "Do you think they go on to their classes as usual? Or has the whole college faded away or blown into dust or collapsed—"

"—or crumbled or snapped out like a light—"

—Just because we've gone? Tony thought. "We are on a carpet," she announced soberly. "It unrolls in front of us, but in back of us it rolls up and there is nothing under it."

"The immediate spot where we are walking is the only immediate spot there is," Natalie said.

"Ace of cups," Tony said, pointing to the fire hydrant.

"House of the true heart," said Natalie. "Joy, fertility."

"Reversed, revolution," Tony said.

"Better still," Natalie said, "suppose they're all just frozen where they were when we left? Like in the *Arabian Nights*, and everything stays like that for a thousand years."

"They are all turned into black and red and gold fish," Tony said, "we must come back and strike three times upon the ground with a staff of brass."

"Ace of wands," said Natalie immediately.

"The origin of all things. Reversed, ruin."

There was so much money in fifteen dollars that they had no need to be lavish all at once, always providing that they were correct in assuming that money was actually a medium of exchange. Perhaps, indeed—they never could know for sure, from one dollar to the next—the green bill or heavy silver coin proffered to the man behind the counter might be met with an incredulous stare, or guffaws, and payment insisted upon in blades of grass, or handfuls of milk, or some unidentified substance which everyone could see and touch but themselves. In a strange country one must be extremely cautious; "Shall we have just coffee to start?" Tony asked.

They were far enough into the center of town to find a drugstore easily. They sat together at the counter, looking at each other and at themselves in the mirror facing them. Natalie, on the right (the one on the right *was* Natalie?) looked very thin and fragile in the black sweater; Tony, (on the left?) seemed dark and saturnine in blue. Neither of them looked at all like the girls in bathing suits who lounged colorfully in the soft drink ads over the mirror. Tony's face was quite pale in the sanitary fluorescent lights of the drugstore, and beyond their two faces, crowding into the picture and immense in their piled variety, were the wares of the shopkeeper: ointments against the sun, dolls—perhaps charms against the evil spirit? were these natives superstitious?—boxes of candy and boxes of candy without sugar, and an infinite number of articles to be used in the control of light: gadgets to make light, gadgets to shut out light, gadgets to improve and distill light, gadgets that operated only upon light or that operated only upon the absence of light, books questioning the source of light and books wondering about the speed of light and books denying the existence of light or recommending its use as food. There were also an infinite number of articles to control air, and articles to control water, and articles to control fire and wind and rain, and many articles, indeed, to control, most effectively, earth. One section of the store—and only a corner of this could be reflected in the mirror—was devoted entirely to nostrums for controlling the human body, and this department, unlike the others, was small and dignified and its transactions

were conducted in low voices. Tony and Natalie in the mirror were exactly at a height, their shoulders touching and beyond their heads the glitter of chromium.

At last Tony said peacefully, "Let's go to the station."

Natalie nodded; because the money was in the pocket of the blue raincoat Tony was wearing, it was Tony who offered money to the man behind the counter and it was accepted without comment.

When they came out of the drugstore the town was beginning to fill up with people on their way to work and Tony said carelessly, as they went down the sidewalk, "Be late for work if we don't move along."

"I've got to do five reports for the old man this morning," Natalie said immediately. "Got to be in the mail this afternoon. Reports to the higher authorities on people caught doing the same things day after day, recommending the ultimate punishment."

"Old lady Langdon caught us smoking in the washroom yesterday," Tony went on, "and said she'd report it to the old man."

"She wouldn't dare," Natalie said. "Anyway, let's quit. Let just not go into the office this morning. Let's go to Sia instead."

"They ought to pension off old Langdon," Tony said. "Le go to Peru."

They passed the town's biggest hotel; workmen on scaff were washing it down with power hoses and Tony and Na stopped shamelessly to watch. The fine spray from the h drifted down onto them through the foggy drizzle, and se small drops in their hair.

"This is the only city I know," Tony said, "where if it's ing already they throw more water on you."

They walked on after a while, moving wherever they p but always bearing toward the railroad station. They s and stared at a cab driver who was trying to clean bir pings off his windshield; they splashed in the wate gutter.

They came at last into the railroad station hand small in the great doorway, dwarfed by the stai

window above their heads. At the top of the great sweeping stairway they paused and looked down on the people below, all so sure of their several destinations; they listened to the message of the train caller standing honorably at his desk beneath the clock and obedient to the will and the distant voices of the trains, translating by permission the great sounds to any who cared to listen.

Natalie and Tony came down the great stairway, down the wide aisle, and slid into seats in one of the rows, listening and watching; they perceived the thin thread of taxicabs which was all that held people in the station to the city outside, the transparent fine barrier of imminent going and coming, of being irresistibly called away or brought back, the conscious virtue of creatures selected to travel with the trains, the harmony of the discipline that controlled his huge, functioning order, where no head was uncounted and no ticket unhonored; they heard the distant paternal urging of the trains.

Oddly enough, Elizabeth Langdon and the rest came here only of necessity, with the intention of leaving this place as soon as they reached it. And yet two people who wanted earnestly to be strangers might sit here for hours and never lose the quick sense of being about to go away, and might probably never see anyone who knew their names, or cared to remember them. After a while Tony and Natalie rose quietly and went down the aisle again and into the station restaurant. They sat down at a table overlooking the nervous movements of the taxicabs and the suitcases set unerringly in the puddles, and ordered ham and eggs and orange juice and toast and griddle-cakes and doughnuts and coffee and sweet rolls. They ate lavishly, passing bits of food to one another, regarding contentedly the glass domes on the coffeepot behind the counter, the glass covers on the stacks of English muffins, the round red seats of the stools. When Tony poured herself a third cup of coffee, Natalie said, "Don't hurry, we have until ten o'clock."

"I do hope our train's not late," Tony said, "We'll be late enough getting in as it is."

"We can telegraph from Denver," Natalie said.

"Or call from Boston," Tony said. "They'll be expecting us

to call, anyway, probably from New Orleans. We have two hours between trains; I thought we might spend it in some bookstore. We have *plenty* of money, after all."

"A week from today we'll be on the boat."

"And two weeks from today," Tony said, "we'll be in Venice."

"In London," Natalie said.

"In Moscow," Tony said. "In Lisbon, in Rome."

"In Stockholm."

"I only hope that train isn't *late*," Tony said.

"Do you think Juan will be there to meet us?" Natalie asked. "And Hans, and Flavia?"

"And Gracia and Stacia and Marcia," Tony said. "And Peter and Christopher and Michael."

"And Langdon," Natalie said. "Dear pathetic old Langdon, she'll be so *glad* to see us, jumping all over everybody and barking."

"I hope they've rememberd to clip her against the heat," Tony said anxiously. "She *does* suffer so."

"She never did quite recover from the spaying," Natalie said, and they began to laugh helplessly, and the waitress behind the long counter looked at them and then automatically at the clock.

Far away they could hear the voice of the train caller. "Albany," he was saying, "New York."

"New York," Tony said softly. They put their hands together on the table and were silent, listening to the voice of the train caller echoing flatly through the station. "New York," he shouted urgently.

"We wouldn't need but one room," Natalie said. "They'd never find us."

"I could get a job." Tony leaned forward eagerly. "I can speak French, after all."

"I could be a waitress, maybe."

"We could open a small bookstore. Only the books we like ourselves."

"And we've *got* fifteen dollars."

They both took cigarettes from the pack on the table, and Tony lighted them; "Can I get you more coffee?" she asked.

Natalie glanced at the clock. "Yes, thank you. We have plenty of time."

"Our train doesn't leave till nearly eleven," Tony said.

You could live quite comfortably in a railroad station; there was the great arching roof for shelter, and food in the restaurant; there was a ladies' room and an enchanted spot where you could find books and magazines and little odd colored toys to amuse the children in Paris, in Lisbon, in Rome. It was better, even, than living in a department store, not quite so good, perhaps, as living in a garret in medieval Spain.

It was nearly twelve when they left the station and they went reluctantly, lingering on the stairway in the face of the drizzling rain outside.

"I understand it's a charming town," Tony said as they came out into the damp day; over their heads the stained-glass window shone briefly in the reflected light of the restaurant neon sign across the street.

"*Very* provincial," Natalie said. "Laughably so."

"But such beautiful old homes."

"And such a modern college."

"And the theaters," Tony said. "And the stores."

"We must try to look up old Langdon while we're here," Natalie said.

Near the station, for some reason, the world was filled with birds flying; all the movement ever made in the world was concentrated, for a minute or so, in one spot, and Tony surrounded by sweeping birds was a marvel of stillness; Natalie laughed and ran away, and the birds followed her briefly and came back to Tony.

"They think you've got fish in your pocket," Natalie called to Tony, and Tony called back, "I wish I had my dear old falcon Langdon."

"*Still she haunts me phantomwise, Alice moving under skies Never seen by waking eyes,*" Natalie said as Tony came running to her.

"Shall we fly?" Tony said, waving back at the birds. "Or would you rather walk?"

"You among the birds," Natalie said. "Page of swords. Vigilance, secrecy."

"Look," Tony said, and held Natalie's arm to stop her before the posters of a theater; the movie now being shown inside was old, and apparently past any redemption by adjective, so that the management had simply, resignedly let the pictures into the frames outside the theater, and were now presumably hiding away somewhere inside, beyond reach of irate patrons. One of the pictures showed a glorious scene between a man in a cowboy hat and uncomfortable pistols, who backed against a door to face a darker, equally weaponful villain; in the background a damsel wrung her hands and all three seemed to turn anxiously to the camera, which alone could justify the violent emotions they ravished themselves to feel. It was plain from the picture that it was near the end of the day; the sun was setting dramatically outside the backdrop window; the hero had the look of one who would shortly remove his guns and his spurs and go home in a car he had bought but could not afford; the heroine seemed to be thinking, under her beautiful look of fear and concern, that perhaps she should keep the children out of school until this chicken-pox scare was over. The villain, too—who, tired now of jokes about his villainy and being treated mockingly by his friends as a potential murderer, had said to himself, "Just this one more time, and then I shall be myself again"—snarled, and sighed, and snarled again; "It must be a lovely movie," said Natalie. "Shall we go in?"

"I would *not* embarrass them by watching them," Tony said, "Look, this one here is a vampire."

It was, indeed, with horns and blood and black cloak and possibly a machine inside which created heartless villainy while sparing its patronizing public any sense of immediacy ("It's *only* a movie; don't be afraid to look.") and which perhaps in some sense of ultimate justice was the kind of machine most moviegoers imagined vaguely would someday take over the world, after their children and their children's children and any posterity they might possibly meet were gone; it was precisely the sort of machine that should take over the world (postulating, of course, that it was a world worth taking over at all, and valuable enough to any machine to justify conquest)—precisely the sort of machine to take over the world: heartless, villainous, unimaginative. "A vampire?" said Natalie. "I think it's a werewolf. Look at its tail."

"More likely one of those hidden personalities, I'd say," said Tony.

"Look over here," said Natalie. "It's got hold of some girl. Girls who get caught by werewolves always look surprised, did you notice?"

"She'd have reason to be surprised if she knew anything about werewolves," Tony said wisely. "Perplexed, she looks to *me*."

"I remember the day Langdon got caught," Natalie said.

"*She* didn't look surprised," Tony said. "No, nor perplexed, neither. She just looked sort of relieved, after chasing *him* for years."

"If we were vampires," Natalie said, falling into step beside Tony, "we would not pick on Langdon."

"I love my love with a V," said Tony, "because he is a vampire. His name is Vestis and he lives in Verakovia. He—"

"I love my love with a W," said Natalie, "because he is a werewolf. His name is William and he lives in Williamstown."

"He is also a waberdasher," Tony said. "*Mine* is a vixter-repairman."

"Not much work for him in Verakovia," Natalie said critically. "I don't believe I saw a single vixter out of order the whole time I was there."

"Ah," said Tony, "but *you* were there in the *rainy* season."

"Still," said Natalie, "what, after all, is there to fixing a vixter? A string here, a screw there—nothing."

"It takes a strong man," Tony said. "Could *you* do it?"

"I used to think," Natalie said, "when I was a child, that I had only a limited stock of 'yeses' and 'nos,' and that when they were used up I couldn't get any more and then I wouldn't be able to answer most of the questions silly people asked me."

"Like, 'What did you learn in school today?' and 'Tell the nice lady your name'?" Tony wanted to know.

"I comforted myself by remembering that I could eke out my stock by things like, 'I don't think so,' and, 'Well, perhaps.'"

"And, 'If you don't mind,' and, 'Much obliged, I'm sure,' and, 'You better be careful what you say or I'll call a cop.'"

"Which is the reason," Natalie went on, "why I don't answer your very pertinent questions about . . ."

"Hanged man," said Tony suddenly. "Hanged man."

"It is *not*," Natalie said indignantly. "It's not fair to use a toy."

"We never *said* it wasn't fair."

Natalie stopped and stared at Tony's hanged man. It was a toy in the shop window, a tiny figure on a trapeze which turned and swung, around and around, endlessly and irritatingly. "Hanged man," Tony insisted.

"The tree of sacrifice is not living wood," Natalie pointed out.

"You can't ever tell," Tony said, peering. "They make extraordinary things for children these days. Dolls that can walk, and birds that can lay eggs, and I suppose animals with real blood for butchering. Not to mention—"

"All *right*," said Natalie sullenly. "Life in death. Joy of constructive death."

"Reversed?"

"Reversed, probably not practical for any smart child," said Natalie, and walked on.

Tony caught up with her laughing. "Let's get something to eat."

"I don't want anything to eat."

"I resign my hanged man," Tony said, still laughing. "It was probably not living wood at all."

They walked on for a minute in silence, and then Natalie said softly, "I used to think, when I was a child, that it was an awful thing to have to go on breathing and breathing, all my life until I was dead, all those thousands of years. And then I used to think that now I was conscious of breathing it would be like everything else where I did it without thinking for a while and then became aware of it, and it would be awkward and difficult to do it as well consciously, and then by the time

I had thought that I used to realize that while I was thinking it I had been breathing."

The cafeteria was filled with people wearing dark clothes and rubbers, moving in sad indecision before bright colorful counters of food. A man in a wet wool overcoat held a slice of cherry pie in his hand; a woman in a coat with a damp fur collar hesitated longingly over a tomato and pepper salad, and below the strawberry shortcake and the sliced ham and the corn muffins and the hot macaroni the floor was trampled and muddy, and the silver of the trays was tarnished and reflected unclearly the plates of food set upon them. Natalie chose cinnamon buns and three kinds of pie; Tony had one kind of pie and one kind of cake and a dish of ice cream and cinnamon buns. They sat down next to the wall, setting their trays squarely on the flat marble table-top, locating the salt and pepper and the mustard and the sugar bowl and the tin container of paper napkins and the used ashtray precisely between them, and their food, colorless and tasteless once it had been separated from its parent counter, awaited them dully on the plates which would be washed and used again when the pie and cake and even the cinnamon buns were consumed.

Their table was long enough to seat eight (crowded in, hot and thirsty after the chase, raising their glasses to salute the lord of the manor, shouting to be heard from below the salt), but they sat alone because they had chosen a table far back, and seemingly destined to be empty except for themselves. Tony said softly, "She *said* she'd be here at twelve sharp, and it's almost twenty after now."

"She might have sent a message," Natalie said. "You know how reliable she always is. Perhaps someone is looking for us with a message now. I'm sure there's a message on its way; it's not like Langdon to be late."

"She wouldn't trust just *any*body, though," Tony said. "Not with a message for us, not Langdon. We'll have to be ready to take the message no matter how strange it sounds. No matter what it sounds like, it will be of course a message for us."

"Do you suppose she got the jewels?" Natalie asked. "And the papers and the guns?"

"Do you suppose that extraordinary woman on the other side is looking for us? What will the message be? 'I have lived long enough, having seen one thing . . .'"

"I believe it's the boy in the black cap; he seems to have lost something. Or the old man there with the cheese sandwich."

"Save those whereout she presses for dead men deadly wine," Tony said happily. "*There's* a message to send someone."

A tray was set down heavily on the table, next to Natalie, and she was silent, although she had started to tell Tony a line which began, "So Satan spake . . ." She looked across at Tony to see the reflection of the newcomer in Tony's eyes; Tony looked up once, briefly, and then down again, and Natalie had to look cautiously sideways, and saw only a checkered jacket and, presumably, a man under it. He was taking things slowly off his tray, putting them down on the table as though he liked food and even this food; he was eating the meat loaf, unbelievably checkered like his jacket, and string beans and mashed potatoes cupping gravy (Ace of cups? Natalie thought; No we've used that.) and vanilla ice cream and coffee; he could not have chosen a more disagreeable lunch, Natalie thought, even if he had said to himself, "Now let's see, what looks positively worst? What will I remember with least pleasure? What am I most likely to have for dinner tonight?" When he leaned over to set the tray on the floor his head touched against Natalie's shoulder and she moved back abruptly.

"Pardon," the man said, and Natalie nodded, assuming that he noticed, and drew even farther away.

"Five of pentacles," Tony said suddenly to Natalie, and Natalie, shocked, stared at her. "What?" Natalie said, thinking, Material trouble, no charity; reversed, earthly love. She looked at Tony and then looked down anxiously at the thick dirty hand maneuvering the coffee cup just beyond her own plates, where the cinnamon bun had suddenly turned stale and sticky.

"Mind?" the man said. Natalie saw that he was holding out a knife. "What?" she said again.

"I'll do it," Tony said abruptly. She reached across the table and, astonishingly, took the knife from the man and pulled his plate of rolls toward her. When Tony had buttered the rolls and pushed the plate back across the table Natalie at last turned openly and stared at the man; he had only one arm.

Of course, Natalie thought, trying not to giggle, he couldn't butter his own rolls, and of course that's why he's eating meat loaf, but you would have thought he'd buy a jacket that didn't look *quite* so much . . .

"Always got to ask for help," the man said genially. He smiled at Natalie around a mouthful of bread and butter. "Rather ask a nice young lady any time."

"Knight of swords reversed," Tony said, seemingly to her coffee.

Quarrel with a fool, Natalie thought. "It's getting late," she said meaninglessly to Tony; it seemed the sort of thing to say to indicate to the man beside her that they were two busy persons, who had better things to do than buttering someone's rolls.

"Salt, please," said the man to Natalie.

She wondered insanely if she would have to salt his meat for him, but, passing the grimy saltcellar, thought, It only takes one hand if he puts down his fork for a minute. "Surprised how obliging most people are," the man said.

"You seem to get along so well," Natalie said, watching Tony.

The man turned around in his chair and smiled at her, as though his armlessness gave him an automatic right to ask anyone he chose for help, and so begin informal relationships at a point usually achieved through many confidences and confessions, but as though, too, it was not often that he were congratulated upon this rare talent.

"It's been a long time," he said. "You get used to it."

"If it's been such a long time," Tony said, "how come you never learned to butter your own bread?"

The man looked across at her and then back to Natalie. "You eat here often?" he asked. "Don't think I've ever seen you here before."

"Not very often," Natalie said nervously.

The man shoved away his plate and took a pack of cigarettes out of his jacket pocket. He offered them to Natalie and, not knowing what else to do (it was a fresh pack and it occurred to her wildly that unless someone took out the first cigarette he would never be able to get it), she took one; when he reached into his pocket again and took out a package of matches Natalie waited politely, but he handed her the matches and said, as before, "Mind?"

"Here," Tony said sharply from across the table. She held out a lighted match, first to Natalie and then to the man.

"Matter with your girl friend?" the man asked, leaning back to look at Tony and exhaling smoke while he talked. "She helpless?"

Natalie also looked at Tony and began immediately to gather her coat around her. The man helped her competently with his one arm and when Natalie rose he waved his hand at her and said, "Come back again sometime, when you haven't got your friend."

"Goodbye," Natalie said politely.

He laughed, and said, "So long, kid."

When they came out of the cafeteria it was unusually dark for early afternoon. It seemed that the light had been withdrawn from the day, as though fearing to face a storm, as though sunlight and clear air, anticipating from several days ago the arrival of enemies, had taken long-planned steps to consolidate their positions elsewhere to visit, perhaps, others of their kingdoms, abandoning this one for a while to the forces of rain and now, this afternoon, to storm. People who ordinarily walked looking down at the sidewalk, perhaps in hopes of finding a penny, now walked looking up at the sky nervously, and the rain which had filled the air inconclusively for almost a week now took on a certain firmness with the knowledge of reinforcements in sight.

Tony and Natalie came out onto the sidewalk wearing their raincoats, but it was for the first time as though they were going somewhere, toward a place now, where before they had only wandered happily. Although they walked with their shoulders together going through the wide main street of the town, it was necessary for Natalie to put her hand under Tony's arm to keep up with her, and neither of them spoke. Natalie did not now know what Tony had thought of the one-armed man, nor did she know why Tony had spoken to him as she did; she did not know, even, where Tony was going. It was, at any rate, away from the cafeteria.

"Well?" said Tony, as they reached the first corner.

Natalie could not decide what to say. There were a number of statements which should be able to bring back their former peaceful state, but saying them consciously and with deliberation was somehow not the same, and then too said consciously and with intention they might not at all bring back the former peaceful state, but introduce rather a new state which would begin by being false. Something new, then? Previously unsaid? Previously unthought? I'm tired, Natalie told herself sadly, and was quiet.

"The question is," Tony said slowly as they stood on the corner, "whether we can still escape, or whether they will have us after all."

"I should think," Natalie said tentatively, "that if we hurried . . ."

Tony laughed. "Don't you see," she said, "if *we're* running and *they're* running, then we're not hurrying at all?"

"No, I don't see."

"Better go slowly, anyway," Tony said. "Not back to the college."

"No, not back to the college."

Tony hesitated. "Are you sure you're not tired?"

"No."

"Will you come somewhere with me? It's a long way."

"Yes," said Natalie.

"You don't even know where it is."

"All right."

"You see," said Tony, her voice still soft so as not to be overheard, but somehow fierce and angry, "it *frightens* me when people try to grab at us like that. I can't sit still and just let people watch me and talk to me and ask me questions. You see," she said again, as though trying to moderate her words and explain, "they want to pull us back, and start us all over again just like them and doing the things they want to do and acting the way they want to act and saying and thinking and wanting all the things they live with every day. And," she added her voice dropping still lower, "I know a place where we can go and no one can trouble us."

"I want to go there, then."

"You won't be afraid?"

"No."

Tony stood on the street corner and looked around, looking even at Natalie. Ahead of them, there was the intersection, with its stores and streets and the natives hurrying about their concerns, gathering their wares together to be finished before sundown, or before the storm came upon them. Behind Natalie and Tony the main street ended abruptly, about two blocks down, in a sudden, insistent stopping of stores, and a beginning of railroads and country lots beyond. To their right was the Hotel Washington, with its murals in the lobby of Washington writing the Declaration of Independence, Washington making peace with the Indians, Washington—a local god— founding the city's first bank. To their left was the far-off tower of the electric company, and the beacon of the radio station. Tony saw all these things, which she had seen before, and looked again at Natalie.

"You ready?"

"Yes."

"Come on, then."

They crossed the main street to the spot where buses drew in and waited asthmatically for passengers. They did not usually ride on things, Tony and Natalie, and it was odd to both of them to push into the crowd of people waiting, to climb up the narrow steps and push farther into the bus even as it moved swiftly, leaving behind it still-hurrying figures on the street, raising imperative gloved hands, brandishing coins, still hurrying.

Natalie, pushing with the rest down the aisle of the bus, fell rather than sat voluntarily; there was an empty seat next to the aisle and before she could catch Tony the crowd of people had pressed her into it and Tony was gone.

For a minute she only sat, trying to draw herself in and avoid the pressures of people on all sides of her. She felt as though she could not breathe, with someone in the seat next to her, someone on the aisle beside her, someone in front of her and someone in back of her and Tony out of sight. The man on the seat next to her was large and seemed to overflow onto Natalie and she could see that he was pressed against the window as well. She thought that she might be less crushed when the bus swung into the middle of the street and the people inside settled into place, but instead they swayed against her from one side or the other. The thought of escaping from the bus came to her, and she wanted to fight and claw and scream when she realized that she could not even stand up, much less wriggle through the people to get to either door. They were holding her by sheer weight, leaning all together around her so that she might move her hands, if she liked, or turn her head, but could only tantalize herself so because beyond that she was paralyzed. She found herself hardly able to breathe and for a minute thought wildly of pushing against the man next to her until his weight broke the window.

It then became perfectly clear to her that this was the reasonable consequence of all her life, from the beginning until now. She had done so much to preserve herself from this kind of captivity and had taken inevitably one of the many roads which would lead her to the same torment; she was helpless among people who hated her and showed it by holding her motionless until they should choose to release her. All her efforts to become separate, all Tony's efforts, had brought Natalie to this bus.

Now, she thought, I must find Tony and get out of here. The thought of escape made her think of prisoners in fortresses, and the long years of small effort required to achieve the last simplicity of release; I could dig out through the floor of the bus, she thought, and would have smiled to herself except that she was certain the man next to her was watching her. She could not see the driver of the bus, nor the way the bus was going, but even though the bus stopped occasionally it did not seem that the pressure around her lessened. She could hear, when the bus stopped, that more people were crowding and pushing in, with ill humor and complaint. Poor things, she thought—do they have to spend all this energy just to surround me? It seemed pitiful that these automatons should be created and wasted, never knowing more than a minor fragment of the pattern in which they were involved, to learn and follow through insensitively a tiny step in the great dance which was seen close up as the destruction of Natalie, and, far off, as the end of the world. They had all earned their deaths, Natalie thought, by a job well done—the woman in the seat ahead who had never needed a face, had perhaps been given for her part only the back of a head and a dark cloth coat collar, the man in the seat next to Natalie, a full-dress part, even the watchchain and the grimy shirt collar—had not this same man, as a matter of fact, been close to Natalie in the station, memorizing her face so that although when next they met she would not know him, he would be able to identify her, winking and gesturing with his head to the others, murmuring perhaps to the bus driver, "*That* one, *there*." The woman in the aisle, whose coat brushed maddeningly against Natalie's face—was she not the one who had held the tomato salad in the cafeteria, watching below her hat brim for Tony and Natalie to come, had she not passed them quickly on the street, glancing with a swift look to make sure of them, had she not stood, ticket in hand, before the train gate, apparently watching the clock? Perhaps, too, it had been this woman peering watchfully out through the eyes of the heroine in the movie poster, whispering, passing on the word: "There they go, *that* way—let *them* know, ahead." And the bus driver must have slipped quickly out of the dress of the train conductor, into the white apron of a cafeteria cook, then into the uniform he wore now, timing himself to the second in order to pull up just in time as Tony and Natalie approached the bus stop. Was the boy in the black cap here on the bus? Perhaps he sat in back of

Natalie and it was his breath she could hear, his knees pressing into the back of the seat. And the one-armed man, then, had been sent to spring the trap as the circle grew closer and closer; the one-armed man had been sent with the message; his speaking to them had identified them finally and been the signal for the circle to close in.

Because she could not turn her head she could not see Tony, who was somewhere in the back of the bus. She thought she could feel Tony watching her. "Is this the Cornford stop?" the woman standing next to her leaned down and asked. "I'm sorry, I don't know," Natalie said, but the man sitting next to her said (with a warning glance?), "No, next stop." "Thank you," said the woman, and moved somehow so that her packages brushed the top of Natalie's head. "Excuse me," Natalie said to the man, "but what is the last stop?" "End of the line," he said, and smiled knowingly at her.

Suddenly a shift took place. The bus, bringing up in a great sweep at a corner, paused for a longer time, and many of the passengers got out. "Change for Linden," the bus driver shouted, half-turning in his seat, and the man next to Natalie said, "Pardon," and slipped out past her and followed the woman in the dark coat down the aisle. Tony sat down unexpectedly in the seat next to Natalie.

"I thought they'd *never* leave," Tony said.

"They were watching me," Natalie said. She turned and tried to look backward out of the window as the bus started to move, but could see nothing in the rain, which was steadily growing heavier, and darkening the day until it seemed now almost like evening, although it could not be later then midafternoon.

"Do you suppose," Natalie said, "That they are each assigned a certain area to guard, and that they have to get back to it to watch for the next ones?"

"A bad job, that," Tony said. "Imagine, always pretending to run a world. Always imitating the sort of people they think they might be if the world were the sort of world it isn't. Pretending to be words like 'normal' and 'wholesome' and 'honest' and 'decent' and 'self-respecting' and all the rest, when even the words aren't real. Imagine, being people."

"The man next to me," Natalie said. "He was an honest self-respecting man. He was supposed to be the sort of small businessman who has not done really well, and who has had to be satisfied with less than he wants because he is not really very capable and knows it. He did it very well, as a matter of fact. I was almost convinced until he made a joke at me."

"They have to give themselves away," Tony said. "They've got to make sure you know them or else there's no point to them at all."

"I don't think they've estimated us correctly," Natalie said. "They seem to think we're weaker than we really are. I personally feel that I have talents for resistance they don't even suspect."

"Perhaps," said Tony dryly, "they have antagonists you have not yet encountered."

Natalie laughed. "If *I* were inventing this world," she said, "—and I may have, at that—I would gauge my opponents more accurately. That is, suppose I wanted to destroy the people who saw it clearly, and refused to join up with all my dull ordinary folk, the ones who plod blindly along. What I would do is not set them against numbers of dull people, but I would invent for each one a single antagonist, who was calculated to be strong in exactly the right points. You see what I mean?"

"The trouble is," Tony said, grinning, "that you've got this world, see? And you've got enemies in it, and they're enemies because they're smarter. So you invent someone smart enough to destroy your enemies, you invent them so smart you've got a new enemy."

"Oh, hell," said Natalie. "Maybe I'd better give up inventing worlds and do without any for a while."

"At least until you've got it figured out better," Tony said.

The bus moved on, stopping meaninglessly now and then to let people get off or on; there was no object to their riding the bus now, these people, beyond the pure formality of spying. The route of the bus was perhaps desperately familiar to the driver, who must have had to travel it many times to be able to do it right when it mattered, and the route was familiar, too, to the people who got on and off, familiar in greater or lesser distance to all of them.

"Imagine," Tony said softly once, "imagine that we live here, just halfway down that block. That house with the wide porch is very well known to us; we live there. You sweep the porch and I dust the living room just inside. We know so well what the house looks like that we go in there by instinct without even looking at it, and we are oddly comfortable in any other house which resembles it. And now we are going past our stop. As far as this point, the bus route is familiar to us, and we know without seeing them every corner and almost every person who gets on and off daily, and every street sign and every store—back there, as a matter of fact, was our grocery, where one or the other of us shops every day. Beyond this corner, everything is wilderness."

"That's why it's so bad to be carried past your stop," Natalie said. "You might never find your way back—you're in someone else's territory, places familiar to the person who gets off at the *next* stop. *Their* grocery stores."

"We're going much farther today, though," Tony said.

More and more people were leaving the bus, glancing occasionally at Tony and Natalie with curiosity and some amusement. The bus had moved through the business section of town, through the better residential section, through the lesser residential section, and was now in a district of dirty small stores and low, dark-windowed buildings, grim and unwelcoming in the dark afternoon.

"This must be the very edge of town," Natalie said. "I've never been here before."

"I've been here before," Tony said. "Long ago, before I knew who you were."

"Do we get out soon?"

"Soon," Tony said.

The bad neighborhood gave way to railroad tracks, and eventually, to spaces of open country. Vacant lots on either side of the road separated small houses and a rare street sign stood

by a squared-off curb, as though at one time optimistic people
had planned houses out here, and streets, and broad sunlit gar-
dens, and had stood perhaps on the eight feet of cement curb-
ing already finished and looked around and thought, We can
catch the bus on this corner and be into town in an hour; the
children will have plenty of space to play. One or two of the
few houses had fences around them, and one of them had wash
hung out in the driving rain.

"We're going to be the last people in the bus," Natalie said.
"If we got out the bus driver could turn around and go on
back home."

"Who else would go this far?" Tony said. "Soon."

"I believe there's a lake somewhere ahead," Natalie said,
peering out through the wet window. "Of course it *could* be
just excessive rain, but it does *look* like a lake."

"It is a lake," Tony said. "Very popular in the summer when
the weather is somewhat more clement than this."

"I can see houses," Natalie said. "What do the people live
on after the hot dogs are gone?"

"Fish, I suppose," Tony said absently.

"We're terribly out of season," Natalie said. Being so near the
lake troubled her; it was a spot where, she could see, warmth
and movement had once abided, where a skeletal roller coaster
presided ghoulishly over the remains of a merry-go-round, a
skating rink, a bath house. She shivered.

"Is *this* where we're going?"

"Do you want to go back?"

Beside the window of the bus, so close that it startled Natalie, a sign moved by, pointing with one imperative arm at the
lake; "Paradise Park," it announced.

"Do you want to go back?" Tony asked again.

Natalie thought of the woman in the dark coat climbing
tiredly onto the bus again at her destined stop, and laughed.
"Suppose—" she began.

"Do you want to go back?" Tony asked again.

"No," Natalie said.

Ahead, the remnants of last summer's pleasure sprawled
darkly, the damp air from the lake carrying along with it the

faint, almost undetectable odors of wet bathing suits, and stale mustard, and rancid popcorn; it was impossible to remember with any clarity the heat of the summer or the taste of sweat or the feeling of clothes confining in the heat, although the sight of the merry-go-round recalled very distantly the sweet jangle of its music. Natalie pressed closer to the glass of the bus window, uncomfortably aware of the dubious warmth of the bus and the clinging wetness of her raincoat against her legs; even Tony, next to her, seemed disagreeably close and pressing and the sudden sight of the thin lines of Tony's face against, through the other window, the leaning timbers of the roller coaster in the gathering darkness made Natalie shiver and say overloudly, " Aren't we ever going to get *out*?"

As though at a signal, the driver swung the bus around in a circle, pulled on the brake, and turned to look at them. "Going back?" he called incongruously down the length of the bus, "or you getting out here?"

Tony rose and started down the aisle, Natalie following her stiffly. "We're getting out here," Tony said.

"Carnival spirit?" said the driver, and he hunched up his shoulders and laughed at them. "Big night on the beach? See the sights, take a swim, look at the girls, win a kewpie doll, take a chance?" He laughed again, snickering, as they stepped gingerly down the slippery steps of the bus. "Take a turn on the merry-go-round for me," he called after them, and the bus door closed behind them.

Natalie stepped quickly to the side of the road as the bus turned awkwardly, because it occurred to her vividly that he might very well try to run them down—who would ever know, on a night like this? He could say it was an accident—and for a moment in the bewildering darkness after the lights of the bus she lost Tony. "Change your mind?" the bus driver shouted, leaning toward her from the window of the bus. "Last chance?" When Natalie did not answer the bus moved, picking up speed as it went down the road, and Natalie watched its lights, thinking, He is going back right now to the lights of the town, to the sounds and the lights and the people.

There was darkness ahead of her, with an odd rich brilliance of water beyond, but no human lights along the lake. "Coming?" said Tony, and she sounded amused. "He was right, you know," she added. "It was probably the last bus."

On the road back to town the signpost pointed evilly down at them with its one arm, still probably saying "Paradise Park," and ahead the roller coaster leaned slightly forward to hear what they said. The only light, apart from the faintly luminous sky, was its reflection on the water; the only sound (beyond perhaps the anxious breathing of the merry-go-round?) was the noise of the waves on the shore. Irresistibly Natalie found herself moving toward the lake, with a human impulse to get to the edge of the world and stop, but Tony took her arm and said, "This way."

"Where in hell are we?" said Natalie; she was cross, and it was colder than she liked, and she was unpleasantly aware that that had probably been the last bus back to town.

"Look," said Tony, and she stood still but did not turn, "if you don't want to come you don't have to. *I'm* going anyway."

"Where else can I go?" Natalie said. "Is it far?"

"No, not very far."

"I'm not going to stay long," Natalie said inadequately. "Unless it's warm."

Tony laughed. "How would you feel about heaven?" she asked. "You wouldn't stay unless it was warm?"

"Look," Natalie said reasonably, "I'm cold. It's wet. I don't know where I am or where I'm going. If I say—"

"You want to go home?"

"Stop it, *will* you?"

"We *could* be on our way to Paris," said Tony. "Or Siam." She laughed again. "And no one can find us," she said. "Someday, suppose we were strangers and we met in London. Would you bow to me on the street, thinking, I used to know someone looked like that, and then I might wave to you, thinking, Doesn't that look like a girl named Natalie I once took down a lonely road? Suppose we were strangers after all this, and we met in London?"

"I would think, 'Tony, Tony,'" Natalie said.

"I know you would," said Tony.

They had gone away from the deserted playground now, and the road they followed had been set out, it seemed, for lovers for whom the Roller Skating Rink was not private enough. Over their heads the trees leaned toward one another, nodding and perhaps whispering ahead that they had come, after so long a delay; underfoot, it was wet and somehow encouraging—each step seemed to urge them forward; one could walk forever in such a vacuum.

Tony stopped suddenly, her feet in the mud, and looked up at the rain which found them still between the trees. "And if I stamped on the ground and called," she said softly, "would anything come rushing to us from the sky, shaking in the world and speaking in a voice . . ."

"Not in *this* mud," Natalie said. "Not in this mud you couldn't stamp."

"All I need," said Tony, "is a desire so strong that the world, all of the world, has got to bend itself and forget itself and break out of its circles and rock itself crazy, all to do what I want, and there's got to be a great crash when the ground under me crashes itself wide open and the fire inside is forced to crawl away from my feet and the sky too turns back so that there is nothing above me and nothing below me and nothing in all time except me and what I want."

"Tony, *stop* it."

"He would take us wherever we wanted to go," Tony said very softly. "We would only need to whisper 'Far away from here,' and he would carry us on his head to someplace where it is hot, and the sun comes down on us, and there is moving blue water and hot hot sand under our feet. Or we might be lying on a curved green hill with our heads in the grass and nothing overhead but clouds or riding on an elephant with strange clashing bells calling us or dancing in the streets of a city where no one is alive but us and the houses are round and red and blue and yellow in the moonlight and the streets are crooked and hung with lanterns and strange, or we can have a world completely flat in all directions and us with our chins resting on the edge and no bodies and with our eyes half-shut can look out peacefully on a world flat in all directions or we can—"

"Then why are we *here*, of all places?"

"We're supposed to be," Tony said. "We have to be here first."

"Have you been here before?"

"Several times."

"Why are we here again, then?"

"Or, if you like, we can be on a cloud, sound asleep in that hot rolling softness close to the sun, or we can be on a mountaintop where the sky is bright blue and the trees are bright green and everything smells of fresh pine and the earth is shining brown and you can see for a hundred miles because even the air is glittering. Or we can say we want to live forever in a palace of blue marble with fountains that flow with purple wine, and flowers growing through the open windows, and hangings of pale-green satin and ceilings of gold, and a repast of fruit and wine set in every room and music of cymbals and lyres, and handmaidens . . ."

"Are you going in *here*? Into the trees?"

"Or choose perhaps a throne higher than the moon, on a black rock, where sitting we can rule the world, where the stars are around our feet and the sun rises when we glance down and beckon, where far below there are contests to make us laugh and above us there is nothing but our own crowns and sitting there forever we can watch and end eternity with a gesture of our finger . . ."

The trees were waiting in the darkness ahead, quietly expectant. A tree is not a human thing, with its feet in the ground and its back hard against the sky; it cannot tolerate the small human tendernesses moving beneath, and, not obeying the whims of moveable creatures, can hardly have more pity for a Natalie than for a field mouse or a pheasant, moving with private pride but falling easily. Beneath the trees it was not dark as a room is dark when the lights are put out, the artificial darkness which comes when an artificial light is gone; it was the deep natural darkness which comes with a forsaking of natural light; Natalie's feet went without sound on the path—made by whom? for what purpose? for whose feet?—and she could not lift her head from contemplation of her own feet on the path, although she knew surely that the trees bent over her, trying, perhaps, to touch her hair. Her feet felt the path and she knew that there was moss there, or something frightfully soft that made no sound.

"Everything is so *easy*," Tony's voice said from ahead of her. "You can remember it all if you try, and all you have to do is lie back against a comforting hand and close your heavy eyes and say, 'I am here, I am where I belong, I have come home.' Just as we've always been doing it, just as it's the natural and quiet and exciting way of doing things . . . as we remember, as through all our wanderings we remember, as we remember . . ."

One foot going before another, it seemed that this was the only way to go in among these trees, and that no one had ever come this way and then turned to go back again, and had perhaps even gone in and out freely. "Tony?" Natalie said. "Tony?"

Tony's voice came more faintly from ahead. "And do you remember the glory? The wonder of dancing and seeing in the firelight the others dancing?" It was as though Tony had removed a little, gone around a tree where the path had not, as though Tony had gone in the darkness a little farther away with each step, still speaking luringly, and was by now so far away that even Tony's voice came only by permission of the trees, relayed in mockery.

"Tony?" Natalie said again more urgently, realizing suddenly, concretely and acutely, that it was indeed very dark and that ahead of her the figure she had mistaken for Tony was only another tree.

"Don't be afraid," said Tony, a voice dying away, now gone out of hearing; was it *that* way? Twigs over her mouth?

"Tony," Natalie said, suddenly very frightened.

There was no answer, and Natalie stopped and stood very still among the trees, feeling dreadfully that they leaned forward to watch her. She put her hand to her face and it was there, she felt her raincoat cautiously and it was still slippery and firm under her hand. The *look*, she told herself, shutting her eyes. We were out for a walk and we came on a bus and we got to the lake and we went past the fairgrounds and we walked along a dark road in the rain, and Tony said—what did Tony say?—and anyway we started as a joke, a *schoolgirl* joke, to follow an odd old path through the trees, and whoever heard of anyone lost in a clump of a dozen trees like this near a lake and an amusement park and even in the rain? Why, people must have been along here a million times, and thought it was funny. Why, probably no one ever before got frightened in this clump of four trees and certainly no one ever before couldn't be more than fifty feet from the road and if it were daylight it would be terribly funny, and even a little bit silly, like children playing ghost. So now turn around, Natalie told herself, and you'll see that there's nothing to be afraid of.

She turned boldly, before she could change her mind, and looked behind her; the path curved out of sight almost immediately, but of course it *was* a path and it led back to the road and certainly the road—if there *was* a road? if there ever had *been* a road?—led back to town. The trees so close to the path that it was hardly possible to pass between them without brushing against bark were of course no more than trees and only the fact that it was difficult to see them clearly in the darkness and the rain made them in any way terrible. And since this was only a clump of trees, after all, the path must go forward out of it and very probably Tony was right now standing just ahead beyond the turn in the path between the trees and waiting and laughing.

And waiting and laughing, Natalie told herself again, and she shivered. And waiting and laughing, and laughing and waiting, and, Natalie told herself sternly, this must stop, and thought, People are only afraid of other people. Waiting and laughing, she thought, and said, timidly, "Tony?"

When there was again no answer, she felt suddenly the elemental fear of some other person who will not speak when spoken to, and denies thus the similiarity of sanities between one person and another, some other person who, waiting and laughing, determines secretly and giggling to feast upon his own kind. "Tony?" she said, and, realizing after she had moved that she was walking, began to go quickly ahead on the path.

Blundering on alone, she came out at last, almost crying (thinking, What is it I know that means steadiness and warmth and a home? Arthur Langdon? Elizabeth? and their names were meaningless) onto a smooth bare place where the dusk, or the light of the lake far behind reflected from the clouds overhead, fell with a brazen and ghastly clarity.

It then occurred to her that she was expected here. This small clearing among the trees had been set up because she could not remain under the trees any longer, and it was necessary for her to find a place to rest. Nothing happens unless it needs to, she told herself, and saw with complacent pleasure a fallen tree across the small clearing and, as she knew she was expected to, sat down upon it. If I take a minute or so to calm down, she said to herself, if I try to relax and not be so nervous about nothing, if I get a perspective on things instead of . . .

Without stumbling, as though permitted, Tony came walking easily through the trees and not by the path, seeming not to put her feet down on the soundless moss. It was a dark unfamiliar figure coming, for a minute, so that Natalie turned suddenly, sitting on the log, and was unable to speak and would almost have run back among the trees except that in time she saw that it was Tony. Tony came closer, in the blue raincoat, hands in the pockets and smiling. "I lost you," Natalie said helplessly.

Tony glanced easily at the trees around them, staring back at them boldly and with amusement. "I was there."

"Only one antagonist . . . only one enemy," Natalie said.

"That's very true," Tony said.

She had done what she was told, then, Natalie thought; she has brought me here with friendship and without force, she has followed her instructions to the letter and will probably be commended. Is she sorry? Does she regret it even for a minute, does a sudden fleeting picture come to her, of the two of us together when it was just beginning? Could she forget the methods she had to use, the small jokes and the little intimacies—or is she wholly a traitor, using any means to achieve the traitorous end, not sparing any thought for the tremendous personal, real emotions that were so undefined in her orders

("Get her here") and yet so inclusive, so desirable, and so secret; will she be required to state in her report that means she used?

Once, try it once, Natalie thought, and said, "Tony, I'm afraid of this place. Please let's go back." Perhaps there might be, somehow, a weakness in the traitor to make this an equal battle, perhaps there might be a small remembered joke which could unlock the chains, bribe the guards, press the hidden panel, perhaps—and only to make it an equal battle, Natalie promised—perhaps there might be—

"Later," Tony said peacefully, the unrepentent traitor, the traitor to traitors. "Later I might let you go back."

Natalie put her head down on her knees and thought, I wish I could go home, and perhaps said it aloud, and Tony, her head back against a tree trunk, familiarly, said, "It's good to be here at last; it's the only possible place."

"Have you been here before?" Natalie asked after a minute, wanting to say, Have there been others? Are you experienced? Am I the first? What did they say? Do? Were they afraid? Did it happen here? Why does it happen at all? Who put you up to it? May I please go home? May I please go back to my own home? Please?—because she did not know any other word that might somehow ask please, no other word than please. "Of course I've been here before," Tony said, surprised. "How did you think I knew how to come?"

And were they all afraid? Natalie wanted to ask, but she said, "Was it always this cold?"

"Cold? Are you cold?" Tony asked, and there was a note of sarcasm, as though she said, And was she cold, the poor thing, was she cold? And did she want her mother, poor thing, poor thing?

"Tony," Natalie said, half-rising, but Tony put her hand on Natalie's arm, almost casually, and held her.

"Wait a while," Tony said. "I'm almost ready." She looked up at Natalie and smiled, and seemed measuring Natalie, because she looked down even at Natalie's feet, and smiled again. "I'm almost ready," she repeated reassuringly. "It won't take long. What are you afraid of?" When Natalie, suddenly helpless, did not answer, she patted Natalie's arm lightly and said, "Don't be afraid," and added, as one reassuring a whimpering child with a familiar rhyme, "Page of pentacles." When Natalie again did not move or answer, she said, "Well, then. A soldier, a child. Reversed, degradation or pillage."

"I thought it was a game," Natalie said.

"Keep thinking of it as a game," Tony said, and put out her cigarette carefully. With Tony's hands on her face, on her back, holding her, Natalie shuddered. *One is one and all alone and evermore will be so*; "I will *not*," said Natalie, and ripped herself away. She *wants* me, Natalie thought with incredulity, and said again, aloud, "I will *not*."

"Of course you won't," said Tony, moving quietly, and Natalie at the last minute saw and stepped back again and said, "I am not afraid of you."

There was a short, an absolute, silence, the trees suddenly alert, listening. Then: "Certainly," Tony said. "If you want to run home, nobody's going to keep you *here*." And she laughed.

I have been found wanting, Natalie thought; I have made myself unacceptable and am not worthy. She hesitated, halfmoving, waiting for the hand or branch to pull her rudely down again and knowing at the same time that she was not worthy, and then she said, "Going?" as though it were a casual thing. Tony looked at her once, and then away at the trees again, and did not speak. Everything's waiting for me, Natalie thought; she half-moved again, and was still. Perhaps even yet? She thought hopefully, but Tony did not stir, and Natalie took a step toward the path. "Tony?" Natalie said. "Going?"

"No."

Everything's waiting for me to go away, Natalie thought. It's time for me to leave, I am innocent, my father has work to do, Elizabeth is going to bed, Tony wants me away. Everything is waiting for me to go off and do something by myself, everything is waiting for me to act without someone else; they are all too busy for me now, even Tony, standing dark under the dark trees. "Tony?" she said again, insistently. "*Please*, Tony."

There was again no answer, and Natalie was at the point where the path entered the trees again. She knew that Tony would not answer her; she knew that she would find her way back by the path without difficulty, the trees drawing back from her as she moved, her feet rustling on the dead leaves and dirt, and, crying now, she went out of the light and into the dark woods, through which she could see the lights, now, of the road back to town.

"Tony?" she called back once, stopping with her hand against a tree, and its rough back lifeless under her fingers, "Tony, come on back with me," but there was no answer.

Her feet again upon the road, with the roller coaster—so soon to be revived for summer traffic—ahead of her, she thought theatrically, I will never see Tony any more; she is gone, and knew that, theatrical or not, it was true. She had defeated her own enemy, she thought, and she would never be required to fight again, and she put her feet down tiredly in the mud and thought, What did I do wrong?

The incredible sight of car headlights stopped her on the road, flat-footed, and as the car came closer it seemed to her frighteningly that it might be her mother and father, come to look for her. Then the car stopped next to her and a voice said, coming louder as the front window was rolled down, "What on earth are you doing out here alone?"

It *is* my mother, Natalie thought, come to take me home. "I'm lost, I think," she said.

"Well, get in," said the woman. She leaned in her seat to open the back door of the car and Natalie obediently climbed in; it was an old car, and the back seat was crowded and cramped with accumulated junk; there were bottles there, she could hear from the rattling, and old papers, and a kind of blanket that felt like the horrible hair of some animal. The car moved as Natalie leaned back and the woman turned halfway around to stare at Natalie. The driver of the car, of whom Natalie could see only a neck and the back of a hat, leaned forward to peer at the road, as though able to see farther with his own eyes than the headlights showed. "Well," said the woman, looking at Natalie in the dark, "*you* were certainly far away from everywhere."

"I was lost," Natalie said.

"Long walk back to town," the driver said.

"You were very kind to pick me up," Natalie said.

"We *always* pick up people," the woman said comfortingly. "Can't stand seeing anyone walk so long's we have a car ourselves. And lucky for *you*."

"It certainly was," Natalie said.

"Where you from?"

"The college."

The woman nodded against the reflected light of the headlights. "College," she confirmed, not at all surprised.

"This is certainly nice of you," Natalie said.

"How old are you? Eighteen?"

"Seventeen."

"*Our* girl's eighteen," the woman said, pointing out some irremediable fault in Natalie. "Goes to business school."

"Stays out of the woods," the man added.

"Well, now, you don't ever know," the woman said consideringly. She turned and looked at him and then back at Natalie. "I guess Moms and Dads never *do* know what the kids are doing, really," she said.

"I guess not," Natalie said.

"I guess *your* Mom would be pretty mad if she saw you walking down that lonely road alone."

"I guess so."

"Can't ever tell what'll happen to a girl alone along there," the man added.

"Attackers," the woman said, and nodded. Beyond her nodding head the first lights of the town showed suddenly. "*Terrible* things," she said in a low voice to Natalie, as one communicating female facts not suitable for the ears of men. "Attackers and all that."

"Where she want to go?" the man asked the woman.

"Back to college?" the woman asked Natalie.

"Extra two miles," the man said.

"The center of town will be fine," Natalie said hastily. "After all, you've saved me a mighty long walk."

"More'n *that*," said the woman, nodding again. "Down that lonely road."

"Tell you," the man said, compromising, "we'll take her as far's the bridge. How's that?"

"That will be wonderful," Natalie said, "I can get back to the college from there in five minutes."

"All lighted streets, too," said the woman with satisfaction. They all watched with silent pleasure as the town took shape around them, filling out its streets with stores, with hotels, with lights. They went down the main street and Natalie saw without surprise that the lampposts were trimmed with wreaths and that strings of lights had been festooned overhead in preparation for Christmas; the yellow and blue and red of neon signs blinked crazily into the car as they went on down the main street to the bridge.

The man brought his car to a slow and accurate stop in the center of the bridge, and the woman reached around to open the door for Natalie. "There, now," she said.

Getting out, Natalie told them both, "Thank you very much, *very* much. I can't tell you how grateful I am."

"Nothing at all," said the woman, and the man said, "All right."

"Thank you again," Natalie said, and closed the door. She waved after them as the man made a cautious, formal turn in the middle of the bridge, and waved again as they went back off the way they had come. Then, somehow puzzled by her quick transition from a lonely wet road to the middle of a lighted bridge, she crossed the sidewalk to the bridge parapet and stood looking down, to make sure where she was, but she saw instead the water below, with the raindrops falling into it.

Why shouldn't I—? she thought with irresistible logic and leaned over farther, and even farther; she put one shoe against the stone to urge herself higher and thought with glory, Mother won't care if I scuff it now; it will be lost before it wears out.

"Going swimming?"

Natalie came down quickly from the wall, feeling to make sure that her skirt was down properly, turning to see who had spoken to her at this irrecoverable moment; it was no more than a figure disappearing into the rain, and turning a wet grinning face back at her over its shoulder; for a second she thought that it might easily be the one-armed man from the restaurant.

More people were nearby on the bridge, but she was not embarrassed to turn away from the parapet and walk quietly toward the college; it occurred to her that unless she actually jumped over the parapet into the river she was of small interest to them. As she passed, she looked into their faces, and they were laughing or talking or walking quietly along, and none of them did more than slide a look past Natalie who was walking quietly along without interest.

The reassuring bulk of the college buildings showed ahead of her, and she looked fondly up at them and smiled. As she had never been before, she was now alone, and grown-up, and powerful, and not at all afraid.

The Haunting of Hill House
Introduction by Laura Miller

Four spirit seekers arrive at a notoriously unfriendly heap called Hill House. At first, their stay seems destined to be merely a spooky encounter with inexplicable phenomena. But Hill House is gathering its powers—and soon it will choose one of them to make its own.

ISBN 978-0-14-303998-3

We Have Always Lived in the Castle
Introduction by Jonathan Lethem

Taking readers deep into a labyrinth of dark neurosis, *We Have Always Lived in the Castle* is a deliciously unsettling novel about a perverse, isolated, and possibly murderous family and the struggle that ensues when a cousin arrives at their estate.

ISBN 978-0-14-303997-6

The Road Through the Wall
Foreword by Ruth Franklin

Pepper Street is a really nice, safe California neighborhood. The only problem is they knocked down the wall at the end of the street to make way for a road to a new housing development. In this novel that launched her career, Jackson satirically explores what happens when a smug suburban neighborhood is breached by awful, unavoidable truths.

ISBN 978-0-14-310705-7

**PENGUIN
CLASSICS**

AVAILABLE FROM PENGUIN CLASSICS

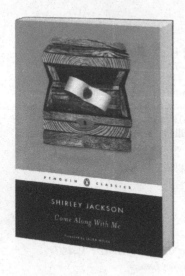

Come Along with Me
Classic Short Stories and an Unfinished Novel
Foreword by Laura Miller

In her gothic visions of small-town America, Jackson, turns an ordinary world into a supernatural nightmare. This eclectic collection goes beyond her horror writing, revealing the full spectrum of her literary genius. In addition to *Come Along with Me*, Jackson's unfinished novel about the quirky inner life of a lonely widow, this book features sixteen short stories and three lectures she delivered during her last years.

ISBN 978-0-14-310711-8

AVAILABLE FROM PENGUIN

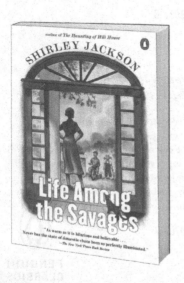

Life Among the Savages

Shirley Jackson was known for her terse, haunting prose. But the writer possessed another side, one which is delightfully exposed in this hilariously charming memoir of her family's life in rural Vermont.

ISBN 978-0-14-026767-9

THE STORY OF PENGUIN CLASSICS

Before 1946 ... "Classics" are mainly the domain of academics and students; readable editions for everyone else are almost unheard of. This all changes when a little-known classicist, E. V. Rieu, presents Penguin founder Allen Lane with the translation of Homer's *Odyssey* that he has been working on in his spare time.

1946 Penguin Classics debuts with *The Odyssey*, which promptly sells three million copies. Suddenly, classics are no longer for the privileged few.

1950s Rieu, now series editor, turns to professional writers for the best modern, readable translations, including Dorothy L. Sayers's *Inferno* and Robert Graves's unexpurgated *Twelve Caesars*.

1960s The Classics are given the distinctive black covers that have remained a constant throughout the life of the series. Rieu retires in 1964, hailing the Penguin Classics list as "the greatest educative force of the twentieth century."

1970s A new generation of translators swells the Penguin Classics ranks, introducing readers of English to classics of world literature from more than twenty languages. The list grows to encompass more history, philosophy, science, religion, and politics.

1980s The Penguin American Library launches with titles such as *Uncle Tom's Cabin* and joins forces with Penguin Classics to provide the most comprehensive library of world literature available from any paperback publisher.

1990s The launch of Penguin Audiobooks brings the classics to a listening audience for the first time, and in 1999 the worldwide launch of the Penguin Classics Web site extends their reach to the global online community.

The 21st Century Penguin Classics are completely redesigned for the first time in nearly twenty years. This world-famous series now consists of more than 1,300 titles, making the widest range of the best books ever written available to millions—and constantly redefining what makes a "classic."

The Odyssey continues ...

The best books ever written

PENGUIN CLASSICS

SINCE 1946

CLICK ON A CLASSIC
www.penguinclassics.com

The world's greatest literature at your fingertips

Constantly updated information on more than a thousand titles,
from Icelandic sagas to ancient Indian epics, Russian drama to
Italian romance, American greats to African masterpieces

•

The latest news on recent additions to the list, updated
editions, and specially commissioned translations

•

Original essays by leading writers

•

A wealth of background material, including biographies
of every classic author from Aristotle to Zamyatin, plot
synopses, readers' and teachers' guides, useful Web links

•

Online desk and examination copy assistance for academics

•

Trivia quizzes, competitions, giveaways, news on
forthcoming screen adaptations

P.O. 0005383006 202

were conducted in low voices. Tony and Natalie in the mirror were exactly at a height, their shoulders touching and beyond their heads the glitter of chromium.

At last Tony said peacefully, "Let's go to the station."

Natalie nodded; because the money was in the pocket of the blue raincoat Tony was wearing, it was Tony who offered money to the man behind the counter and it was accepted without comment.

When they came out of the drugstore the town was beginning to fill up with people on their way to work and Tony said carelessly, as they went down the sidewalk, "Be late for work if we don't move along."

"I've got to do five reports for the old man this morning," Natalie said immediately. "Got to be in the mail this afternoon. Reports to the higher authorities on people caught doing the same things day after day, recommending the ultimate punishment."

"Old lady Langdon caught us smoking in the washroom yesterday," Tony went on, "and said she'd report it to the old man."

"She wouldn't dare," Natalie said. "Anyway, let's quit. Let's just not go into the office this morning. Let's go to Siam instead."

"They ought to pension off old Langdon," Tony said. "Let's go to Peru."

They passed the town's biggest hotel; workmen on scaffolds were washing it down with power hoses and Tony and Natalie stopped shamelessly to watch. The fine spray from the hoses drifted down onto them through the foggy drizzle, and settled small drops in their hair.

"This is the only city I know," Tony said, "where if it's raining already they throw more water on you."

They walked on after a while, moving wherever they pleased but always bearing toward the railroad station. They stopped and stared at a cab driver who was trying to clean bird droppings off his windshield; they splashed in the water in the gutter.

They came at last into the railroad station hand in hand, small in the great doorway, dwarfed by the stained-glass window above their heads. At the top of the great sweeping stairway they paused and looked down on the people below, all so sure of their several destinations; they listened to the message of the train caller standing honorably at his desk beneath the clock and obedient to the will and the distant voices of the trains, translating by permission the great sounds to any who cared to listen.

Natalie and Tony came down the great stairway, down the wide aisle, and slid into seats in one of the rows, listening and watching; they perceived the thin thread of taxicabs which was all that held people in the station to the city outside, the transparent fine barrier of imminent going and coming, of being irresistibly called away or brought back, the conscious virtue of creatures selected to travel with the trains, the harmony of the discipline that controlled his huge, functioning order, where no head was uncounted and no ticket unhonored; they heard the distant paternal urging of the trains.

Oddly enough, Elizabeth Langdon and the rest came here only of necessity, with the intention of leaving this place as soon as they reached it. And yet two people who wanted earnestly to be strangers might sit here for hours and never lose the quick sense of being about to go away, and might probably never see anyone who knew their names, or cared to remember them. After a while Tony and Natalie rose quietly and went down the aisle again and into the station restaurant. They sat down at a table overlooking the nervous movements of the taxicabs and the suitcases set unerringly in the puddles, and ordered ham and eggs and orange juice and toast and griddle-cakes and doughnuts and coffee and sweet rolls. They ate lavishly, passing bits of food to one another, regarding contentedly the glass domes on the coffeepot behind the counter, the glass covers on the stacks of English muffins, the round red seats of the stools. When Tony poured herself a third cup of coffee, Natalie said, "Don't hurry, we have until ten o'clock."

"I do hope our train's not late," Tony said, "We'll be late enough getting in as it is."

"We can telegraph from Denver," Natalie said.

"Or call from Boston," Tony said. "They'll be expecting us